THE LOST SAINTS

of Tennessee

THE LOST SAINTS

Amy Franklin-Willis

Atlantic Monthly Press
New York

FEB 1 0 2012

Copyright © 2012 by Amy Franklin-Willis

Printed in the United States of America
Published simultaneously in Canada

FIRST EDITION

ISBN-13: 978-0-8021-2005-2

Atlantic Monthly Press
an imprint of Grove/Atlantic, Inc.
841 Broadway
New York, NY 10003

Distributed by Publishers Group West

www.groveatlantic.com

12 13 14   10 9 8 7 6 5 4 3 2 1

To Wendy—with all my love and thanks.

To Georgia, Gracie, and Giovanna—the best trilogy I will ever have a hand in creating. I love you, my three Gs.

Sometimes being a brother is even better than
being a superhero.
—Marc Brown

Are the saints perfect people?
No. They persevere.
And *that's* what makes them saints.
—Reverend Mark Spaulding, rector,
Holy Cross Episcopal Church

~ PART I ~

EZEKIEL

Why is light given to a man whose way is hid?
Job 3:23

❧ One ❧

1985

The late August air lies still, its weight pressing down on me in a way it didn't when I was a boy. Fords, Oldsmobiles, and the occasional late-model Chevy crowd the parking lot of Grayson's Café. I sit in the truck working my way through one cigarette, then another and another. Sweat melds the back of my shirt to the seat. Each time a newcomer opens the restaurant's door laughter spills out. The Mabry High School class of 1960 gathers inside for its twenty-fifth reunion. They are drawing together in a moment, happy to see one another, to talk of times past. When I go in they will avoid saying anything about our classmate and my former wife getting married last weekend. They will fail to mention my brother Carter's name, even though he drowned almost ten years ago. And none will have the guts to ask the obvious question—how did the smart boy with a full scholarship to the University of Virginia end up living in a converted shed in his mother's backyard and working on the line at the Dover elevator plant?

A loud tap on the passenger-side window startles me. Tucker snorts awake on the seat, raises his head at the sound. It's Jackie. The chance to see her is the only reason I'm here tonight. Without a word, she opens the door and climbs up. The "ex" before wife does not stop her.

"Scoot over, Tucker." She holds a sweating Bartles and Jaymes bottle in one hand and pushes eighty-nine pounds of dog toward me with the other. "Dinner's almost done, you know. The beef tips didn't taste good warm. They surely aren't going to taste good now."

Her voice floats over me, sweet and slow. I grip the steering wheel a little harder and look at her out of the corner of my eye. A mistake, of course. Looking at Jackie makes me want to touch her. Tonight she wears a bright blue dress. The front dips two inches into the cleavage she is so proud of. She likes to say those breasts didn't cost her a penny. All it took was two pregnancies, fifty hours of labor, and a push-up bra.

The scent of wild honeysuckle growing next to the road drifts through the truck, carrying memories of rained-out baseball games, walks through the woods behind Mother's house, and Jackie's perfume.

I nod in the direction of Grayson's. "How is it?"

"How do you think it is? Bunch of forty-something fat people." She picks at the label on the wine cooler, pulling until it rips off. "Everybody keeps asking where you are. Jesus."

Jackie spies the Marlboros and eases one out of the pack, leaning toward me for a light. Her fingers brush mine. As she settles back against the seat, her gaze rests on the MoonPie wrappers and old *Auto Trader* magazines covering the truck's floor, sharing space with empty cans of barbecued Vienna sausages, the contents gone but their smell still present beneath the Tucker odor.

"Where's Curtis?" I ask.

Jackie married him last Saturday at the Mabry Methodist Church. Our daughters were the flower girls. Louisa showed me a picture when I took her and her sister out for a burger last night. *We looked nice, didn't we, Dad?*

"Curtis couldn't make it. Dealership conference in Memphis." Jackie shrugs. The shiny material of the dress moves with her shoulders. I wonder when I kissed them last. Christmas Eve a year ago. Before Curtis popped the question on Christmas Day. Before the divorce, legal for two years by then, felt final to either of us.

"Aren't you going to tell me congratulations?"

She is trying to pick a fight.

"No honeymoon?"

"We spent two days in Memphis. I didn't want to be away from the girls too long. And then there was the reunion and all." The thumbnail of her left hand goes into her mouth, giving her away. There is more than she is telling.

It would be helpful if I couldn't read these signs anymore. If the knowledge accumulated over the years of who she is, of what she likes—kisses on the soft flesh at the back of her knees—and what she's afraid of—water moccasins—if it could all be erased.

"Congratulations."

The word tastes like dust. Jackie is now someone else's wife. Despite efforts to consume more after-work beers than previously believed possible, it is a fact I can't make go away.

Somewhere between Sunday's end-of-the-weekend drinks and the early hours of Monday, the notion of suicide floated past my mind for the first time in forty-two years of living. Sobriety did not make it disappear. My daily choices have evolved from whether to have chili or a Swanson's Hungry Man dinner to kicking around suicide methods.

Gun to the head is too messy. And what if you miss? A person could end up with half a face and be a vegetable for life. Hanging oneself seems tricky. If the drop isn't far enough to break the neck instantly, a person can suffocate for as long as seven minutes. That's six and a half minutes longer than I'm up for.

It's clear the best way is a drug overdose. If it was good enough for Elvis, it's good enough for me. I've got a stash of pain pills in the house, saved up after the accident at work. The doctor raised an eyebrow the two times I went in for a checkup and asked for a refill on codeine.

So far, the only member of the Cooper family to rob God of his right to terminate a life was Uncle Leroy back in 1956. He did it with a 12-gauge shotgun in the barn. On Christmas Eve, the selfish bastard. His ten-year-old son found him on Christmas morning. Story goes there wasn't even a head left, just pieces of gray stuff stuck in the blood-soaked hay. That ten-year-old boy is now thirty-nine and spends his time in a Mississippi jail serving twenty-five years for killing a guy in a bar fight. We all knew Uncle Leroy had good reasons for doing what he did. But when a person decides to check out, the rules should be no major holidays, birthdays, or anniversaries. No messy clean-up for the loved ones.

Most people seem to follow a road map for their life—do this and you'll be here. Do that and you'll live happily ever after. Get married. Have kids. Work. Go to church. I got a map, early on, and followed it. Got good grades. Went to college. And then the Smith boys got ahold of Carter and the map changed.

Scratch that. The map disappeared.

Tucker decides Jackie is ignoring him and struggles to sit up, making awful wheezing sounds as he does.

"What is that?" she asks.

"Reverse sneezes."

Jackie cocks her head to one side, the motion exposing the length of her neck.

I stroke the soft space between Tucker's eyes, tell him to take it easy. "The vet says it's something about the sneeze getting caught. Sounds like he's having an asthma attack but he isn't. No harm in them."

"If I ever saw a dead dog walking, it's Tucker."

Her words hit me and I turn my face to the door so she can't see the pain register. *Keep it up and I'll be glad you divorced my ass.*

She can't have forgotten who found Tucker. Rescued him from a ditch on the side of Highway 57 thirteen years ago, brought the dog back to our house cradled in his arms with tears running down his face. "He's broken. Legs don't work," my brother said. "Found him all tucked up in a ditch."

Turned out the puppy was almost dead of starvation. Legs worked fine after we put some weight on him. He's long past his Puppy Chow days now, with clumps of hair falling out on a regular basis, cataracts in both eyes, and arthritis so bad he limps more than walks.

Jackie covers her face, massages the temples. The fading sun catches the diamond on her left hand and glints of light bounce around the cab, the stone easily ten times the size of the one I put there two decades ago. Business at Curtis's Ford lot must be good.

"I didn't mean that about Tucker."

She strokes the dog's gray fur, whispers into his ear. His mouth hangs open, the tongue unfurled in the dog version of a smile. It's possible he misses Jackie as much as I do. Despite her constant complaints about his smell and general good-for-nothingness, she never failed to return from the grocery store without a bone from the butcher or a new box of dog biscuits. She is the one who first let Tucker sleep on our bed, unable to take his puppy whining from the designated dog area in the garage.

"Well, I did mean it," she says, "because he's getting old, you know. But I didn't mean to be mean. Okay?"

I take a drink from the bottle she offers. The taste is too sweet, like Kool-Aid, but the cold feels good as it slides down the back of my throat. A car pulls in beside the truck and its occupants, a couple I don't recognize, move through Grayson's front door. Jackie takes the cigarette from her mouth and smashes it into the truck's crowded ashtray.

Without looking at me, she asks, "Are you going in or not?"

She knows I'm scared and will be understanding, up to a point.

"Come on, Zeke. Come with me. It'll be like old times. Right?"

Jackie laughs, and this, more than anything else about her, has changed. The laugh used to come up from deep in her belly and sound like it could go on for days. Now it stops in her chest, almost as if something is blocking the way, forcing it out harsh and loud.

"You okay?" I ask.

The air around her shifts, electrifies. Her ribs expand beneath the dress as she takes a breath, slices out an answer. "I'm fine."

She climbs out of the truck fast, taking all the air with her.

"Jacklynn, wait."

She stops, leans against the passenger side door. Her body faces away from me. We spent hours in similar positions during the months before the split, talking at each other's backs. Five years ago she asked for a divorce in the tone she reserved for telling me news like the washer is broken or Honora's braces have to stay on another year. She said, *Ezekiel, you can't love anybody right since Carter died; the girls and I deserve better.*

"Follow me." She calls the words over a shoulder as she begins walking away.

"Not sure if I'm up for it." I slide across the seat to the passenger window, calling out to her. "Just seems kind of pointless, don't you think? Everybody sizing each other up."

Jackie stops. She turns around, tilting her head as if the words don't make sense. She retraces her steps. Our faces are inches apart. The sight of small wrinkles framing her mouth and the corners of her eyes strikes me as unfair. Age was not supposed to find her.

"No one's going to call you a loser, if that's what you're worried about," she says.

"Maybe not to my face."

"Come on."

Her eyes hold mine. There is no anger in her gaze, not even a flicker of disappointment. It has been years since she looked at me without an accumulation of hurt piled up. She wants me to go inside with her. Is it love or just an unwillingness to walk back into the party alone? If I lean forward the slightest bit, our mouths will touch.

Jackie steps back, out of reach now.

"Can't do it, can you?" She shakes her head. "Can't even walk in the door to see people you see every day and who've known you since you were born?"

I want to say, *Yes, yes, I can, if we go together,* but she is already on a roll. Her look morphs from the tender Jackie I married twenty years ago to the more current royally pissed-off version. She speaks in a low tone that gradually rises in volume.

"Ezekiel, you're not special. What happened to you and your brother is not all that different from a hundred horrible things that happen every day. That's the part you can't stand, isn't it? You hold on to all that pain like it's a kind of treasure."

"Shut up, Jackie."

The shriek of a fire engine goes past, cutting the silence between us. Jackie lowers her head for a moment.

"Last chance," she says, adjusting her hair in the side mirror. "I'm going inside."

"Be there in a minute," I say.

The wine cooler rests against the seat. After draining it, I drop the bottle to the floor. It rolls around and falls into the door well, slamming against the metal with each curve along the familiar seven miles back home to Clayton. At mile three it hits me that the divorce was Jackie's final attempt to make me better.

∼ Two ∼

1985

I call in sick to work. Say it's the flu. By the third day the boss grumbles about needing me to come in, but I lie and tell him I can't keep any food down, how it's coming out both ends. Bad. Chickasaw Lake is the place I spend my days, staring at the pyramid-shaped sweet gum and weeping willow trees and fishing for bream. On Thursday a cloudless sky invites me up to the Tipton Trail Tower. I climb all seventy-three feet of it, my breath coming faster than I'd like.

My brother said the angels sang up here. I listen. Wait. A wind melody ruffles the trees. The shushing of a crow's wings brush the air. The crow loops a wide circle before landing with a sureness I envy on the highest branch of a pine tree. The cry of a whip-poor-will echoes across the quiet.

That night the cry weaves through my dreams, carrying images of Carter as he changes into the bird and back again. In the morning, bright sun sears the shade of the bedroom window. First light used to be my favorite time of the day. While

Jackie and the girls slept, I got up and made coffee. Carter would amble out from his room, still wearing pajamas, and we'd sit at the table drinking from chipped mugs—the sun slowly rising, the soft light warming our backs. Now the only thing that fills me with any kind of warmth is cracking open the first beer of the night.

Leaving isn't something I do much. I seem to be better at being left. Jackie marrying Curtis last week killed any re-union fantasies I might have had. Not ten days ago she told me I needed to let go, get on with things. I told her to worry about telling Curtis what to do. She's right, though. As usual. Neither Carter's death nor losing Jackie has moved through me, settling in the space reserved for "bad things that have happened in the past." They are right here, in the middle of my chest, heavy and tired and present.

By Friday afternoon I decide to try work. When Jackie and the girls left, I moved from first shift, which ended when they got out of school, to second shift. Tucker was the only one to mind my getting home around midnight. On the drive to the plant I pass our old house on Tyler Road. The truck seems to stop on its own, pulling over to the side of the road next to the driveway and making me remember what our lives together were like. How Honora and Louisa found a litter of calico kittens living under the house one spring. How Carter liked to clomp down the hallway in work boots at night, yelling, *Uncle Carter's going to get you,* while Honora squealed into bed. How Jackie and I made love in every room of the house the first weekend we moved in. *To christen it,* she said.

A different wife now cooks at the stove I bought Jackie the year I got a raise. The new family includes a father, a mother, two little boys, and the rangiest hunting dog in Hardeman County. The wife spies my truck. She comes out into the front yard with the dog skulking by her side.

"Anything I can help you with?" she asks with a look that is anything but helpful.

I shake my head and drive back home. How do you tell a stranger she's got the life you thought you had?

Where to go seems less important than the going. It doesn't take long to throw a few things in a duffel bag. The bottles of pain pills, the spiral notebook next to the phone. Notes will need to be written.

I get into the truck, then climb right out again to grab the Folgers coffee can from above the fridge and pull out three hundred dollars, all in twenties. Savings for the girls' Christmas presents this year. I had planned to buy Louisa a leather sketchbook and pastels set at Mulligan's Hardware. For Honora I had imagined wrapping as many packages of double-A batteries as I could afford, to keep her Sony Walkman running. The thought of never seeing my girls again makes me hesitate. I should go find them at school and tell them good-bye.

But I can't. There's no way I could look at them and still leave. This way is better.

A book on the couch catches my eye. It is an ancient paperback, the front cover lost a hundred summers ago, leaving the opening pages wavy from decades of humidity. *The Adventures of Huckleberry Finn* is placed carefully in the bag between the socks and T-shirts.

Tucker waits by the truck, suspicious. If he could, the dog would climb up to prevent any chance of being left behind. But the thirteen-year-old body requires help now. When

I place him on the seat, he leans down and gives my hand a quick lick.

Movement stirs at the side window of Mother's house. My own home, though "home" seems a grand word for it, is the shed right behind her house. Originally a tool shed, my father and I renovated it in 1961 so Carter and I could live there together. The curtain falls back into place and I know Mother has seen me packing up. Probably been watching from the back bedroom window, too. As the truck nears the end of the long driveway we share, she steps out onto the front porch, arms crossed against her chest. The years have added heft to her figure and softened the bones of her face. She has taken to wearing her hair short for the first time. It doesn't suit her.

"Where are you going, Ezekiel?" Her voice carries across the yard. "It's too late for you to be going in to work."

Tucker begins to whine next to me. He loves Mother. Always has. Must be the scraps she feeds him at the back door.

"Headed out of town." I don't stop the truck until she comes down from the porch and blocks the driveway. "Christ, Mom. Get out of the way, will you?"

She is wearing a sleeveless housedress with big flowers on it, something she swore she'd never do. *Housedresses,* she used to say, *are for three kinds of women: fat, old, or too tired to care.*

The outside air has already warmed up. Possible thunderstorms tonight. Another reason to get on the road. The paper said they would be coming our way from Memphis, so heading east seems reasonable. Picking a direction, general as it might be, makes me happy.

"You're not going to tell me, are you?" She scowls, shakes her head. "You know it'll be ten years next week that your brother drowned? We're supposed to have a nice memorial at church this Sunday. And here you are leaving."

She wants to say more but a coughing fit prevents it. It is a deep, cavernous rumbling. Last week my sister Violet had to take her to the emergency room while I was at work. They diagnosed her with walking pneumonia and a touch of emphysema. When I ask if she needs a drink of water, she waves the question away.

I know all about the plans for Carter's memorial. Preacher Wilson caught me in the bread aisle at the Mabry Piggly Wiggly last week to tell me how we'd have the whole congregation singing Carter's praises and thanking the Lord for carrying him into the gates of heaven. I nodded but all I could think was how grateful I was for getting enough notice to ask for the Sunday shift at work.

What I want to say to Mother is *It's nice you're so worried about making a fuss over Carter. Shame you couldn't manage it while he was alive.*

"Please move," I say instead.

She steps back, shrinking into herself a bit, and I try not to notice. Try instead to remember my brother and how she almost threw him away.

"Give your sisters a call and let them know you're okay. You hear?"

I wave out the window and watch in the rearview mirror as she picks her way back up the stairs, favoring the bad left knee. She lowers herself onto the top step, tugging the dress down over her legs so only the thin ankles are visible. She looks small and alone and tired. Perhaps more so than I have ever seen her.

Mother's fierce presence guided her family. Prodding. Shouting. Loving. When Lillian Parker Cooper entered a room, there was a sense of the wind shifting, the very air seduced to come her way by her intoxicating combination of beauty, specialness, and sweet regret. Mother made you want to stand close to catch a bit of that breeze, to feel it filling the space around you.

A while ago I gave up wanting to be near her. I can speak politely to Mother for as long as it takes to say thank you for dinner or I'll fix the chimney next week. Anything more leads us back down the path to Carter.

∾ Three ∾

1946

Growing up, everybody used to string Carter's and my names together whenever they needed to find one of us—"CarterZeke!" echoing through our house and out onto Five Hills Road. Being the boys in a family with three girls was part of why we were close, but being twins seems more important. There was only one other set of twins in Clayton—Mary and Carrie Olney, five years older than us. They were identical and wore their hair, the color of darkest night, in two long braids down their backs. The girls were inseparable to the point of buying homes right next door to each other after they married.

Unlike the Olneys, when my brother and I looked in the mirror we saw the differences in each other: his dark eyes versus my light ones, the tops of my shoulders only grazing his triceps. But we knew what it was like to want the other within arm's reach. Mother used to tell us stories about how she'd be busy cooking or cleaning and my brother would come running in to pull her away. This was before Carter could talk. He took longer than any of us, giving Mother good reason to worry. She said Carter would get this look on his face, his brow all crinkled up, and she knew it meant I was in trouble, could see it as plainly as if he'd told her.

This was a truth about Carter. His face showed whatever he was feeling, the moment he felt it. Worst bluffer in the history of poker. I asked Mother once if we ever had one of those "twin languages" you hear about. The Olney girls made up their own sign language when they were toddlers and somehow remembered it their whole lives. Mother had thrown back her head and laughed at the question. *Ezekiel, honey, you two never did need to speak to each other much. What does a person say to the other side of his heart?*

Four years old when our dad first brought us to Chickasaw Lake, we couldn't believe the sheer size of it—the water rippling across the floor of Lavice Valley until it looked like it might swallow up the shortleaf pines tracing the eastern shoreline. Generations of boys like us grew up fishing the lake, hoping to catch one of the abundant bluegill or catfish or maybe a leftover skeleton from the nearby Battle of Davis Bridge site. Carter captured a small female bluegill that day with our father, the October sun glittering against its brilliant yellow underside.

When I sulked over him catching a fish first, he held it out to me. I touched it, the gills still fluttering with gasps of air.

"You caught a pretty one."

Carter pushed the fish into my hands. More than anything I wanted to take it and pretend *I* had felt the tug on the line and reeled it in. But I knew the beautiful fish wasn't mine, no matter how much Carter or I wanted it to be.

I gave it back and turned my gaze from the lake to the valley surrounding it. Second-growth oaks, cedars, and willow elms formed a blanket of the deepest green across each hill as if God had unfurled Lavice Valley like a woman shaking out the bedclothes.

"You'll catch your own soon enough," our father said, ruffling the back of my hair in a way that meant I had done the right thing.

As we grew older, Carter and I spent all of our free time at the lake, only a ten-minute walk through the woods from our house. The water reflected the valley's annual color transformations from green to gold with splashes of garnet to bare silver as clearly as it captured the growing images of us. Carter's reflection always stretched taller than mine, even when I tried to outsmart it by wearing my Cleveland Indians cap high on my head. For a while, our trips to the lake included me helping Carter learn to read. In between tugs on the line, I read aloud from whatever comic book I had and spelled the occasional word in the soft sand of the shore—*See, Carter,* I would say as I sketched with a fallen twig, *this is how you spell "Shazam."*

One June day when the summer's heat had yet to wrap itself around Clayton, Mother sent Carter and me out back to weed the vegetable garden. Mother spent hours in the garden every year, coaxing the best tomatoes in Clayton out of it. Aunt Charlotte couldn't understand why her garden plot, only three houses down from ours, produced mealy tomatoes and her sister's county-fair winners. Pulling weeds was our primary chore and it always took longer than we thought it should. Time we knew could be better spent.

"If you do a good job," Mother said, "I'll let you have a couple of the lemon cookies I'm baking for the church picnic tomorrow."

This was motivation. Thin and crispy, Mother's lemon cookies tasted sweet and tangy all at the same time. She made them only twice a year—for Easter and the annual church picnic.

Saturdays changed our yard next to the well into a laundry area. Our oldest sister, Violet, stood over the big wash tub, scrubbing the clothes on the board while Daisy cranked the clothes through the wringer. She stuck her tongue out at me as we walked by. I'd weed the garden any day over doing the wash.

For a good while, Carter and I went through the garden rows, following each one, pulling a weed here and a weed there like we were supposed to until my brother launched into our favorite garden game.

"Soldiers!" he yelled.

We threw ourselves down on the ground, flattening the pole beans we'd never liked anyway. I was Lieutenant Cooper and Carter was a Nazi SS officer. I always made him the Nazi. Dirt flew as we tore out most of the tomatoes and cucumbers, throwing them at one another like grenades.

Carter ran out of ammunition first. He stood, raising both hands in the air. "*Nicht schießen! Nicht schießen!*"

I taught him to say that after reading it in *Our Army at War*. The rules said I had to honor Carter's don't-shoot request. But the sun caught the glint of a brilliant green cucumber inches to my left. It was perfect, shaped like a fat little grenade. I grabbed it.

After taking a few steps back, I ran full out and let it fly in Carter's direction.

At least I thought I let it fly in Carter's direction.

"Incoming!" I yelled.

Carter hit the ground.

Inside the kitchen, Mother stood at the sink rinsing dishes. She looked up just as the perfect cucumber grenade sailed toward her. Toward the kitchen window. Through the bottom pane it flew, landing in the sink neatly sliced in half.

I ducked my head. Carter ran over to me. He kept looking over his shoulder to where Mother's angry face loomed in front of the now-broken window.

"No lemon cookies, Zeke," Carter said with a sorrowful look, shaking his head.

Mother stormed down the back stairs strangling a dish towel in her hands. I wanted to run but knew it would only postpone the punishment.

"You just broke a brand-new window your daddy put in last week. Last week, do you hear me?"

She strode toward us, the wide skirt of her dress whipping against her legs. When she saw the garden, she stopped— the rows were no longer rows, and broken tomatoes spilled red goo over the ground.

"You break my window and ruin my garden? The whole family will go without vegetables for a month. I work hard so my children will have something on their plates that isn't brown or white."

Violet pointed out that there were a few tomatoes left on the vines.

"Not many," Daisy said, always helpful.

"Girls, hush up. I'll deal with these two." She pointed at the back door. "Inside. Now."

"We're going to get whupped, aren't we?" Carter whispered.

And we did, the sting of Daddy's leather belt across our backsides easier to bear when the two of us took it together.

My brother was different in a slippery sort of way. As a little boy, he looked normal and most of the time acted normally, if a little quiet. But things changed when we started school. Lucille Ryder taught first through eighth grade in Clayton's one-room schoolhouse on the east side of Highway 57. Miss Ryder made you pick the switch to be hit with from the hickory tree in the yard if you got in trouble.

On the second day of school, Carter and I sat at our desks working on the morning's writing assignment. Violet and Daisy had stayed at home with a bad case of poison ivy. The girls got it while picking blackberries the day before. Daisy wanted to make the biggest berry pie ever and ignored her older sister's warnings to mind the plants with the three leaves. When it was too late and Daisy picked a leaf off just such a plant because it looked pretty, she got mad and ran up to Violet, rubbing her hands across Vi's cheeks so Daisy wouldn't be the only one miserable.

My brother was having trouble writing his name—it would be two more years before he could print it legibly—so I scribbled it for him at the top of the page, dotting the letters so Carter could trace over them with his pencil. Miss Ryder caught sight of this.

"Ezekiel Cooper, come here."

The last place anyone wanted to go near was Miss Ryder's desk. She smelled of old shoes and rotting bananas. I put down my pencil and stood up. As I walked to the front of the class, the boys started chanting, "Trouble, trouble."

Miss Ryder grabbed my right hand. "Did you or did you not write on your brother's assignment?"

I nodded. She wrenched my wrist.

"Yes, *ma'am*. I did."

Her eyes narrowed. "Why?"

When I told her my brother was having trouble writing his name, a strange smile spread over her face. She released my hand, leaving a red welt around the wrist.

"Go sit. Mr. Carter Cooper, come here."

My mind scrambled for a way to get Carter out of there without earning both of us a whupping. He walked slowly up to the front and we passed each other in the aisle.

As our shoulders brushed, I whispered, "Keep your eyes down. Don't look at her. You'll be okay."

One of the older girls, Betty Streit, hissed, "Stupid, stupid," as Carter passed her desk. Miss Ryder told him to go to the chalkboard. My heart began to beat so fast I could hear its thrumming in my ears. The urge to throw up pricked at the back of my throat.

"Carter, please write your name on the board ten times. You will not be excused from class today until you finish." She grimaced in a way that was supposed to be a smile before adding, "I'll even give you a brand-new piece of chalk. How's that?"

He looked back at me, his eyes big. I pretended to write in the air to show him what to do. Miss Ryder pushed back from the desk. Her chair scraped against the floor, causing the hairs on my arms to stand up. She gave Carter the chalk.

By now, half the class was giggling. In the moments before Carter's hand began to move, I squeezed my eyes shut and prayed harder than I ever had. *Dear God, please help him. Please make him write his name.* It would be a miracle if he did, but Preacher Dawson was always going on in church about miracles happening every day.

Carter drew row after row of *o,* the only letter he knew how to write properly.

Snickers spread through the class. Our friend Tommy Jackson told them to shut up. The teacher smirked.

"Well, now, Carter," she said, "that's the strangest spelling of a name I believe I've ever seen. Son, why don't you go on along home? Come back when you're ready to do your own work."

The chalk dropped from my brother's hand, splintering into powdery pieces across the dark wood floor. He ran for the back entrance, not even looking my way. I took off, ignoring Miss Ryder's threats of a whupping tomorrow. The air outside cooled the heat on my cheeks—flushed from rage and from the double dose of shame over Carter's ignorance and my own momentary wish that he was not my brother.

His figure sprinted down Main Street. After chasing him three blocks, I finally caught up by the crossroads. Tear tracks made dusty pathways down his face. His chest heaved with loud, hiccuping breaths.

"It's okay," I said.

The words sounded empty. My brother understood more than I may have realized. Life might have been easier if he had been less intelligent. He would not have grasped that there was a whole world out there he would never join, a world sure to pull me away from him.

Carter placed his hands on the back of his neck, cradling his head between his arms, as if shielding himself from an attack.

"Won't be okay," he said. "No, sir."

∾ Four ∾

1985

Clayton's only gas station is empty when the dog and I swing by on the way out of town.

"You're late, Zeke. Boss is going to chew your ass," Gerald Watson says, easing off a stool behind the counter to ring me up.

Gerald graduated from Mabry three years after me. He was drafted into Vietnam, something Carter and I avoided due to our age. When Gerald came home, he had lost part of his left leg and gained a weird sense of humor. When President Reagan made the joke about outlawing Russia, Gerald put the punch line—"We begin bombing in five minutes"—on the store sign for weeks, right underneath "Bread! 2 for 1."

I pay for the gas and walk back to the truck. After settling behind the steering wheel, I move to turn the key. Starting the truck leads to putting it in gear, which leads to driving. The moment of leaving is upon me and suddenly I can't do it. My hands drop from the wheel.

Tucker pins me with a pitiful look. Snacks. We'll need sustenance for this trip, wherever we're going. I head back to the store.

Moses Washington's old Chevy pulls in on the other side of the pump. Behind his truck a thousand dust particles rise up in a small cyclone of sparkling bits. I duck in the front door before Moses climbs out. If he sees the bags in the truck there will be questions. He knows I'm supposed to be at the plant. Sometimes I think he knows everything.

Moses and his wife, Pearlene, have been around me my whole life. Pearlene delivered Carter and me when we came too quickly for Mother to get to the hospital. Some people say Moses has lived in Clayton long enough to have seen Yankee General Edward Ord march his soldiers over Davis Bridge.

The inside of Gerald's Gas consists of three aisles whose crammed shelves contain every item a person might need. Bread. Extension cords. Tylenol. Fish bait. I grab two six-packs—one RC Cola and one Budweiser. Barbeque pork rinds are a favorite of Tucker's. Five bags of those go on the counter. MoonPies for me. Beef jerky.

The bells above the door announce an arrival. Moses walks in. There is nowhere to hide. He takes in the large load on the counter.

"Looks like you and the dog are going on a trip. Where you headed?"

"Leaving is all," I say.

Moses nods, like he understands. This will not be the end of the conversation. Besides serving as town handyman, he's also the closest thing Clayton has to a Father Confessor. We don't have a Catholic around here for miles but most folks like to talk. And Moses likes to listen.

Gerald takes his time ringing up my items. I hand over a twenty.

"Well, hell," Gerald says, spitting a wad of chewing tobacco into an old Maxwell House can. "I'm out of ones, Zeke. Hang on a second while I go grab some out of the safe."

Moses stands alongside me holding a bottle of chocolate Yoo-hoo and pressing the other hand into his hip, claiming the arthritis is acting up again. The morning gas rush, such as it is, has long passed and we are the only customers.

I keep my eyes focused out the window. Jessie Canthrop pulls into the dairy bar across the street and orders her first ice-cream cone of the day. Most folks put her weight somewhere between three and four hundred pounds. Last year, Jessie's Girl Scout cookie order alone was enough to send the Clayton troop on an all-expenses-paid trip to Dollywood. Tucker sits in the truck, his eyes tracking me, unsure of how this day is unfolding.

"I don't think I caught where you were headed," Moses says in a friendly tone.

When I play deaf he shifts his weight beside me, clearing his throat. "You running away from something?"

Sweat pools in the small of my back, dampening the elastic on my briefs. The idea of leaving had seemed so easy at home—get in the truck and go.

"I'm not running." This is a lie. I know it and he knows it.

Part of me wants to tell him, to say the words out loud and hear them vibrate off the air. *I'm going to kill myself, Moses.*

"Pearlene and I been talking about doing the same thing for years. Moving ourselves over to Memphis where we can pass more black folks than white folks in the street."

Moses and his wife are several shades darker than the darkest white person in town. For a fact, everybody in Clayton knows that at least one person in his family has a little bit of Cherokee or black or both. And everybody, except Moses and Pearlene, pretends like they don't know.

"We never have left, though. At least not yet. We still got some time, I imagine."

I stay quiet.

He reaches a big-knuckled, scarred hand in my direction. Pats my shoulder. "Don't you go and be a chicken shit."

How does he know?

A smile covers his face but the pressure of his hand increases until I have to try hard not to squirm. "You've got two sweet girls," he says. "They don't need a daddy leaving town."

It won't help to tell him I'm not even sure the girls will miss me.

"I've known you your whole life, son, and you've had a rough go of it lately. But with those blue eyes like your mother's, just a matter of time before another good woman lands in your arms, and you got that smart head to figure out what you need to be doing with yourself. You just need a new beginning is all."

Gerald's large gut precedes him through the back door. "Damn safe is a bear to open."

He heaves himself back up onto the stool with the help of a cane and counts out my change.

I turn to Moses to say good-bye. The old man and I stare at each other. The thing about looking at Moses is his whole life story can be glimpsed through his eyes—the warmth in them telegraphs all the love he's given his wife and surviving child over the years, but also there's a resigned sadness, evidence of the grief he and Pearlene endured in losing two of their three children, a daughter when she was five years old and a son when he was twenty. Even with all that, suicide has probably never crossed Moses's mind. He's strong. No one in this town would argue he's the better man here.

"You remember what I said?" he asks.

I nod and start the truck up, knowing this will be the last time I see him.

Moses stands in the doorway watching me go, slowly shaking his head like he knows I'm going to be a chicken shit.

I head east on Highway 57. The sky is stripped blue. Tucker hangs his big head out the window, ears flat back in the wind, nose on full alert sniffing the hot air. As the miles increase between Clayton and me, I can feel my shoulders start to let down. No one knows where I am right now. No one would think I should be here.

At Eastview, I turn north toward Jackson. The Johnny Cash eight-track blasts out of the truck's speakers. *I hear the train a comin'* . . . "Folsom Prison Blues" is Tucker's favorite song. As soon as Johnny says, "I hang my head and cry," the dog gives me a look that says he's happy, even though our routine is all off-kilter and he doesn't know where we're headed.

Another pickup passes us on the left and the old man driving gives me a thumbs-up—for the song or for the dog or for both. My brother took to wearing all black in the last years of his life. We had a running joke where I would ask, *Whose funeral you going to?* and he'd shout, *Yours!* Then he'd tackle me.

The beginning years in the Tyler Road house were good ones. Love had run freely between Jackie and me, babies were being made, and my brother felt safe again. He had a real home with us, not just the shed where he and I lived in the five years between 1960 and when Jackie and I married.

When Honora was born, Jackie and I almost went crazy those first few months. The baby had colic, and every afternoon she'd start crying and keep going until we thought she'd run out of tears. I started working double shifts just to get some peace. One day she cried nonstop from the time I left the house at five thirty that morning until bedtime. Nothing Jackie tried calmed Honora—not even taking her for a ride on pothole-filled Redbud Road, which usually caused her to fall asleep. It's a miracle we didn't damage the old Impala's chassis as many times as we drove it up and down Redbud that year.

By eight thirty that night Jackie had all she could take. She went and put the still-screaming baby in the crib and walked out to our tiny front porch and had herself a good cry. She believed she was a terrible mother. We'd tried for five years to have a baby and now finally here she was and Jackie wanted to give her back.

For most of the day, Carter had stayed in his room or outside, away from the caterwauling. Jackie and I had chosen the house, in part, because of its small third bedroom on the back, perfect for my brother. She didn't even flinch when I proposed to her and said I wanted her to marry me with all my heart but I also needed her to promise it would always be okay for my brother to live with us. Jackie said she didn't know how long she'd been out on the porch before she stopped crying enough to notice the baby was quiet.

Noises came from the kitchen. She blew her nose one last time and went inside. In the gentle gray of the early night, Jackie watched from the doorway while Carter swayed back and forth making scrambled eggs on the stove with one hand, the tiny infant held over his shoulder with the other.

The baby's eyes grew heavy and she at last surrendered to sleep. Carter heard Jackie move behind him and motioned for her to sit at the table. The eggs and a piece of unbuttered toast were set before her along with a glass of milk. He left her alone to eat while he took the baby in the living room. When Jackie finished, she found them asleep in the rocking chair. She covered them with an old afghan and watched them from the couch until her own eyes closed.

The way I miss Carter and the way I miss what Jackie and I had are all tangled up. Maybe if it had been one or the other . . . If I could trade my marriage for my brother, maybe that would be enough. But the sum of the two losses together is too much.

Two hours later I'm thirty miles outside of Nashville. Thirty miles from Rosie, the baby sister who had been Carter's and my constant pestering shadow, following us into snake-filled creeks and happy to play soldiers all day. And while we complained about a girl tagging along, it was mostly for show. Of all the people who will be left behind, she will miss me the most.

I pull over at a Stuckey's to call, hoping to catch her before she heads out for lunch with an up-and-coming country music singer. Her clients are always up-and-coming. They are almost never anybody I've actually heard on the radio. The only female agent at KMG, Rosie started as a secretary fifteen years ago, doing everything anybody ever asked her to do, plus a thousand other things they didn't. After the boss gave up trying to screw her, he promoted her.

I step into the phone booth, drop a quarter into the slot and push the numbers scrawled in my address book under "Rosie work." A receptionist answers and puts me through. The noon sun beats down through the booth's grimy panes of glass. *Fags get AIDS* is written in blue marker across the black plastic cover of the phone book.

"This is Rosie."

Her voice echoes out at me like she's sitting in a cave, which means I'm on the speaker-phone thing, and she sounds so grown-up. I think of Rosie with ponytails and scraped knees. Doesn't matter that she's almost forty now.

"Hey, Rosie, it's your brother."

"Surprise. Surprise." I can hear her grinning. "Momma called this morning. Said you looked like you were running away from home. Where are you?"

"I'm about a half hour outside Nashville."

"Half hour? Half hour! Give a girl some notice. Hang on a second."

I hear footsteps and murmurings between Rosie and her secretary. "Damn" comes across loud and clear.

"Why didn't you tell me you were coming? I've got a lunch date with the senior vice president. My boss's boss. I can't not go. Stay with me tonight. I'll take you out to dinner."

Her words tumble at me, one on top of the other. Always in a hurry this girl is. Maybe because she is the youngest of the five of us or maybe because she was born that way, Rosie is tough. When the girl decides something, whether it's having fried okra for breakfast or working with famous country music people, get out of her way. Mother thought Rosie was crazy for hauling herself up to Nashville. Kept telling her, *Going to get your heart broke, my girl, you are.* Mother knew what it was like to want something so bad and end up not getting it.

"Don't worry," I say, trying not to sound disappointed. "I've got farther down the road to go tonight, so can't stick around for dinner. Just calling to say hi. You okay?"

"Don't change the subject. Where are you going? Did you tell the girls you were leaving? Did you tell Jackie?"

Two teenagers in a rusted-out Pontiac pull up next to the truck. They stare at me, then roll their eyes at each other. My own daughters are too young to drive. At least by themselves. Honora turned fifteen this summer. Jackie asked me to teach her to drive, said it could be something my girl and I could do together. Mend some fences that have been all broken down since the divorce. I took Honora out once a week to First Baptist's parking lot. She didn't appreciate the truck's manual transmission. *Why can't you have an automatic like everybody else?* The first lesson ended with both of us mad, but by the third one, she got the hang of it. Last week I took her out for a drive on the highway. She shifted all the way into fifth gear. Made her proud. *I like going fast, Daddy,* she said.

Rosie's voice calls out to me from the phone. "Did you hear me?"

"I got to go. Somebody's waiting for the phone." I pause for a second, torn between telling her everything and worried she might talk me out of it.

"Listen, I love you, okay?" This is a compromise. This is the only thing Rosie needs to know.

She yells at me not to hang up. Tucker waits with his head out the truck window, panting like he's about to pass out. After I give him some water, we head east again. The Smokies rise up outside the truck's windows by sunset. The last time I saw the mountains was with Jacklynn on our honeymoon. It was October and wide bands of red, green, and yellow cut across the mountains. Jacklynn was twenty-two and I was twenty-three. Happiness loomed large.

As darkness falls, I stop in Pigeon Forge at a motel done up to look like a real log cabin, though it's actually logs painted on vinyl siding. The nightly room rate is half my daily take-home, so I go for the weekly rate, figuring I'll have a kind of a vacation before doing what I've come here to do.

The McDonald's around the corner provides dinner. I eat in front of my room's TV. Every five minutes the top of the set requires a whack to make the picture come in clear. The static is a friendly background buzz while I try to fall asleep, but the sheets scratch my skin and headlights from cars on the main road keep sweeping through the thin curtains. My daughters wouldn't mind. They like having at least one light on when they go to bed. When Honora and Louisa were small, Jackie was in charge of baths and teeth and hair brushing. My job was to tuck each daughter in the way she liked it. Lou wanted the covers pulled all the way up to the chin but she always left one leg on top, in case she needed to escape. *You never know, Daddy, monsters could come.* In the glow of the pink-shaded lamp that sat on the nightstand between their beds, I read to them. The titles changed from *Goodnight Moon* to *Cat in the Hat* to *Little House on the Prairie. Lights out,* I'd say. *Just one more, Daddy. Please. Last one,* I'd say.

Tucker lies on the floor by the bed, already snoring after finishing off the burger and fries.

The far-off sound of a train's whistle echoes over the droning of the air conditioner. I close my eyes and listen, hear the whistle get closer and closer until the train must be heading straight for the room. It takes me back to Clayton. To Carter and me waiting every Tuesday night for the five-thirty freight train from Memphis to whistle through town so we could race across the tracks before heading home to dinner.

❧ Five ❧

1948

My mother had no great hopes for my sisters, knew their futures promised little difference from her own, even suspected that their girlhoods might prove the high-water mark of their lives. Not so for her boys. When my brother and I had landed in her arms on a clear October night, she thanked God. Two sons. Two children with chances to get out of Clayton. Go to college. Wrestle from the world everything we might want.

Only two years after our birth, measles swept through Clayton, taking Mother's dream with it. Vi, Daisy, Carter, and I got it, the rubeola vaccine still nearly two decades away. But only my brother almost died. His fever climbed so high he went into convulsions; then encephalitis swelled his still-forming brain, pushing him into a coma for two weeks. When Carter pulled through, neither our parents nor the doctors worried much about the possibility of permanent brain damage—my parents because they didn't question the miracle of their son's survival and the doctors because they had little knowledge about long-term effects.

The first night Mother told me I was different from Carter, she must have been convinced it was the only way to salvage her dream for us, knowing that the greatest chance for its success now rested with me.

The sound of my sisters' murmurings, soft secrets shared among the three of them, carried out through the open window to the front porch step where Mother and I sat trying to get cool after the day's heat. She smoked her last Lucky Strike of the day and drank iced tea laced with more sugar than I could stand. Sugar and a fair bit of vodka. The number 36 train barreled through the Clayton crossing, rattling panes of glass in the living-room windows and announcing bedtime. As stars pierced the dark velvet of the Tennessee sky, Mother leaned down to me, her mouth brushing my ear. When she spoke, the noise of the words was no louder than that of a water moccasin gliding past me in Shelby Creek.

"You see those lights up in the sky, Ezekiel? You see the brightest one?" she said. "That, my boy, is you. Don't let anybody tell you different. You're one of the chosen ones. God will strengthen you. That's what your name means."

This was new information. Up until then, I had known two things about the origin of my name—Mother heard it on one of her favorite radio shows—*The Shadow*—and somewhere in the middle of the Bible was a section with *Ezekiel* on it.

I turned to stare up at her. She was the prettiest mother in Clayton; everybody said so. And when she smiled wide, when the smiling reached all the way into the deepest blue of her eyes, I got this feeling like everything was going to be okay.

Tonight she did not smile wide. Instead, her eyes glowed with a far-off light that made me uneasy. I liked the idea of being the brightest star, but what about Carter? Wasn't he one of the chosen ones, too?

A small amount of tea lingered in Mother's glass. Her voice grew louder. I sneaked a glance in Carter's direction to make sure he wasn't close by, because I sensed that whatever Mother was going to say next, he shouldn't hear.

"You're different, Ezekiel. You're not like your brother, sweetheart. Not like our poor Carter."

There were a few things I'd begun to notice about my brother by this point—how he still didn't know his ABCs and I had been reading since I was four. How he didn't talk much. Sometimes he stared right through me, looking off into a place no one else could see. Ever since we'd taken him to the Memphis doctor earlier that summer, Mother never stopped smoking. No one told Carter and me what the doctor said. When I asked, Mother said not to worry about it. So I didn't. At least not much. It would be a few more months before she would share the doctor's prognosis with me. I don't think she ever told Carter.

In the fading light, Carter handed a socket wrench to our father as he changed the spark plugs under the hood of the 1945 Chevy half ton. My brother's nearly seven-year-old frame already stretched two inches taller than mine. *Older and taller,* he'd say to me. Older by ten minutes.

The play-by-play of the Cleveland/St. Louis Browns game came over the radio in Daddy's Ford. A hit crackled toward us as Kenny Keltner knocked another one out of the park with guys on second and third. Daddy stopped hammering long enough to listen as all three runners scored.

"You wait and see, boys," he told us, "Cleveland's going all the way this year."

It was the most he'd said about baseball since Babe Ruth died. Daddy had sworn he wouldn't listen to any more baseball that year, as a memorial to Babe. He broke down when Cleveland started winning.

"You realize that—" When Mother started a sentence with "you realize," it never led to anything good. "—I am missing the *Prince Albert Show* on WSM. Mr. Hank Williams is probably singing right this minute and here we are listening to a bunch of nothing about men running around a triangle."

Daddy kept right on hammering. I held my breath. If he was tired and grumpy, he'd look at her mean and say something like, *Don't you carry on tonight.* If he was tired and happy, he'd let it slide.

"It's a diamond, Lillian. Not a triangle." He sat down heavily on the old oak stump, letting the hammer fall to the ground. "What we should be listening to is the news, to see what that fool Strom Thurmond is up to."

Daddy coughed and spit a big one into the dirt, talked about how Thurmond ran out of the Democratic National Convention with his States' Rights Party and how they were going to get people to vote for them.

"If President Truman loses, does anybody think Thomas Dewey and the Republicans are going to care if I've got a job or not?"

"I care, Daddy," Carter said. Our father held out an arm and my brother walked into it, easy as you please. Carter had the same barrel chest, brown eyes, and square jaw as our father. I had Mother's slight build, light coloring, and the unmistakable Parker family dimples—one in each cheek and one in the chin—which earned me years of school-yard teasing.

Daddy pushed Carter off with a pat and went back to hammering. My brother walked up the steps and plopped down next to me, our legs almost touching.

"Sure is hot still," he said.

I nodded. Neither of us wanted to go to bed yet. It was cooler outside.

Mother threw us a glance that said bedtime was only a minute away. She kept staring at us until she looked like she was going to cry. Then she got up all quick, knocking over her glass, and ran inside the house. The tea glass tumbled down one stair, then the next, and the next, until it landed in the dirt and spun around. Daddy didn't even look up.

I didn't know for sure what made her upset that night but it was an easy guess it had something to do with the fact that life—in this case, plans for Carter—was not working out. Again.

∾ Six ∾

1985

Tucker and I walk the streets of Pigeon Forge every morning and every night for six days, stopping in shops where most of the "genuine" souvenirs are made in China instead of Tennessee. We eat at McDonald's so much the girl on the drive-through morning shift starts recognizing my voice.

Through the speaker, she says, "Good morning, darlin'. Sausage biscuit, hash browns, and coffee for you?"

She winks at me as she hands over the food. I put her age at somewhere over fifteen and under twenty. Her lips are full and buried beneath layers of lipstick; she is pretty in a hard kind of way. On Thursday morning, I feel disappointed when a stranger takes the order.

At a downtown fudge shop, I buy a postcard from the three-for-a-dollar rack that I have no intention of mailing to anyone. What would I write? *Greetings from the Town of my Suicide!* The scene on the front shows a farm surrounded by the Smokies. I stare at the picture until it conjures another farm, in Virginia this time, surrounded by another set of blue-tinted mountains. Cousin Georgia and her husband, Osborne, and me around the dinner table, sharing stories of our day together. My room overlooking the apple orchard. A whole world opening up to me at the University of Virginia. And then it all disappeared. I slip the postcard into the back pocket of my jeans.

By the time we reach the six-foot-tall wood bears flanking the Logland Inn office, I know tonight is the night. The money is about to run out and my nerve will float away the more Big Macs and beer I consume. Tucker limps into the hotel room behind me and I wonder if he knows something, if he can smell the decision on me. Tonight will be another kind of leaving day.

Calling Jackie is the responsible thing to do. To hear her voice one last time and to say, without really saying it, why I need to do what I'm about to do. As soon as I say hello, she starts yelling. When I try to explain how I had to get out of Clayton, she cuts me off.

"Please, Ezekiel. We all need to get out. But you've got a family here. You've got a job here. At least you *had* a job here."

She says my sisters are going out of their minds worrying. When I ask to speak to the girls she says they're busy with homework.

"Put them on the phone, Jackie."

"No."

The line goes dead.

Son of a bitch. It's pointless to call back. On principal, Jackie won't give in. Even if I said, *Hey, you tightly wound nothing-is-ever-good-enough ex-wife, put my daughters on the phone, because after tonight I'll never be able to speak to them again,* she would probably assume I had been drinking and hang up again.

Guilt makes me dial my sister Violet's number. Instead of yelling, she begins to cry.

"Jesus, Vi, I'm sorry. God, don't cry. I'm fine. Really. I'm fine."

She takes a big breath, blows her nose. "Are you fine? When are you coming home?"

"I don't know."

"Is this because of the reunion, Zeke?" Forty-six now, her voice still has the breathy, childlike quality it did when she was a girl.

The motel manager fixed the TV in my room this morning, looking the other way when he spotted the dog's water bowl next to the door. An old episode of *Gunsmoke* fills the screen. Watching it is more appealing than talking to Violet.

Silence stretches between us.

"I need to ask you something."

"I got to go, Vi."

"Hold on. Please. I'm so worried about you. Is this about Carter? Because if it is, you need to talk to somebody, sweetheart. And there's something you should know about Mother. I took her to the doctor this week and she didn't want me to tell you but—"

I cut her off. "Tell Daisy I'm okay. Love to everybody."

When Carter drowned the month before our thirty-third birthday, Violet and Daisy were all over me about getting my feelings out, talking it through, letting them help me. Little Rosie was the only one who said anything that made sense. After my brother's dark brown coffin was lowered into the earth, she pulled me aside and said, *I don't understand how there can be you without him or me without both of you.*

And this is precisely my point—how can there be me without him?

The bottles are lined up at attention like miniature orange-colored soldiers along the sink. The notes are stacked next to the phone on the bedside table. Jackie's is first. I copied a passage from *Huckleberry Finn,* the one I've been rereading every day since coming to Pigeon Forge, about going out in the woods and hearing the sound a ghost makes when it has something to say but can't communicate it. The ghost can't go peacefully to its grave until it's understood, so every night it wanders around grieving.

I pray Jackie won't burn Honora's and Louisa's notes in anger. Not that I would blame her, but the girls will need to see them. My daughters are the most beautiful proof of my ever having breathed.

Tucker's last meal consists of chicken-fried steak and French fries from the diner next door. The dog can smell the food and his tail thuds in happy anticipation. I open the pills and sprinkle their contents on top like parmesan cheese. If I've timed everything right, we should both lose consciousness at the same time. But the truth is I've got no idea what I'm doing. Drugs have never been my thing. Alcohol, on the other hand, I have some experience with. It seems logical that I've got to get the dog set before I start downing the pills because what if I pass out too quickly? We're in this together. The two of us.

The dog looks up at me with brown eyes, runny from some Smoky Mountain tree pollen. After Carter died, Tucker waited by the front door every night for a year. The dog would begin to whine, pawing at the door, as it grew darker outside. We had to be careful because if someone came in, Tucker would bolt out, convinced *he* could find Carter if no one else could.

"Listen, old man," I say, sitting on the floor next to him, "you're about to have a great dinner and then you're going to get sleepy. When we both wake up we'll be somewhere else. If things work out, we might even see Carter."

Tucker's ears prick up at the sound of Carter's name. He pokes his nose against the bowl, impatient for food.

"Hang on. We should take a moment before we start all this, don't you think?"

He bumps the bowl again. I grab him by the collar and heave him over to the bed so that we are both facing it. The swirling pattern on the avocado green bedspread makes me dizzy. Praying is something I do once a year, maybe twice. The dog's tail thuds against the carpet dotted with cigarette burns. He thinks this is a game.

Someone walks into the room next door and turns on the TV. Suitcases are dragged across the carpet. The door slams.

"Dear God," I begin, stopping right away because Tucker walks over to the window and moves the curtain back with his nose to get a look at who is making the racket.

"Don't worry about it," I say, pulling him back over to the bed. I start the prayer again.

"What we're about to do is not going to make you happy. It's one of your big rules not to do this. But it's the only thing left to do. And if anyone needs to burn in hell for all eternity, take me, not the dog. He hates to be hot and this is not his idea."

The dog yawns.

"Help my girls and Jackie understand why I needed to do this." I am asking God to explain something I can't.

Tucker pants next to me, mouth hanging wide open, and the smell of his breath is so foul I cover my nose.

"Old man, if there is a heaven, there is no way in hell God's going to let you in smelling like that."

I put the food bowl on the ground and Tucker devours the entire meal within two minutes, nearly choking as he takes huge mouthfuls, saliva studding the gray of his muzzle like diamonds.

"Jesus, Tucker." *Slow the hell down, man.*

Now it's my turn. The first twenty pills go down okay. I swallow them in groups of five, broken up with sips of Coke. Coke seemed better than Budweiser, though I consumed two of those before dinner. The whole thing is so easy. No wonder people do this.

The gag reflex kicks in on the second twenty. I keep trying—closing my eyes and swallowing as hard as I can, rubbing my throat with one hand like I do when I'm trying to force a heartworm dose down Tucker's trap. Another five go down. But just barely. Tuckers watches from the floor, his head resting on his paws, content with the bulging contents of his belly. His eyes float down and then spring awake when I gag. He is annoyed.

Another five minutes and every single pill ends up in the toilet, shriveled indigo-colored capsules floating among chunks of hamburger. The whole thing looks so disgusting I heave again.

Two more bottles remain on the sink. Twenty pills. Two

hundred milligrams short of what I need to do the job. If I take them I'll probably only end up with some kind of side effect like irreversible erectile dysfunction.

Tucker groans softly on the floor next to me. The dog. The dog has done this better than me. He has managed to keep the crap down. The dog is going to die.

~ Seven ~

1985

"I need a vet. Can you tell me where I can find a vet?"

"Who is this?" The voice is not the regular Logland Inn night manager.

"Room eighteen. My dog is sick. Really sick."

"Sir, I'm sure you know it's the policy of this motel that no pets are to be brought on the premises and if you've violated that policy you will be liable for a minimum fine of two hundred and fifty dollars and any additional cleaning—"

I hang up, ripping out the phone book from the nightstand, keeping an eye on Tucker the whole time. He keeps nodding off.

"Wake the fuck up, Tucker."

I go over to him, prodding him in the belly, scratching behind his ears, lugging him up onto the bed with me so I can hold him while I dial the Smoky Mountain Emergency Pet Hospital.

A friendly, vaguely familiar female voice answers. When I explain a modified version of the situation, she says I need to come right away, every minute can make a difference. I scribble down the directions before carrying Tucker out to the truck.

"Hang in there, okay?" I tell him. "We're going to get some help."

His head lolls in its usual way when he sleeps, but I take it as a sign of impending death.

"Wake up, Tucker!" I elbow him in the side with my free arm, trying to keep him with me.

It takes three illegal U-turns and ten minutes in the dim twilight to find the place, located on an isolated side street. As we pull into the driveway, a young woman in a white lab coat walks out to meet us. The porch light illuminates her. It is the McDonald's drive-through girl. My heart lifts the slightest bit. She is a nice girl. She will help us.

"Hey, I know you," she says with a half smile. "Sausage biscuit, hash browns, and coffee, right? This is my night job." She opens the passenger side door to get Tucker. "Let's get this big guy out."

I step in front of her and carry the dog inside, rambling on about how I left him in the motel room and he got into the pain medication.

The vet charges into the exam room, rolling up his shirtsleeves as he comes through the door. He kneels down next to Tucker, placing a stethoscope on his chest. A perfectly round bald spot makes a crop circle on the back of the vet's head.

An eight-by-ten framed photo of Benji looks down on us from the wall. Benji tilts his head to the side in the way that made everyone say "how cute" during the movie. A black paw print is stamped in the lower right corner of the photo.

Autographed by the star himself. Tucker lies on my feet, doing his best to ignore Dr. Hickman.

"Respiration is slow," he says, flashing a light in each of Tucker's eyes. "How much and what kind?"

"What?"

"How much did the dog ingest? And what type of pain medication was it?" Before I can answer he asks another question, one that sounds discriminatory. "How old is he?"

He steps out of the room and yells down the hall. "Gina set up an IV."

"Twenty pills of codeine, thirty milligrams each."

The vet nods, frowning. "Has he vomited any of it?"

Tucker raises his head up, nailing me with a look. "No," I reply.

"Can he walk?"

I stand up, gently pulling on the dog's collar. "Come on, Tuck. You can do it." He makes it onto all fours but it takes a lot of effort. When he tries to walk, it's like the rear-wheel drive is blown out. His haunches collapse beneath him and he ends up in a heap on the floor.

Alarm bells explode in my head. *The dog can't walk. What have I done?*

"He's already showing signs of an overdose—ataxia, miosis, and some mild respiratory depression. We're going to induce vomiting and then force-feed him charcoal to absorb the drug in his system."

Tucker lets out a groan. Dr. Hickman pats his head. At least the man cares.

"It's going to be a rough night," he says, looking at me directly. "If his breathing gets too slow or he loses consciousness, we'll need to put him on an artificial respirator. Lucky for you I took a second mortgage out on my house last year to buy one for this place. We're the only animal hospital for two hundred miles that has one. We'll do everything we can to save the dog, but I need you to know that what this old guy ingested was enough to kill a teenage girl."

I nod, trying to keep my face together, and hug Tucker's neck before they take my boy away.

The waiting area has three metal folding chairs and pet magazines from 1981. I take a cigarette out. My hand shakes as I light it. Darkness has dropped down outside. An open window lets the sweet night air in, its fresh smell knocking against the antiseptic and animal smells of the clinic. A fat tabby cat with one eye wanders into the room, hopping on top of the front desk. The clock above it reads nine thirty. Tucker and I were supposed to be dead by now.

The hours crawl past. A few minutes before midnight Gina appears by my side. She looks as worn down as I feel.

"Here. You need this." She holds out a cup of coffee and a Snickers bar. "The dog's hanging in there."

She does not meet my eyes as she speaks, glancing down at the scuffed running shoes on her feet instead. My stomach cramps as I swallow the bitter liquid. The girl lingers for a moment, as if she wants to make sure I drink it all.

"So, he's going to be okay?" I ask.

Her eyelids flutter down again. "Dr. Hickman is a good vet. He stabilized Tucker's breathing, but now we're working to get the drug out of him. Tucker's tough, but this is hard stuff, you know? Nobody likes to throw up. I better get back in there."

Her small form disappears down the hallway, slipping behind the door where my dog is puking his guts out. She's right. Tucker hates to throw up. He once ate the better part of two dozen raw chocolate chip cookies, stole them right off the baking sheets before Jackie put them in the oven. As it all reappeared over my one good pair of pants, he stared up at me between heaves with a scowl that said it was my fault.

The coffee cup warms my hands, cold despite the humid warmth of the clinic. The words almost escaped my lips while Gina stood there. *I did it to the dog. I fed him the drugs. It wasn't supposed to happen like this.* But if I say that, they will take the dog away from me. And either way this goes, if he dies or if he lives, Tucker is coming with me.

A hand presses gently on my arm. "Zeke?"

I wake with a start and glance at the clock. One thirty. Gina stands next to the chair.

"Something happened a few minutes ago. Dr. Hickman wanted me to come out and give you an update."

She wraps her arms around her chest before continuing. A loud buzzing sound in my ears threatens to drown out what comes next. I hold my breath.

"Tucker lost consciousness around one fifteen. He's on the artificial respirator right now to regulate his breathing."

"Jesus."

The one-eyed cat hops into my lap, preening and rubbing against my chest. The warmth is comforting but I swat it away.

"Come on, Jack." Gina scoops the cat into her arms. "I'll keep you posted, okay? It's going to be a long morning. Do you want to go back home and I'll call you?"

"No." I am not leaving without the dog.

"Maybe you'd like to borrow the phone over there." She points to the desk. "To call someone?"

Gina thinks Tucker is as good as dead and wants to have backup in case I lose it. My mind gears up, sorting through people to call. The only person I can imagine sitting through this with me is Rosie. *Rosie.* Nashville is three and a half hours from Pigeon Forge.

~ Eight ~

1985

A little after 5 AM Rosie bursts through the door of the Smoky Mountain Emergency Pet Hospital dressed in plaid pajama pants stuffed into purple cowboy boots. She wears sunglasses despite the lack of sun outside.

"Jesus Christ, this place is hard to find." She pushes the glasses on top of her head and wraps me in the scents of Virginia Slims and perfume that smells like freshly cut grass. "What's going on, Zeke?"

She pulls back and grips my shoulders. "How's the dog?"

A sense of relief floods through me, warming the muscles cramped from hours spent in the metal chair. I am not alone. The whole ugly story wants to spill out. But I won't let it. Not yet.

"He's unconscious. They've got him on an artificial respirator."

Rosie's eyes, the same topaz color as Carter's and our father's, widen. "Well, shit."

I turn my head away for a moment, trying to keep it together.

The closing of a door in the back echoes out to the waiting area. Dr. Hickman walks down the hallway toward us. His green scrubs shirt is splattered with stains—a multicolored collage of yellow, black, and dark red. Rosie reaches for my hand, squeezing it hard.

"Tucker woke up. About five minutes ago." The vet wears a bemused expression. "Surprised the hell out of me."

The earth tilts and I fall, caught by the same chair I sat in expecting news of Tucker's death. Questions float in my mind but I can't form them out loud.

"Will he be okay?" Rosie asks.

"I don't see anything at the moment that makes me worry. But we need to keep him here today for observation." He runs a hand down his face, trying to wipe the exhaustion off of it. "You're one lucky owner. I didn't have a lot of faith the dog was going to pull through."

"I didn't think either of us was going to make it through," I say. My whole body aches, the nerve endings tingling and raw. Rosie's hand makes small comforting circles on my back.

My words of thanks to the vet sound hopelessly insufficient.

"Thank me after you see the bill. Gina will be out with it in a minute." Dr. Hickman's expression softens. "Tucker's a good dog. Keep that codeine locked up, okay?"

Rosie's questioning gaze burns down on me.

"Not now, okay, Rosie? Right now I need to see Tucker and then I really need to sleep."

My sister inherited our mother's laser look—the one where she could narrow her eyes at you and cut through everything. I keep my gaze steady on the floor.

"I need some sleep, too," she says finally. "See the dog and then let's get out of here."

Gina emerges from the back and walks behind the counter, punching numbers into a calculator. Punching a lot of numbers into the calculator.

"It all comes to $2,750."

Tired as my brain is, it quickly figures the one credit card in my wallet cannot take a hit as big as that.

"We take Visa," Gina says, trying to be helpful.

I slowly remove the wallet from my back pocket and go through the motions of looking through it. Before I'm done, Rosie slides her own Visa card onto the counter.

"I can't let you do that."

"It's done." She waves a hand to dismiss it. "Your little unapproved Smoky Mountain getaway has cost you your job back home, so pay me back when you get another one. It's a good thing I like that dog." She nudges me with her elbow. "Go see Tucker."

The dog lies stretched out on a stainless-steel table, not moving, looking dead. Bits of black are stuck in the soft fur of his muzzle. The charcoal. When I place my head near his, it is wonderfully warm. Alive. My boy made it through. We take in a couple of big breaths together. Inhale. Exhale. That's all it is. Inhale, exhale. We're still here together. The crater in my chest contracts, gratitude filling the hole part way.

The dog's eyes open. He tries to get up, ready to leave this strange place with its bad smells and horrible medicine.

"Take it easy, buddy," I say, patting him back down. "The vet says you need to stay here a little bit longer, okay? You're going to be all right, though. Everything's turned out fine."

• • •

Rosie and I grab breakfast at the Pigeon Forge Diner next to the motel. After we both eat large helpings of bacon and biscuits and gravy, she nails me.

"You going to tell me what the codeine was about, Zeke?"

The restaurant bustles with the early morning crowd. The thunk of ceramic coffee mugs hitting Formica tabletops. The scrape of spatulas against the grill as the cook manages a batch of hash browns. Truckers in baseball caps pulled low over their eyes curl over their cups, loading up on caffeine before heading out on the road. Our waitress returns to the table asking if we need anything else.

"You want some more coffee, Rosie?" I say, welcoming the distraction.

"Honey," she says to the waitress, "I don't need anything else right now except for my brother to answer the question I asked him."

"Afraid I can't help you with that," the waitress says with a half smile, placing the check on the table.

Rosie sits back and crosses her arms over her chest. Her focus is legendary in our family. When she was nine, she spent six months selling boxes of Mrs. Leland's Golden Butter Bits candy door-to-door just to get the "500 boxes prize"—a transistor radio that broke a week after she got it. She has been known to wait weeks, sometimes years, to reach a goal when properly motivated. Her slow rise at KMG is a case in point. Getting to the bottom of big brother's latest disaster will be one of those goals.

A mother with two young daughters sits at the booth opposite ours. She looks in her twenties, nearing thirty. The girls could be six and four. The smallest one starts to whine for milk and the mother meets my eyes, shrugging, before signaling to the waitress. For a year in each of Honora's and

Louisa's lives Jackie and I decided eating out was too much trouble. After a few meals where everything on their plates ended up on restaurant floors, we said we'd wait until they had reasonable table manners.

Those problems seemed so easy. Kid can't behave at a restaurant? Don't eat out. Kid not ready to sit on a potty? Keep her in diapers another six months. Now the complexities of keeping them safe, of keeping them whole, overwhelm me. Mommy's divorcing Daddy. Daddy's sad all the time.

There are two choices. Door number one: Spill the whole thing to my sister. Door number two: Sell her the same story I told the vet's office. Maybe I should be honest. Tell her suicide is not for sissies. The scale of this latest failure reinforces my belief that there is nothing I can't screw up. My brother used to be confused by the word *sissies*. He didn't understand how it could be hurled at you as an insult and also be the name of three people he loved most in the world.

When I look back at what our family had—what worked versus what didn't—it was an unspoken belief that each of us was valuable. That each kid had something to offer. Not in the "you will be president" kind of way, though maybe Mother did mean it like that for me, but mostly in a basic, human way. You are loved. You are valued. This was an elemental truth of our childhood. When Mother fractured that truth in the fall of 1960, all but throwing Carter away, it splintered through the family—traveling from Carter, to me, to our father, and our sisters.

"Zeke?" Rosie claps her hands in front of my face, causing me to blink. "It's Saturday, okay? I can sit here all damn day. I've got no other place to be. So you can talk to me now or you can talk to me after lunch or dinner. But you're not leaving until you say something."

I take a sip of lukewarm coffee. "Thanks for coming."

"You're welcome. Get on with it."

"Remember when I got hurt at work last year?" *Door number two it will be.*

She nods.

"Boss moved me from doing trim work to installing the Formica floors and I slipped. Banged the hell out of my shoulder." This part was all true. "The doctor prescribed codeine for the pain. The shoulder got better but it's still not quite right. So I take a painkiller now and again. I brought them on this trip and did a dumb thing."

She grabs a piece of bacon off her plate and munches, looking skeptical.

"Last night I came here for dinner and left the pills out on the nightstand with the top off. You know Tucker. The dog eats cow shit, for God's sake. I came back and found him lying on the floor with the chewed-up bottle next to him, all of the pills gone."

My sister sifts through the words, calculating their accuracy. "That's a good story," she says.

"What? You don't believe me?" I work on sounding outraged. "I don't need you to believe me, Rosie. Okay? What? You think I tried to do something else with the codeine? Like what? Go ahead. Say it."

A few heads turn in the direction of our table. I feel bad for the mom and two kids who don't need to hear this.

Rosie leans over the table, voice low. "You want to know what I think? I think you came here to kill yourself. I think you called me to say good-bye. I think you took those pills yourself and maybe gave some to Tucker so he wouldn't be left without you, too."

I laugh, throwing my hands up. "Then why I am here? Shouldn't I be dead?" I yell now, pointing at my chest. "I. Am. Here."

She shrugs. "I don't know, Zeke. Christ. Will you calm the hell down? What's the matter with you?"

"You're calling me a liar, Rosie. And suggesting I tried to kill my own dog. Anything else?"

I throw money on the table and stomp out of the restaurant. Not bad acting. *Hill Street Blues* here I come.

"Zeke, wait!" My sister hurries to cover the ground between the front door and the truck. I forget she hasn't slept much in the past twenty-four hours, either.

The morning clouds drift past, carried by a light wind. Saturday. The dog and I have made it to another Saturday. For some reason the thought makes me smile.

"Tell me one thing, okay?" She puts a hand on my arm. "What are you doing here? Why did you leave Clayton?"

"That's two things."

Her hand drops. "This isn't fucking funny."

"You want to know why I came to beautiful Pigeon Forge?"

She nods.

Simple question. I stall and put my hands in the back pockets of my jeans, thinking of how to answer. My right hand hits the hard edge of something in the pocket. I pull it out. It's the postcard from the fudge shop.

I hold it out to her. "*This* is why I came here."

Rosie takes the card and stares at it. "That's a picture of a farm in the Smoky Mountains. You came here to buy a farm?"

"I didn't come to Pigeon Forge to stay here. I'm on my way to somewhere else."

"Really?" She is far from convinced.

"To Virginia. I'm going back to Lacey Farms. To see Cousin Georgia and Osborne. They sent me a letter a while ago and said they could use some help."

Might as well make it sound good.

She hands the postcard back. "Why didn't you tell anybody that?"

I duck my head and try to look sheepish. "I should have. But I needed to get away from Clayton and think it through, you know? Clean mountain air and chocolate fudge never hurt anybody, right?"

"I guess." A look of confusion still clouds her face. Against her intuition, she is inclined to believe me.

"I don't know about you but I've got to get some sleep. There are two beds in the motel room if you want to take a break."

We leave the truck in the diner's parking lot and walk over to the Logland Inn. Rosie collapses on the first bed she sees and falls asleep with her boots still on. She's too tired to notice the stack of good-bye notes next to the phone, and I quietly pick them up and stash them in the bottom of the duffel bag, planning to throw them away somewhere down the road. In the bathroom I open the remaining pill bottles and watch their contents spiral down the drain. Today I see another possibility. Though it would be less risky if the Laceys *had* actually sent me a letter asking for help with the farm.

After a shower, I lie on the bed and let my eyes close at last.

❧ Nine ❧

1955

By second grade, the Clayton School got a new teacher straight from the teacher's college and she took a liking to Carter. Miss Weaver stayed after school three days a week to help him learn his letters until, by the end of fifth grade, he could read. Not long books at first. Just the Dick and Jane readers. He still liked me reading to him best. But he learned to write, too. Proved that Memphis doctor about as wrong as he could be. Things went along fine for a while until our oldest sister Violet came home late one night with some news. Some bad news.

Three weeks later, on the night before Violet's wedding, Mother spoke to Carter and me about it. It seemed odd to have Violet getting married. She was only four years older than Carter and me. We were all still kids.

"Your sister's going to make you children uncles before you're thirteen," she said, shaking her head and making a clucking noise with her tongue against her teeth, a noise she made only when one of us did something dumb. Violet was a

year older than Mother was when she got pregnant with Vi.
There was no comfort in knowing that history was repeating
itself.

I kept quiet until she left the room. Then I told Carter
being an uncle *could* be fun.

"If the baby's a boy, Carter, we could teach him to play
basketball and stuff."

"What about a girl?"

"Forget it. What are we going to teach a girl?"

The wedding day brought cold January rain. All of us kids got
dressed up—shoe shines, baths the night before, new clothes.
I'd been trying to explain to Carter why Violet was getting
married. He and I were sitting in the rough old oak pews waiting for Vi to come down the aisle on Daddy's arm when he
leaned over to me. My brother looked good that day with his
hair slicked back and a blue tie on.

"Vi's not going to be living with us anymore, is she?"

"That's right. She's going to live in a small house up the
road from us. With Louis."

"And she's going to be a momma?"

"Around summertime."

He nodded and then folded his hands in his lap, waiting
for it all to begin.

After the ceremony, there was punch and wedding cake
in the church hall. Daddy stood up and said how proud he was
of Louis and Violet. Mother shot him a look like she was going
to pitch a fit, but Daddy kept going.

"The Cooper family welcomes the Rydell family. Violet
is our eldest child and I think it's always hardest to say the first
good-bye to one of your children. But her mother and I—"

He stopped and smiled at Mother, who smiled back, even though it was a no-teeth-showing kind of smile.

"Lillian and I are happy to see the joining of our families."

Violet looked pale, the whiteness of her dress reflected in her face. Mother had given her no rest about wearing white, said the dress should be red, but Daddy came to her rescue and Vi got white.

I watched her say hello to all the guests, shaking hands and hugging. She seemed happy enough. Worn out but happy.

Halfway through the wedding reception Daisy came up to me looking irritated, though this was nothing unusual.

"Have you seen Rosie?"

I shook my head.

"We're supposed to be watching her. Help me look. Momma's going to kill us if she's lost."

"She's eight now, for God's sake, Daisy. She can look out for herself."

"Be quiet and help," she said, pulling me along. We searched the hall and then the church. No Rosie. I don't know what made me go out back, by the creek, but it seemed like a place she might want to go. Crazy about water, Rosie would swim in anything she could—bathwater, creek water, lake water. Daisy and I walked toward the tall poplars lining the creek. When we were six feet from the edge, I heard Mother's voice. Daisy went to call out to her but I put a finger to my lips. My skin had that itchy feeling it got whenever something scary or bad might happen. We walked a little closer, still hidden from Mother by the trees.

She was sitting on a tree stump and Uncle Leroy sat beside her on the ground. We couldn't hear what they were saying and just as we were about to get close enough to be seen, Leroy got up on his knees and kissed Mother. I waited for her to pull away and slap him across the face, like women did in the movies, but she didn't. She kissed him back.

I had yet to put my lips on anybody who wasn't a relative, but I could tell it wasn't the first time Mother and Leroy had kissed. They did it easily, like it had happened a lot of times before. When it ended, Leroy pulled Mother close to his chest and she rested her head on it, like we'd seen her do with Daddy. Daisy's hand flew to her mouth and she turned around, running back to the church. I watched for a moment longer, still not quite convinced my eyes were seeing right. They kissed again, and when Leroy's hand moved to touch my mother's breast, I turned and ran back to the church, too.

We found Rosie hiding in the coat closet and yelled at her for disappearing. I never said anything to Mother about Leroy. What could I have said? *Mother, what the hell are you doing kissing Daddy's brother?* A child doesn't tell his mother how to act.

A few days after the wedding, Carter and I were playing basketball in the backyard when Daisy came out to hang laundry on the line. I went over to talk about Mother and Leroy.

"Don't bother me, Zeke."

"Listen, I just want to ask you about . . . you know, the creek thing."

She whipped out a bedsheet, making a loud crack in the air as she did, and pinned the sheet to the line. The rains had stopped and the sun shone stronger than it had in months. Daisy wanted to get the wash hung as quickly as she could in case the weather decided to turn cold again.

"Don't know what you're talking about."

"What do you mean you don't know what I'm talking about? Come *on.* You know."

She ignored me. I stationed myself between her and the clothesline, forcing her to look at me.

"You're lying," I said.

"I'm busy, Ezekiel. Go bother your brother."

I never have figured out how people think something's not happening if they're not talking about it. It's happening all the same.

We ate a lot of beans that spring. Pole beans. Green beans. Butter beans. The price of cotton had started to fall and our father knew the time was coming when he wouldn't be able to cover the house note. The state put out a call for strong men to work on the highways that summer, so Daddy signed up and was gone almost two months. I asked Mother one night if she missed him when he was gone.

"Of course I do, Zeke," she said, looking up from the sewing in her lap. "Don't you?"

"You don't act like it sometimes," I said. This was as bold as I could be without coming right out and accusing her of messing around.

Her needle paused in midair over the faded pink dress she was mending.

Mother stared at me for a moment before speaking. I wanted her to see what I knew. *Willed* her to see the knowledge on my face of what had happened at the creek.

"I love your father very much, Ezekiel. If I don't act like it sometimes, it's only because I'm tired and it's hard when he's gone. Understand?"

She reached out to touch my arm but I turned on my heel and left, unconvinced.

When Daddy was gone, Uncle Leroy came by every night to check on us and I couldn't stand the sight of him. He performed his usual hello by grabbing me by the scruff of the neck, holding on until I begged him to let go. Not once that summer did I beg. I stayed silent until he'd get antsy.

"What's the matter with you, boy? Getting too big for your uncle to be carrying on with you? You a big man now?"

"No, sir," I'd say, hands curled into fists at my side, aching to hit.

∾ Ten ∾

1985

The morning dawns hazy and warm. Today is the tenth an-
niversary of my brother's death. I say a prayer for him. For
myself. For the place calling to me now, a place where more
good things seem possible than bad.

By six thirty, I clear out of the motel room and throw
my bag in the back of the truck. Tucker stands in the doorway,
glancing between the truck and the room. He has gotten com-
fortable again at the Logland Inn after his stay at the pet clinic.

"In the truck, Tuck. Come on."

With one last look at the bed, he hobbles out and accepts
help up. "I'll get us both a sausage biscuit on the way out of
town. How 'bout that? You want bacon, too? Today you can
have bacon."

His tail twitches. Bacon it will be.

Gina stands at the McDonald's drive-through window.
A thick coating of lipstick the color of cotton candy makes her
look younger than she is. I let her know I won't be stopping by

tomorrow or the next day. Don't want her worrying. Her hand rests on the window ledge—the fingernails are chewed down to raw, fleshy stubs. Another customer calls to her through the speaker.

"Just a minute, please," she says into the microphone, then turns back to me. "I'm glad everything went okay with the dog. Wish I was on my way out of here, too."

Her look tells me she knows she will never go anywhere but where she is. I consider telling her to hop in. We could get out of Pigeon Forge together. She hands over the bag of food.

The car behind me honks. I put the shift lever in drive and wave as her image fades in the rearview mirror.

Before Rosie got on the road back to Nashville yesterday, she told me Mother has lung cancer. Mother has been smoking two packs a day as far back as I can remember. Lucky Strikes. Nothing else.

"Do you know what the average life expectancy is for lung cancer?" Rosie said. "Less than a year."

How could our strong mother have cancer? I felt a tug back to Clayton. She would need our help. But Vi was there. And Daisy. Surgery was the recommended treatment. Before they would operate, though, Mother had to fully recover from the pneumonia. The doctors said she was "lucky" the illness had brought her into the ER, where the chest X-ray revealed a shadow on her left lung.

I told Rosie I was sorry about the news but I couldn't go back to Clayton. Not yet. *It's a matter of life or death,* I added silently, sure she wouldn't appreciate the sentiment. If things got really serious, I promised my baby sister I'd come home.

The fastest way to Virginia is to head north and take Interstate 81, but the thought of being boxed in by semis for hours makes scenic win over speed. The southern route takes

Highway 441 south to Gatlinburg, crisscrossing through the bottom of Tennessee on 321, tracing the northern boundary of Great Smoky National Park, and finally meeting up with I-81 close to the Virginia border. The truck will have to make it through the Smokies and a piece of the Appalachians.

The last time I went to Virginia I was eighteen. Navigating was left to the train engineer. As the familiar hills of Tennessee disappeared out the window, it hit me that I'd left home, left my brother and my girlfriend, to live with a relative I'd never met, in a state I'd never set foot in, to attend a university where I wouldn't know a single person. Today, I'm just as scared. Scared of what I'll find there. Scared they'll tell me to turn around and go home. More scared nothing will be better there, either. And then what? Codeine take two?

The sound of Dolly Parton's voice croons out at me from the truck's radio. She's singing about if teardrops were pennies and heartaches were gold. After climbing steadily on Highway 321, I turn in to a scenic pullout. Dad used to stop at every one of them on family car trips. Said it broke up the drive. Mother didn't have time for them.

"Carter, we're running late," she'd say. "We don't need to be reading signs and looking at things." Daddy would just wave a hand at her and let all of us kids pile out and look.

My truck is the only vehicle in the parking lot. From the bottom of the duffel bag, I dig out the good-bye notes written back at the Logland Inn. The noise of the truck door slamming stops a woodpecker's *rat-a-tat-tat* on a nearby birch. Tucker goes off to the bushes to do his business. The strong smell of damp earth mixed with crushed pine needles releases under my feet as I walk.

The September morning cloaks the mountains in mist. The sign says the Cherokees called this region *Shaconage,* which means "place of blue smoke." Looking out across the forest of beech and birch with Fraser fir and red spruce up higher, the Cherokees got it right. A haze hangs in the lightest hue of a robin's egg and dances like gossamer above it all. The view appears so fragile that if I turn my back it may all disappear, evaporating into the mist.

Carter should be here to see this. He would have said, *Let's move right here, make a camp and hunt for our food. Like Huck and Jim did.* During the summer we turned twelve, we worked our way through the *Adventures of Tom Sawyer* and the *Adventures of Huckleberry Finn.* At night I read to Carter in our bed by flashlight, and by day we'd collapse under the shade of the biggest oak tree we could find and read until Mother called us in for dinner.

Maybe I should have become a park ranger and gotten us a little cabin in the woods where Carter wouldn't have had to deal with many people. I could have taken Jackie and the girls. My brother might still be alive if I'd done that.

It seems like the wanting to see him or tell him about my day should be done. Ten years is a while. Jackie says you never stop missing someone you love. This is the most depressing thing I've ever heard and I hope to God she is wrong.

But Jackie is rarely wrong. Marrying Curtis Baxter was a mistake. She thinks he can give her what I couldn't, which, according to her, is the love and attention she deserves. But what she thinks is love is no more than Curtis wanting to add one more precious thing to his collection of Mustangs and vintage Smith & Wessons.

I tear the three notes into pieces, throwing them over the edge. It isn't clear to me whether I will try the final exit route again. It won't be today. And I'm pretty sure it won't be tomorrow. The wind grabs hold and carries them out toward the mountains, pieces of confetti dancing snowlike among the trees.

A pristine Cadillac pulls in beside my truck and a man wearing a long-sleeved shirt and pants with suspenders gets out. He blows his nose with a red bandana pulled from a back pocket.

I nod hello as I walk back to the truck, ready to move on.

"Hell of a view, isn't it?" he says.

My hand stops over the door handle. "Yes, sir. It's a fine view."

"Where you headed?" Before I can respond he continues. "I'm Washington, DC–bound. Taking the long way round to get there. Wife died three months ago. God rest her soul. I'm ready to see the country. Know what I mean?"

What must it be like to be eighty-something and starting out the rest of your life alone? Maybe not much different from being almost forty-three and alone. Only the prospect of fewer years of solitude waiting for you.

"Look at me forgetting my manners." He reaches out a hand. "Grayson L. Kenilworth. The second." He winks. "Might as well tell you all my secrets."

We shake hands. A semi barrels past in the northbound lanes.

"Son of a bitch, those suckers are loud." Mr. Kenilworth shakes his head as if trying to clear out the sound. He looks heavenward. "Mrs. Kenilworth didn't approve of swearing. But we won't tell, right?"

He asks again where I'm headed. I wait a few seconds before replying, wanting to make sure he's done talking first.

"Virginia. Outside Charlottesville. Little place called Bailey."

"I know Bailey. Sure do. Pretty country out there." A fly lands on Mr. Kenilworth's large left ear and he swats at it.

"Bailey is old Virginia. Wouldn't figure you for the fox-hunting type," he says. "And I mean that as a compliment, son."

Tucker wanders into view, eliciting a laugh from Mr. Kenilworth. "That's surely not a hunting dog. No way, no how."

The dog ignores him and stands by my side, unsure. The man is right about Bailey. From what I remember, everybody on Tall Oaks Road owned enough horses to run their own Kentucky Derby. Cousin Georgia and Osborne were two of the few residents who didn't participate in the hunt. They got up on horses only when they wanted to explore the farm. Cousin Georgia said she could think of no bigger waste of time than chasing a poor fox like mad through the trees with a bunch of half-drunk snobs who thought they were better than everybody else because their great-great-great-great-grandfather settled Jamestown.

"I've got family out there. Cousins."

"Horsey types?"

I shake my head. "They've got a farm. It's a working farm. At least it was when I was last there."

"When was that, son?"

"Nineteen sixty."

He lets out a sound that is either a belch or a laugh. Or both. "Nineteen sixty? You've got some catching up to do once you get there, don't you?"

At five minutes after nine o'clock, we pull into a Motel 6 outside of Charlottesville. By the time I settle in the room, it's too late to call Cousin Georgia. I grab the fat phone book off the nightstand and search for her number. It doesn't take long to find Osborne Lacey. The last time I spoke to either one of them was after Louisa was born. They sent a baby outfit, and after weeks of Jackie nagging me, I called Georgia to say thank you. She kept saying I should bring the family out for a visit. Told me she and Osborne still thought about me every time they passed by my old room. We never went, though. Too busy mostly, but I also think I wasn't ready to go back. Lacey Farms marked the spot for what life had been like before—when the University of Virginia was my future—and what came after.

Thunderstorms move in and make trouble all night. Scared to death of them since he was a puppy, Tucker leans himself against me the whole night and whimpers nonstop. Sleep never quite comes for either of us, so when the sun touches the room's dingy brown curtains, I go ahead and get up. Outside, the only sign of the night's weather is a few random tree branches scattered across the parking lot. By six thirty I'm showered and shaved. If Cousin Georgia keeps the same hours she used to, she should be up. But I don't want to risk waking her or Osborne, so I eat breakfast at the Waffle House next door. The coffee is scalding hot, and the biscuits and gravy make my stomach cramp up. Afterward, I walk back and forth in front of the motel room door trying to settle my insides and get calm enough to walk in there and call. *This is a bad idea. Maybe she's died. Maybe Osborne's died. If they aren't dead, the last thing two old people need is a shiftless relative and a stinky dog on their doorstep.*

Tucker yawns and licks the biscuit crumbs from his chops. My legs will not walk inside the room to make the call. I climb back in the truck. Smoke my fifth cigarette of the day. Watch people come out of their rooms, some still dressed in pajamas, looking tired and hopeless. One guy walks out in his boxers, scratches his balls, and yells back toward the open door of his room.

"Bitch, you better get out here and clean out this car before I leave your ass."

The dog and I trade a look. *Fuck.*

I call at straight-up nine o'clock. She answers after the second ring.

"Cousin Georgia, this is Zeke Cooper."

"Excuse me?"

She's forgotten who I am. Jesus.

"Cooper, Cousin Georgia. From Tennessee."

A pause. "Cooper?"

"Yes, ma'am." I speak louder. "Ezekiel Cooper, ma'am."

"Oh," she says.

Uh oh, I think. "It's Zeke, Cousin Georgia. From Clayton. My mother's Lillian Parker Cooper."

There is an intake of breath. "Oh, Ezekiel. Forgive me. Of course. How are you?"

I clear my throat before telling her I'm in Charlottesville.

"Charlottesville?" She sounds confused and tired, not at all like the energetic woman I remember. She yells for Osborne to come quick. "When are you going to come see us?"

"Whenever it's all right for me to stop by."

"Anytime's fine by us, Ezekiel. It's been a while, hasn't it?"

"Yes, ma'am. Too long."

She asks if the girls are with me.

"No, they're back home with their mother," I say.

"That's too bad. Another time."

"I'd be happy to drive over right now, if you and Osborne are home."

His heavy footsteps near the phone. He mutters something to Georgia about losing her mind before Georgia hands the phone over to him.

"Hello?" Osborne's deep voice rumbles. "Ezekiel?"

"Yes, sir. This is Ezekiel."

He asks if I need a ride. I thank him but say I've got the truck.

"You get on over here, then. We're going out on the front porch right now to wait for you."

The phone clicks off.

∾ Eleven ∾

1985

The twisting branches of live oaks arc across both sides of the Lacey Farms entry road, offering shelter as I steer the truck to the house. When I lived here twenty-five years ago, life offered a thousand possible destinations. Good destinations. Now, when it comes to possibilities, I tend to think of what can go wrong instead of what can go right. Maybe that's part of getting older, like going gray. I smooth my hair in the rearview mirror, and though a touch of salt sprouts on the top, the rest remains the light brown of my youth. This gives me hope.

The main house rises in the distance, a testament to solid antebellum glory. Five chimney towers stretch toward the sky. The first time I saw the house I didn't even know what Greek Revival was. But I knew a mansion when I saw one. Knew I'd be happy if they let me sleep on the porch.

A weed-filled front lawn and a sagging split-rail fence that looks like it hasn't been whitewashed in two decades frame the house. Its shutters have faded from a glossy black to a peeling gray. Tucker perks up on the seat. He puts his paws up on the dash and looks out the window. Cousin Georgia and Osborne make their way down the front steps as we pull into the circular driveway. Osborne looks frail, the skin papery over his bones. Cousin Georgia is rounder in the middle and her now-all-white hair is piled on top of her head. But her eyes smile at me with the warmth I remember.

She flies over to the truck, opening the door. As soon as my feet touch the pavement, she pulls me in, engulfing me in the smells of lemon verbena and the morning's breakfast biscuits. Osborne stands next to her and gives a formal handshake, though his left hand reaches out, a small tremor evident, to clasp my shoulder.

"Welcome back, welcome back!" Georgia says, "I told Oz it's been so long since we've seen you. Lord, we must look ancient! But look at you. Still so good-looking with those blue eyes and dimples."

She catches sight of my suitcase in the back of the truck. "You can leave it," I say.

Georgia tosses her husband a look. He keeps his mouth clamped shut. The secret code of their marriage is indecipherable. Could my appearance have sparked an argument?

"You're welcome to stay here as long as you like, Ezekiel," Georgia says. "Your room is still your room. I hoped you'd return to it someday."

Quiet drops down. This is my moment to say, *Yes, I need it.*

Cousin Georgia stares down at her hands, the fingers interlaced together. They are such small hands. Suitable for kneading biscuit dough, doing needlepoint, and perfect for picking the hard-to-reach apples from the trees in the orchard. It strikes me that she is waiting for me to say I will stop here for a while. For some reason, it will make her happy.

"I believe I'd like to stay. Thank you," I say.

Osborne grabs the suitcase out of the truck with surprising ease and marches up the front porch. Tucker casts a wary glance at the house, unsure of his welcome in this new place.

"The dog can come, too, of course," she says.

"For God's sake, Georgia," Osborne grumbles.

The dog hobbles out of the truck by himself and nearly jogs his way up the stairs.

After settling my things in the old room on the second floor, Georgia suggests that Osborne and I take a walk around the lake. "Trying to get rid of us," Osborne whispers. "You caught her without having a meal prepared and it's killing her." Georgia presses a glass filled with sweet tea into my hand on our way out.

Osborne and I walk to the lake nestled on the lower half of the property. The cloudy, late-morning sky melts into a dull gray against the deep green of the Blue Ridge foothills. A light breeze carries the scent of ripening apples.

"You're not getting to see the farm in the prettiest light," Osborne says. "Now, if you'd come at sunrise this morning . . ." He lets out a low whistle. "Never more beautiful than after a thunderstorm. The whole front of the house glowed with that morning sun. The light is starting to change now. Getting that fall slant to it. More to my liking. "

He walks in long, fluid strides for one who looks so frail. Along the curving path, a magnificent magnolia tree towers over a line of crape myrtles capped in brilliant reds, pinks, and purples. Osborne points to the garnet-colored foliage on the flowering dogwoods as further proof of fall's arrival. The lake comes into view, rimmed on the east by a stand of weeping willows and on the west by loblolly pines stretching to the sky, their clean scent filling the air. We stop at the water's edge. The silver flash of a trout dances beneath the water. The sense of having been in this same spot before with Osborne tugs at me.

"Brought you here first thing when you showed up on our doorstep twenty-five years ago. How old were you then? Seventeen? Georgia told me you liked to fish, so this seemed like the right place to show you straightaway. Make you feel at home."

When I saw it for the first time all those years ago, I marveled at my good fortune—to have a lake stocked with rainbow trout and the familiar bluegill only steps away from the place I would call home. Who could believe it? I wrote to Carter, telling him to have Mother bring him for a visit as soon as possible—we would fish by moonlight, by sunrise, when-ever we wanted. Only later did I find out Mother never gave him that first letter or any of the ones that followed.

Osborne bends down next to the water, floats a hand along the top. "One of my favorite places around here. Good thinking spot. None of those damned apples or peaches staring at me with all of their problems."

"I was happy then." It surprises me to hear the words out loud.

"And now?" The question is asked with Osborne's back to me; the tone pleasant, curious.

A glossy black stone catches a glint of sun and I pick it up, the rock's weight barely registering. With a practiced flick of the wrist, I skip it across the water—watch it bounce once, twice, three times before disappearing beneath the surface.

"Happy probably doesn't cover it."

• • •

We leave the lake and trace the perimeter of the main house. Osborne's father had the place measured when I was here last, after the Bailey Historical Society told him that the Lacey home missed being the biggest house in the county by ten square feet. After the remeasurement, an additional twenty-five square feet were found. Osborne points out the work done and not done. Three years ago they almost lost the whole thing to termites.

"'Course that gave our Georgia something to go on about since she'd been telling me for years to get it checked for termites. Half the county came out to see the tent go up over the house. You should've seen it."

The southern half of the house, where Osborne's parents used to live, is closed off now. "They wouldn't let us touch a crack on the wall over there for ten years, so there's no telling what needs to be done. And I'm too old to do it." He shakes his head. "Can't hardly keep up with the orchards anymore, much less the house."

A small disk of chewing tobacco appears from his back pocket and he places a pinch between his cheek and gum.

"What just happened didn't. Okay?"

"Fine by me," I say.

No need for a wife to know everything. Most things, yes. Jacklynn and I were friends with a couple who had taken an "honesty oath" after almost breaking up over the husband's longing for blondes in short skirts. The poor guy couldn't take a crap without reporting back to the wife what color it was.

The sky darkens and a light rain begins to fall. We wander back up the front stairs into the shaded coolness of the front sitting room. Ceiling fans push the air through, forcing out the morning's humidity. Osborne motions for me to sit on the couch and lowers himself into a faded recliner.

THE LOST SAINTS OF TENNESSEE

"Feel that? The air is heavy, like it's too tired or full to move. Those poor folks in North Carolina are getting hammered by another hurricane. Thought we'd miss all of it but maybe not. Maybe not."

He begins to cough, a little at first, and then more until it's not clear whether he's getting any air in. I get up, unsure what to do. He waves me back down. Georgia appears, like magic, with a glass of water.

"It's the emphysema," she says, shaking her head. "Do you smoke, Ezekiel?"

I nod.

"It's an awful habit. A deadly one. Osborne quit last year on doctor's orders. On *my* orders. Does your mother still smoke? She started so young. We must have only been eleven."

Mother was puffing away on a Lucky Strike the morning I left. Nothing could get her to stop smoking. Even now with the lung cancer diagnosis. She'd say life was too short not to have a cigarette now and then. And a drink. Mother is not a drunk. Even I won't call her that. But she needs a "glass of tea" or two or three a day like some people need coffee or television.

After dinner, tired sets in so bad Cousin Georgia sends me up to bed with a slice of my favorite hummingbird cake. *Wasn't that lucky?* she said. *I came across the recipe yesterday and decided to make it. You just never know.* Tucker and I stand together at the bottom of the stairs, looking up. An awful lot of stairs separate us from our bed. The dog looks hopefully in my direction.

"Can't do it, buddy. Got my hands full and I'm too tired tonight to carry you up there. Come on. We'll go together."

And so we do. One slow step at a time. The muscles in my back protest, cramped from the long drive.

A nagging thought pushes at me through the exhaustion. Jackie. I should call and check in. Mother, too. After Tucker collapses on the rug next to the bed, I pull the phone off the night table and dial, asking the operator to reverse the charges so Curtis will pay for the call.

"Does it feel strange to be back?" Jackie asks.

This is a good question. I lie back on the bed, the phone cradled against my ear. "Strange isn't the right word."

"Well?"

Through the tiredness, a welcome sense of relief hovers. As if coming here may have been the right choice. The best choice.

"It feels something like home."

"Clayton is your home, Zeke."

I change the subject to our daughters. This produces a long sigh from Jackie. Honora has dyed her hair again. A ghoulish shade of black this time. And there's a boy. A senior. *A senior?*

"He's asked her to the homecoming dance. Sophomore girls hardly ever get asked to homecoming. And he's a cutie, let me tell you."

"What's his name?"

"He's a new kid. Moved to Mabry this year with his mother after his parents divorced."

"I thought we agreed she wouldn't date until she's sixteen. She's not sixteen."

"She's almost sixteen, Zeke. It's just a dance, anyway. And you're not around to tell her no, so I said yes. You want to tell her no, come back and tell her. When, by the way, were you planning on coming home?"

"Listen, I've got to go to bed."

The phone is silent for a moment, misleading me into thinking she's sympathizing with how tired I must be.

"It's always about you, isn't it? Zeke's tired. Better go to bed. Zeke's having a midlife crisis. Better run away from home. Why don't you buy a convertible, too? And take up with a big-breasted twenty-year-old while you're out there?"

She pauses, gathering steam.

"And there's something you should know about your mother. I ran into Daisy yesterday and she told me—"

"Jackie, I know about the lung cancer. Rosie told me. I'm really tired."

The line goes dead.

I run a hand over my face. *Jesus.* Convertible? Midlife crisis? Is that what this is? Do I want to take up with a big-breasted twenty-something?

Too damn tired. My boots fall to the floor with a clatter and I can't be bothered to take off anything else. The old house emits creaking sounds like it, too, is yawning before settling down to bed. The gentle noise of Georgia and Osborne in conversation sifts under the door.

The events of the past few days feel overwhelming. Honora and Louisa believe I have abandoned them. Again. Doug Mitchell's fired me. Probably already hired another guy. Mother is fighting cancer.

Coming to Lacey Farms feels like the best and worst decision. Barring the overdose route, there was no place else to go. A sleeping Tucker begins to whimper as one of his forelegs jerks. Must be chasing the barn cats he glimpsed in the yard.

Mother answers after the second ring. She sounds out of breath.

"It's me. You okay? You don't sound good," I say.

Her voice is muffled for a moment, and I know she is settling herself on the gossip bench that holds the phone in the dining room.

"I'm fine, Ezekiel. Don't worry. I was out in the porch swing when the phone rang, so I hurried in here. I knew it was you. So you're at Georgia's?"

"Yes."

A pause. I should say something about the cancer. Something supportive and nice.

"How's Georgia look? Old yet? Must be nice for you to be back there."

"Georgia looks pretty good. Osborne seems a lot older. They kept my room just like it was before."

There is no need to say before what.

She sighs. "Doesn't surprise me. You're the closest thing they've got to a kid of their own."

Through the phone I can hear her still trying to catch her breath.

"Listen, I should let you go," I say.

"No." She clears her throat. "I'm okay, son. I'm fine."

This is one of the longest phone conversations we have ever had and she wants to prolong it. But the feel of the soft bed beneath me is too tempting.

"You should get some rest. I'm pretty worn out, too, so I'll say good night."

"Oh."

She wants me to keep talking but I can't. Not tonight.

"Good night, Mother."

"'Night, Ezekiel." Her voice is low. "I love you."

~ Twelve ~

1959

Georgia Parker Lacey and my mother, Lillian Parker Cooper, grew up over in Alabama together. Their families lived only a few feet apart on the land Granddaddy Parker owned in Colbert County. Of the ten acres, he parceled out all but a half acre to relatives. Mother liked having cousins to chase through the tall rows of cotton, but there never seemed to be quite enough food or space in the small houses built out of tar paper and Alabama pine.

When she was ten, Mother's family moved the one hundred miles to Clayton. She and Cousin Georgia stayed in touch through letters and saw each other at the annual Parker family picnic. Georgia stayed on in Alabama, running the house and taking care of her mother when she took sick with cancer, until one day she met Osborne Lacey in the general store at Montgomery Landing. Osborne was passing through on his way back home to Virginia, where his family owned more land than anybody else except the state.

Cousin Georgia's letter to Mother after meeting Osborne was extra long. She described how he invited her out to his truck to try a Lacey Farms peach, "the best darned peaches in the South." Cousin Georgia thought Osborne must be full of himself, but there was something gentle in his eyes she liked, so she followed him outside.

"We grow these on our farm back home," he said, pulling a perfectly round peach from a sack on the front seat. "Apples, too."

Georgia bit into the peach and a rush of juice spilled down her chin. Osborne pulled a handkerchief out of his pocket and reached over to wipe the juice.

"I'll do it myself, thank you," Georgia said, taking the handkerchief. "The peaches are real sweet. You're right about that."

He gave her the sack to take home. In return, he asked for her name and address and wrote to her every day for three months until he proposed, by letter, and she accepted, by letter.

Mother went to the wedding in Virginia and swore she'd never go back again. I suspect she was jealous of Georgia and her new role as daughter-in-law of the well-off Laceys, far from Mother's situation as the wife of a failed farmer. For the next decade, Mother only heard about Georgia through news from the Alabama Parkers.

When my tenth-grade history teacher told Mother I was smart enough to get a scholarship to college, she recalled that a fine institution of higher education, the University of Virginia, lay only a few miles from Lacey Farms. During the three years that would pass before my high school graduation, Mother and Georgia exchanged weekly letters. Georgia was not the type to hold a grudge and was glad to be in touch with our family again. Mother never said much about their letters other than an occasional comment to Daddy like *How nice it must be to have a washing machine, Carter,* or *What I wouldn't give to go on vacation.* She did not reveal the grand plan she and Georgia had constructed on my behalf until the fall of my senior year.

I arrived home after a bad basketball practice. Coach Tyler had yelled, *He shoots, he misses, he shoots, he misses,* every time I got near the basket. The only thing on my mind was eating dinner and going to bed. Instead, Mother sat me down on the front porch swing and stood over me, waving a letter in my face like it was the starting flag for the Indy 500.

The source of the letter was obvious from the fineness of the paper. It was so thin the evening shadows danced through the words.

"Cousin Georgia will feed and house you during the four years it will take you to graduate from UVA. The farm's only fifteen miles from Charlottesville. They even have an old car you can use to drive back and forth to school. What do you think of that?"

Her face was transformed, its usual strained or annoyed or tired expression replaced with a look of pure elation. It was the most excited I had seen her.

"And," she went on, "Georgia says every one of those spoiled Lacey men from Osborne back to his great-great-grandfather went to the university, so there should be no problem getting a slot for you. Probably a scholarship for tuition and books, too. Didn't I say you were going to get out of Clayton, Ezekiel?"

She jabbed me in the ribs with a finger. "Haven't I said that every day of your life, son? I swear, the Lord has answered our prayers. He surely has."

I stayed quiet for a bit, mindful of the type of response she'd tolerate. Her plans didn't come as a complete surprise.

The topic of UVA had come up over the years. I knew it was a good school. I also knew I didn't want to go there.

"That's nice of her, Momma," I offered, "but I want to go to UT. They'll give me a scholarship, too. And Jackie and Tommy—"

Mother pulled herself upright. In the space of no more than a minute, her expression changed from disbelief to anger to resolve. The last one was, by far, the most intimidating.

"That's not your choice, Ezekiel."

"Why not?"

I knew I risked a fight, but this was my life.

She kneeled down next to me, reaching for my hand. Hers looked lost on the wide expanse of mine.

"You know UVA is where you should be, son. I've told you and told you how you're the brightest star. You're different from Jackie and Tommy."

She stroked my hair, something she used to do every night when I was a child and couldn't fall asleep. I ducked my head.

There was quiet between us, both of us planning what to say next. When she turned to face me, tears welled in her eyes and I knew I was done. The path I had chosen was being blocked by a force as immovable as one of the century-old hickories near our house.

"Who else in this family can go to UVA? Violet didn't finish high school. Daisy and Rosie will get married soon enough. Your brother couldn't even finish eighth grade."

Daddy's old bluetick, Walker, wandered up on the porch looking for a pat. I scratched behind his ears, the uncomplicated love welcome. The air was filled with the smells of wood smoke and burning piles of leaves.

When Mother spoke again, the words emerged slowly, each one dropping with dead-on accuracy.

"I need you to do this, Ezekiel. For me."

Though only seventeen at the time, I understood that she needed me to be a success more than she needed anything else. All of us kids had heard the stories of Mother's singing, how the sweetness of her voice used to make people cry in church. How she longed to sing on a stage, how she never even made it to the Mabry High annual musical, thanks to getting pregnant with Violet. Mother's failures were many in her eyes and her chances for redemption few.

Carter's voice boomed from the backyard, yelling for me to come play basketball. The solid whack of the ball hitting the side of the house echoed onto the porch. I eased myself out of the swing.

"You go on along," she said. "You'll be leaving your brother soon enough."

∾ Thirteen ∾

1985

The smells of bacon frying and coffee brewing wake me. It is the first time since the divorce that someone has prepared breakfast for me. I lie in bed, content to let the sounds of the morning wash over me. Downstairs, the oven door opens and slams shut, Cousin Georgia baking a pan of biscuits, most likely. I hear a shower turning off somewhere.

The seams of the star quilt covering the bed are fragile beneath my fingers. The individual squares are beginning to fray and pull apart at the edges, showing the same signs of age as everything else at the farm. Tucker stirs awake on the rug, passing gas that smells of the junk he's been eating the past week.

"Man," I complain.

He yawns.

Osborne's heavy footsteps pause outside my room. A light knock on the door sets Tucker to barking.

"Come on in," I say, standing up with a stretch. Judging by the kinks in my neck and the soreness of my back, the mattress must be a holdover from my previous stay.

Dressed in jeans and a long-sleeved white shirt with the Lacey Farms logo—an apple and a peach in a basket—on the pocket, Osborne appears younger this morning. He wears a Smith's Feed and Fuel baseball cap. Backward. It makes him look like the grandfather of one of those singer types who talk more than sing, the ones Honora listens to on her Walkman.

"Sleep all right?" He gives Tucker a pat.

"Out for the count, sir. And you?"

He walks over to the window, lifting the yellow curtains to the side. "I believe this room has one of the nicest views."

My eighteen-year-old self spent more than a few Sundays looking out across the farm instead of studying. Miles of split-rail fence trace the property line until it meets the horizon. It had been hard to grasp how the Laceys owned more land than a person could see with his own eyes. The orchards lie to the north, the barn to the west, with the square of the riding ring in front of it.

"That's the window I'd look out when I couldn't sleep at night. The dark threw a funny purple color across the property. Took me a while to get used to the quiet here. Back home, I was used to trains passing through and making a lot of racket to get me off to sleep."

"You had trouble sleeping? If Georgia knew about it, she would have called Amtrak and got them to divert a train through here."

The thought pleases me.

"No one else has stayed in this room since you left," Osborne says. "Georgia wouldn't have it."

This makes me skittish. The room is a shrine to the boy I was then, not the man I have become.

"I'm sorry Georgia felt that way." I bend down to tug on my boots. "This room no more belongs to me than it does the dog."

"You were like a son to her, Ezekiel. To both of us. You still are."

Pointing to the bed, he says, "That quilt there? Georgia started sewing it the first time your mother sent a letter asking about the university. You weren't more than fifteen. But Georgia told me she felt in her heart you were going to come live with us and she wanted to make you a proper quilt for your bed. She said it had to be a star quilt because that's what your momma was always saying about you—you were the brightest star in the sky."

"Mother said a lot of things." The words come out harsh and dance too close to the edge of whining. "Things didn't turn out quite like Mother planned."

"Seldom do." Osborne's hand wanders up to scratch the back of his head and he seems surprised to feel the bill of the hat. He turns it around to face forward, transforming himself back into the old farmer.

"Georgia will be waiting breakfast on us."

Tucker's ears perk up and he trots out the door behind Osborne.

After the meal Cousin Georgia kisses Osborne good-bye as he heads off to town. She winks at me over his shoulder. As soon as the solid shut of the mahogany front door echoes through the house, she unties the blue apron from around her waist and says the dishes can wait.

"Fill up your coffee cup and follow me."

Tucker is content to sleep off his breakfast in the kitchen. A smoke with coffee feels necessary, but I refrain. Cousin Georgia takes off in the direction of the apple orchard. The morning air settles on us, heavy with humidity. "Thunderstorms later today. That hurricane on the coast is causing all sorts of trouble."

A cow lows out to us from the barn.

"Dairy cow?"

She shakes her head. "Regular old stinky longhorn. Longhorn! About fifteen years ago a semi wrecked on I-64 with a full load of cows. Most of them were killed, but a few survived. The Humane Society put out a call to the farmers around here to take in the rest, since the rancher who owned them couldn't be bothered to come fetch them. We took in three. Down to the last one now."

She pauses at the edge of the riding ring. A gauzy mist floats over the fields. Beyond them, the hills rise up until they grow into proper mountains.

"I need a cigarette, Ezekiel. Have you got one?"

Her mouth sits in a straight line.

"What about the emphysema?"

"I don't have it. Osborne does. I can't smoke around him."

I try to hide a smile as I pull the pack from my shirt pocket and help her light up. Grab a smoke for myself, too. Georgia inhales deeply, as if she's been underwater for hours and just came up for air.

"The man is driving me crazy. Crazy, Ezekiel. I don't know how much more I can stand."

This is not good news. Are there no happily married couples left in the world?

"His nephew took over managing the family's real estate holdings last year. Told Osborne he was welcome to drop by whenever he wanted. Drop by? Oz has run the company for the past twenty years. They thought he was getting too old, which he is, but that's not how you treat a person. Then Mother Lacey died in June, crazy as a june bug by the end. Father Lacey didn't last much longer. He passed in December from a burst aorta."

She tosses the remainder of her coffee into the grass. "Osborne's got what his mother had and he's scared to death. Early Alzheimers, the doctors say. We were so caught up in caring for his father we didn't pay attention to his own forgetfulness. But right after the funeral, when our days stretched out with no one to take care of but ourselves, the symptoms got worse. He'd leave the house only to turn around because he forgot where he was going. Or he'd go to the grocery store with a list I gave him and buy nothing from it, only sweet things he used to eat as a boy."

We finish our smoke in silence. One of Mother's aunts got Alzheimer's when we were kids, though they didn't call it that then. Mother forced us to go see Aunt Ginny at the nursing home every Christmas and Easter. I hated the place with its smells of pee and bad food. Hated the starving looks the residents gave us when we walked by their rooms. I'd get sick to my stomach as soon as we pulled in the parking lot.

Georgia lets out a small, unsure laugh. "Listen to me. Your first morning here and I'm going to have you on the road before lunchtime with my nonsense. Come on." She grabs my hand in hers. "Let's go see the apples."

The sight of row after row of stalwart apple trees brightens her mood. A light breeze carries the heady smell of ripening fruit. Shiny apples wink out from the trees' nooks and crannies.

"Good crop?"

She surveys the orchard, placing a hand on the closest one and glancing up. "The Pippins look really good. In six weeks time, they'll be ready."

After wandering through several rows, she stops to tug a small apple from a tree's lower branch. A pocketknife appears from Georgia's housedress and she slices off a wedge of fruit. The interior is dull green but fading to red. Faint russet-colored dots can be seen on the meat.

"See?" she says. "It's not juicy yet. The flesh is this nice creamy yellow color, but taste it. Not sweet. A few more weeks. These Golden Pearmains are my favorite. We're one of the few orchards left in the state that still grows them. The big orchards won't, because the apples spoil before they can get them to the grocery store. But they make the best cider in the world. The McNatts buy bushels of them from us and press them to sell at their fruit stand."

The sound of a car coming up the drive interrupts us. Georgia frowns.

"The boys must not have been too talkative this morning. Let's walk back."

Fat raindrops begin to fall, slowly at first, then in rapid streams. I pull off my top shirt and hold it over Georgia's head as we hurry back to the house. Osborne stands on the front steps getting drenched, and even I can tell that something is not right. Cousin Georgia rushes to him. Tucker appears and looks from me to the Laceys as if he's not sure who to let cross the threshold.

"Come in the house now," she says to Osborne. "What's the matter? You're so pale."

He shakes his head. She grabs one of his hands and pulls him inside. Sensing they need to be alone, I back down the steps.

"Ezekiel," he calls, "don't go. It's nothing you can't hear."

Georgia's impatience with him appears to grow at the same rate as her worry. Water trails down Osborne's clothes, puddling in small circles around his work boots.

The sharp buzzing noise of an electric hedger comes from the back. Osborne looks up.

"It's Jimmy in the back, darling. That's all."

"What's he doing?"

"Trimming the holly bushes. You know how they like to take over that side of the house."

A dark look crosses Osborne's face. "Now, Georgia, what are those holly bushes trying to take over?"

"Nothing. Nothing. Hush. Tell us what's gotten you so upset this morning."

"It's Joe Cummins. He dropped dead of a heart attack right at my feet while we were having coffee at the Feed and Fuel. Just fell out of his chair, grabbing at his chest, and then he was gone." He snaps his fingers. "No more Joe."

Georgia's hands fly to her mouth and she shuts her eyes for a moment before wrapping her arms around him. Osborne throws off her embrace.

"We all knew he had a bad heart. But I've never seen a man die before. Right at my feet. And one of my oldest friends. I don't want to tell you about it. I just want to walk for a while."

"It's raining," she says.

He steps out the front door. Georgia grabs a slicker from the coat tree. "At least wear this."

With slow movements, Osborne does as she asks and takes off in the direction of the lake, turning back long enough to say they should go see Joe's wife when he returns. We stand in the hallway, Georgia and I, for a good five minutes, watching Osborne. I don't know what to say.

"Why don't I go into town today? You don't need a houseguest right now."

A world of hurt and worry settles on her face, deepening the lines around her eyes. And then it vanishes. "Don't be silly. Come help me with the horses. We better get them fed before the weather gets worse. Our stable boy is down in Florida at Disney World this week with his family."

Rain jackets are procured. The stables are situated down the knoll from the main house. Osborne Sr. developed a taste for horse racing and bought two racehorses right about the time I was leaving the farm. Though there are ten stalls, only three of them are occupied now. Cousin Georgia hands me a bucket filled with oats and I follow behind. We feed a pinto first, then a sleek, black Thoroughbred, and lastly an old white horse who tosses his head when he sees me until Cousin Georgia whacks him on the butt and tells him to cut it out.

"Grab a brush from the tack room and brush Darcy. She's the pinto. Another one of Osborne's rescue animals. You don't even want to hear that poor creature's story. Watch out for her back feet, though. If you catch a big tangle on her tail, she'll stomp you."

In the next stall Georgia brushes the large black horse with strong sure strokes and I try to copy her as best as I can. We work our way from the head to the tail. The sweet smell of hay mingles with the warm, strong scent of the horses and the leather of the saddles.

"It's a wife's nightmare, you know." She speaks while spreading an armful of fresh hay in Darcy's stall. "I'm sure Joe got up this morning, ate his two eggs and bacon, and kissed Eliza good-bye just like he did every day."

Darcy stomps the moment I near her tail with the brush. If I hadn't been standing as far as possible from her hindquarters, she would have neatly crushed my foot. Georgia laughs, sounding like a girl of eighteen, not a woman in her seventies.

"It's funny how horses have such predictable personalities, isn't it? She's been doing that since the day Osborne brought her home from the rescue farm in Lynchburg. Broke two of Oz's toes that first year."

"Thanks for letting me brush her."

"You're tough. Now go give old Whitey a good brushing. She's too tired to try anything."

While Whitey does not try to stomp me, she does keep reaching her mouth back to bite my hand. Her teeth are huge and yellow.

"If I remember right, people around here foxhunt," I say. "Do you ever use the horses for hunting?"

Georgia snorts. "Do any of these motley beasts look like they're ready for hunting? Well, maybe Diamond here."

She gives him an apologetic pat. "Foxhunting is not something Oz or I will ever do. Can you think of anything more ridiculous, really? We ride the horses, of course. Not much else to be done with them. Though Osborne and I have stopped taking a nightly ride around the property. He fell off Whitey this summer, I don't know who was more embarrassed—Osborne or Whitey. We haven't gone out since."

After shutting the horses up snug in the barn, we head back to the house. Georgia stops and shades her eyes with a hand, looking off toward the eastern fields. Osborne's figure is headed for a dense grove of cedars and hickories.

"Will he be okay, do you think?" I ask.

She pauses for a second, her gaze fixed on her husband. "No, I don't suppose he will."

～ Fourteen ～

1959

I told no one of the plan to attend UVA. In our junior year of high school Jackie and I had decided we would both go to the University of Tennessee. After four years in Knoxville, we'd get married and settle wherever we wanted. Atlanta, maybe. Or Washington, DC. But Mother was an expert at making a person doubt himself. She kept saying Virginia was the only way to make something of myself. Virginia held opportunity. When she said the word, she emphasized each syllable: op-por-tu-ni-ty. And when this approach did not have the desired effect, she'd say, *There's always the military for our Clayton boys, if you want to go off and get yourself killed while you see the world.*

The day before the homecoming game, Jackie and I walked out to the courtyard behind the school to have lunch away from the cafeteria crowd. The poplar trees lining the back of the school were deep yellow. Jackie's hand slipped easily into mine.

"I need to tell you something," I said.

She seemed distracted and murmured something I couldn't hear.

"What?" I said.

"I need to tell you something, too." A shaky sort of smile followed this statement. My Jackie is beautiful now, but back then there wasn't a girl for a hundred miles who looked as good as she did in a sweater and skirt—all rounded shoulders and soft breasts and ankles so small I could touch my thumb and forefinger around their circumference.

"Mother's cousin Georgia in Virginia said I could come and live with her and go to school at the university there. Thinks I'll get a scholarship, too."

The words tumbled out in one breath. The tone was upbeat and a tad proud, as if this might inspire Jackie to respond likewise.

Her mouth formed the shape of a small *o*. She said nothing for as long as it took the blue jays to find the crumbs from our pimento cheese sandwiches. Next thing I knew she hurled herself at me, hitting me first on the shoulder, then the back, screaming the whole time about what a selfish bastard I was and how dare I leave her now, especially now, and that she hated me, just hated me.

I grabbed her by the wrists. "Calm down."

"I won't. You don't really love me, do you? You've been planning this for a while now. Leaving. Me."

Her breath came in short bursts. I loosened my grip, afraid I might be hurting her. The wind caught the paper bags from our lunch and they made a scritch-scratch sound as they scattered across the pavement.

"It's not like that, Jackie."

She turned her back to me. I reached for her arm.

"Please. Look at me."

She shook her head.

"Okay, then, I'll talk this way. My mother just told me about Virginia." Of course this wasn't completely true. "I may not even get in. Who knows? It doesn't change us."

When Jackie finally turned around, the look on her face scared me more than any words she could say. It was hopelessness, pure and simple.

Her news beat mine. She was pregnant, about two months along. We had begun making love the year before. And after we started, stopping didn't seem possible, though we tried. We both had plans. Jackie wanted to become a dress designer. I wanted to go to college and to visit places like New York and Mexico, to see what it was like to live where people crowded you on all sides in subways and trains and buildings rose up like steeples toward the sky. Springfield, Massachusetts, was also on the list because Carter wanted to check out the Basketball Hall of Fame.

Jackie hadn't been feeling well lately. Last week she'd gotten sick out our back door when Mother was frying a chicken. I remembered the searching look Mother gave me that night but hadn't paid it any mind. Now she would have Violet and me disgrace the family.

"There's a doctor in Memphis, Zeke. Rachel Blackson went to him last year to—" She couldn't finish the sentence. "You know."

Still reeling, I didn't catch her meaning. "To what?"

The pained expression on her face told me. I had never felt so out of my depth. Of course everyone knows he can get a girl pregnant by having sex with her. But no one thinks it will actually happen. And we had been careful—most of the time.

"Is that what you want to do, Jackie? Go to this doctor in Memphis?"

"I don't know what I want." She walked away from me, headed to the football field, her shoulders heaving. I caught up and turned her around, tilting her face up to me.

"We'll figure it out, okay? Just give me a little time."

"We don't have a lot of time."

"Maybe you and the baby can come live with me at Cousin Georgia's. She's got a big old mansion. What difference would you and a little baby make? They'd probably love it because they couldn't ever have kids."

This stopped the sobs. She pulled a handkerchief from her pocket and blew her nose. "Maybe I could go to school there, too?"

"Must be a girl's school nearby. Has to be."

"I could take a class a semester and maybe your cousin could watch the baby?" she said.

It could work. With the sound of the second lunch bell ringing around us and the sidewalk filling with students, we latched on to the plan. Somehow, the future we dreamed about in the backseat of Tommy Jackson's Buick only a month before might still be possible.

"Jacklynn's pregnant." Not able to look my parents in the eye, I stared at the bare wood floor, scraping the toe of my shoe in the light coat of dust.

The air in the living room went still. Daisy and Rosie could be heard in the kitchen fighting over whose turn it was to do the dishes. Carter had a cold and was lying down in the bedroom.

"Say it again," Mother said.

I looked up. Her hands cradled her face, as if in shock. To repeat the words seemed too awful.

"Do it," she said.

This time I spoke softly, so only she could hear me. She covered her mouth and tore out of the room, leaving my father and me alone.

"Goddamn it to hell, son."

He lit a Marlboro, hesitated, then gave me one. I tried not to cough as the smoke drifted into my lungs. The raw, burning sensation spread through my chest, a distraction at least from the look in my father's eyes.

The sounds of Mother's crying carried in from the porch. Daddy cursed and slammed the front door.

"Crying's not going to do anybody good, now is it?"

"No, sir."

His broad shoulders curved forward, making him look older and worn down.

He smashed the cigarette into a metal ashtray. "You'll do right by her, of course."

I nodded, though not sure exactly what he meant. I figured marry her, which I wanted to do anyway. Seemed like I had always wanted her to be Jacklynn Cooper.

"I'd marry her in a heartbeat, Daddy. I would."

He grunted. "You will. How far along?"

"Two months."

"Go on to bed now. I'll talk to your mother."

He didn't have to say it twice. I headed off to the back bedroom as quick as Uncle Leroy used to grab a shotgun on the first day of squirrel hunting season. The only people who knew Jackie and I had been fooling around were Tommy Jackson and his girlfriend, Mary Alice. We would all go park by the lake. Tommy and Mary Alice walked in the woods for a bit while Jackie and I stayed in the car; then we'd do the same for them. Making love to Jackie, even in the backseat with cracked leather pressing into us, felt like the closest thing to touching God I could imagine. When I was inside her, and she put her arms around my neck and whispered my name, there wasn't a person alive who could have told me what we were doing was bad.

∾ Fifteen ∾

1985

By one o'clock, Osborne and Cousin Georgia leave to spend the night with Joe Cummins's widow. Georgia kisses me on the cheek as they walk out, saying she's put dinner on a plate in the fridge, just warm it up in the oven, and keep the radio on.

"This might be a bad storm. You and the dog sit tight. The horses are in the barn so they'll be okay. Flashlights and candles are in the top of the hall closet in case we lose power. I'll call you later to check in."

A loud crash of thunder reinforces her words as their car eases down the driveway. Tucker decides the bathtub is the safest place and manages somehow to get in without my help.

The echo of the doorbell sets off Tucker's barking. The afternoon has faded into twilight without my noticing. The storm is in full force—buckets of rain thrash at the windows, and lightning tears across the dark sky every ten minutes, followed by a boom of thunder. Through the curtains of the front-room window I glimpse a person dressed in jeans and a hooded green raincoat at the door. The dog barks as if Grant is advancing on Shiloh.

"Shut up, dog." If he's that worried about it, he can get out of the damned tub and stand guard.

Caution makes me call out, "Who is it?" The wind takes most of the response, but I catch the word "neighbor" and ease the door open.

The stranger rushes in, kicking the door shut with a muddy boot.

"God, it's awful out there. I'm Elle Chambers. I live on the farm across the road. Georgia called and asked me to check on you. So, here I am."

She is tall, with a nose a little too big for her face, and dark, curly hair that clings to her head like a tight cap. She looks to be in her early thirties. A large knapsack appears from her back and she reaches into it. What could be so important that it needs toting in the middle of a storm?

Three glass jars emerge. Their contents glow an amber color tinged with pink.

"Applesauce," she explains. "Made it fresh today. I heard about Joe Cummins keeling over. Mr. Lacey loves homemade applesauce."

She hands over each jar, placing them in my arms. They hold a lingering warmth and the scent of cinnamon.

"You'll want to put those in the fridge."

"Right."

When I return, Elle is sitting on the couch with her legs tucked up beneath her, boots left by the front door. She has found the battery-operated radio and tuned it to the local station, setting it on the coffee table.

"There's a tornado watch out. You need to keep this thing on. My horses are about to go crazy, so I've got a bad feeling about tonight."

She gestures at a photo on one of the side tables. "I would have known you were Zeke even if Mrs. Lacey hadn't told me. You look just as you did then, give or take a few wrinkles."

The silver frame holds a picture of me, Cousin Georgia, and Osborne out in the orchard, each one of us holding up an apple. Osborne's father had taken the photo, telling us to look damn proud of those apples, the best damned apples in the state of Virginia.

"Mrs. Lacey is thrilled you're here. How long are you planning on staying?"

Her red T-shirt is snug, and the soft outline of her breasts distracts me, as do her hands—the fingers are long and tapered, elegant, the nails short and unpainted. The ring finger is bare. She catches me staring and the corners of her mouth curve upward.

"Staying long?"

"To tell you the truth, I'm not sure."

"You won't find a prettier place to stay, that's for sure. Do you know what Thomas Jefferson said about those hills out there?" She points out the window, where, at the moment, nothing but rivulets of water can be seen. "He said they are the 'Eden of the United States.' I've lived at my farm for four years. Never want to move anywhere else again."

She exudes confidence bordering on arrogance, an unfamiliar trait in a woman for me. It has been a long time since

I made simple conversation with a woman not related to me. Too long. I sit, hands in lap, struck dumb.

"Do you like to ride?" she asks.

"Depends on what."

"Horses. What else is there?"

"Don't know how."

"Big guy like you, doesn't know how to ride a little old horse?"

She is teasing, knocking me off balance so I don't know whether to tease back or walk over to the couch and put my hands in her hair and kiss her until morning.

Curiosity gets the better of Tucker and he wanders in to check out the enemy. He determines zero threat and comes near for a pat. Elle obliges, stroking his fur in such a pleasing way that he takes up residence on her foot.

"Starved for affection. Poor animal."

I bristle. "Yes, poor thing."

She stands up and heads for the door. "I'll meet you at nine o'clock tomorrow morning at the stables here. By noon tomorrow—"

Neither of us has noticed how the rain has suddenly stopped outside and the wind can't be heard. Silence surrounds us except for an insistent beeping coming from the radio. Elle stops and turns up the volume. An F3 tornado has touched down three miles west of Bailey. All surrounding towns are to take shelter immediately.

"Where's the storm cellar, Zeke?" Her teasing manner is gone, replaced by a sense of calm urgency. Clayton has never seen a tornado. Our part of the world suffers severe thunderstorms and an occasional ice storm.

"I don't remember." I head for the back door, convinced it must be within a few feet of the house. Her hand reaches out for my arm, pulling me back. The strength of the pull surprises me.

"We don't have time."

It occurs to me that I might, at last, have found a place where life feels promising again only to face certain death by a funnel cloud the size of Rhode Island. A sound somewhere between a laugh and strangulation escapes my lips.

"Jesus." She mumbles something under her breath. "Thank God I put the horses in the barn. They should be all right. What about the Laceys' horses? Do you know if they're in the barn?"

I want to say, *Who gives a shit about the horses—What about us?* "Yes, we put them in the barn earlier."

Elle scoops up the radio and races into the middle of the first-floor hallway, throwing open closet doors along the way. The doors slam against the smooth surface of the wall and I wonder if they will leave marks, if I will be here in the morning to check, if Georgia and Osborne will mind if they do. A closet meets with her approval and she begins throwing boxes out of it.

"Find a flashlight. Two if you can."

The flashlights are in the top of the hall closet, just as Georgia said they were, and I pray the batteries are not the same ones from my last visit to Lacey Farms. In an attempt to appear in control of the situation, I question Elle's choice of closet and suggest alternate ones.

"Shut up, Zeke. Help me so we can make room for the three of us."

In five minutes, we manage to empty all of the closet's contents into the hallway, clearing a four-foot-by-four-foot space. Tucker goes in first, tail tucked between his legs and eyes wild. An escalating whining noise enters the house from outside, disturbing the previous stillness. The lights flicker once, twice, go black. A look passes between Elle and me.

"It's coming," she says.

We sit facing each other in the closet. Elle shuts the door and darkness closes around us.

～ Sixteen ～

1959

The Friday after Jacklynn told me about the baby, Tommy Jackson and I were waiting for her after gym class like we always did. We were talking about how we got creamed the night before by Chickasaw's basketball team when Jackie's best friend, Kate Wright, came running up to us. She was crying and panting so hard we couldn't make out her words.

"What's wrong?" I asked.

"Just come," she said, pulling me by the hand. "Jackie keeled right over in algebra class, holding her stomach like she was about to die. Bill Smyte and Curtis Brown carried her to the nurse. She couldn't walk, it hurt so bad. And Nurse Kelly called an ambulance. They're outside right now."

The three of us ran out to the front of the school. We made it in time to see the ambulance pulling away. Tommy immediately went to the principal's office and convinced Mr. Downey's secretary to give us all a ride over to the hospital.

Kate held my hand the whole way. I wondered if she knew about the baby, and I guessed, by the look on her face, that she did. Mrs. Riley chattered at us, telling me it was probably nothing but a bad stomach flu or maybe appendicitis—did I know whether Jackie still had her appendix?

The school had called Jackie's mother, and she drove up to the hospital at the same time we did. We all ran inside. A nurse spotted Mrs. Chatham and asked if she was Jackie's mother.

"Come on then," the nurse said. "And what's your name, son?"

"Ezekiel."

"The patient wants you, too. Follow me." We trailed her down a hallway, the smell of floor polish and stale sickness strong enough to make my stomach turn, until she stopped at a group of metal chairs. She told us to take a seat; the doctor would be in shortly.

Mrs. Chatham wouldn't sit. "Tell me how my daughter is. What's wrong with her?"

"Ma'am, I'm Nurse Charlotte and I'm telling you your daughter will be fine. I promise."

She smiled so surely before leaving us that it made me feel better. I wanted to tell Mrs. Chatham everything then— about the baby, and how I'd marry Jackie and we'd go live with Cousin Georgia while I got my degree, so I could make good money for us—but I couldn't manage to speak a word, it all got caught in my throat. Mrs. Chatham sat with her hands clasped over her red purse while I slouched in my seat and prayed hard for the first time since I was little. Prayed for Jackie to be all right; prayed for the baby to be okay. I knew any baby made between us would be a beautiful one. I thought about seeing it for the first time and holding it, having the baby grab hold of my finger with his own.

A short man came down the hallway toward us, hurried strides closing the distance quickly. *Dr. Campbell* was embroidered in neat black letters on his white coat.

"Your daughter is in the process of miscarrying right now, Mrs. Chatham. She's bleeding heavily and the cramping's severe. I want to admit her to the hospital."

Mrs. Chatham was shaking her head as if she didn't understand. Not all of the words made sense but I knew what miscarrying meant. No more baby.

"I think I'd know if my daughter was pregnant, Doctor."

Dr. Campbell placed the tips of his index fingers to his nose and cast a sideways look in my direction.

"She's pregnant with my baby."

The words were barely out of my mouth before she slapped me. There was no time to dodge it. For a small woman, she packed enough weight behind the slap to make my cheek blaze with the sting.

"You did this, Ezekiel Cooper! My baby girl's going to die because of you!"

The doctor cleared his throat. "Ma'am, your daughter won't die. And her chances of a future healthy pregnancy are good, given her age and general good health."

Nurse Charlotte came up behind him. She said Jackie was asking to see me. I looked over at Mrs. Chatham. It didn't seem right that I should see Jackie before her. But she waved me away. Said she needed to phone Mr. Chatham. The nurse led me back down the hallway to Jackie.

Nurse Charlotte stopped before a closed curtain and

turned to me. "Your girl looks pretty bad right now. You going to be able to handle that?"

How bad was bad? Would there be blood pouring out of her, spilling onto the floor? My mind kept spinning round and round.

Jackie looked dead. Her eyes were closed and her face blanched so white it was hard to tell where she ended and the bedsheets began. I couldn't keep a "Jesus" from escaping my mouth.

Nurse Charlotte glowered. "Go over and say something. Hold her hand. Go on." She nudged me in the back.

I searched for Jackie's hand beneath the sheet. It felt so cold and small in my own. I brushed the hair back from her forehead and leaned down to kiss her. When she opened her eyes, I could see all of the light had gone out of them.

She began to speak and I had to bend down to hear.

"This solves everything, doesn't it?"

"*Shh*. I love you."

She closed her eyes again. Delicate blue veins stretched across the eyelids and I traced them ever so lightly until her face creased with pain.

"What it is?"

Nurse Charlotte drew me back from the bed. "She probably needs more pain medicine. You run along now."

The miscarriage did, in a way, solve things. I could go to Virginia as planned. All alone, as Mother liked to remind me. "Don't be trying to sneak that girl onto the train. This is a blessing, Zeke. A blessing."

My father had been kinder, telling me he was sorry for both Jackie and me. Within a few days, Jackie was out of the hospital. She spent another week at home resting. I tried to come see her every day but her mother said she didn't want visitors.

On Jackie's first day back at school, I gave her a clutch of corn poppies to cheer her up. She said thank you, all polite-like. There was talk running around school about why Jackie went to the hospital. But since none of us—not me, not Kate, and not Tommy—would say anything about it, nobody could say for sure Jackie had been pregnant. They also couldn't say for sure she hadn't been.

Jackie and I met for lunch, the first time we'd been alone since it happened. I asked if she wanted to go to Grayson's Café and she shook her head, said there would be too many people. She wasn't hungry, so we ended up walking around the campus.

"I'm so sorry this happened," I said. "I feel responsible."

She held my hand as we walked but didn't lace her fingers through mine like normal. Instead, she grasped just a few of my fingers, the hold less sure.

"You look so sad, Jackie. I can't take it."

She stopped walking, let go of my hand. "You know what the worst part is? I feel like I did this. I didn't know if I wanted this baby, Zeke. I prayed that it would just go away and everything could be like it was."

Jackie hid her face from me and I watched her shoulders shake as she cried. I tried to put my arms around her but she pushed me away.

"God doesn't work that way, sweet girl. It wasn't your fault. The baby just wasn't strong enough to be born. I talked with Preacher Dawson last Sunday and he told me God has a special place in heaven for all of the lost unborn babies. A real special place."

I put my arm around her waist, trying to bring her close.

"Please. Don't touch me." She walked ahead, putting distance between us. "Don't you understand?"

I followed her to the athletic fields. The noon sun beat down on the running track. I fished out my Cleveland cap from my jeans and pulled the brim low over my eyes.

"It's getting hot early, don't you think?" A stupid thing to say.

"I don't feel the heat," she said. "I don't feel anything."

I stood there with my hands in my pockets and watched Jackie walk away. I wanted to go after her, to tell her I loved her, but my feet stayed planted where they were. Her sadness scared me. I didn't know how to be that sad. Didn't want to know. It would be another fifteen years before Carter's death left me with more grief than I could carry.

May rolled around and everybody in the senior class was making plans for prom and graduation. Tommy kept bugging me to ask Jackie to the prom. I told him to shut up. In the second week of May I caught Jackie outside of homeroom.

"We need to talk. About graduation. About prom."

She clasped her books to her chest and rested her chin on top of them. Her eyes were soft as she looked at me.

"We'll go to the prom together," she said. "The other stuff we'll talk about later, okay?"

"I got a letter from UVA. Full scholarship."

The bell rang and I couldn't tell if she'd heard me or not. Before I could ask she disappeared into class. The teacher shut the door in my face, leaving me to stare at its chipped white paint.

The night of the prom Jackie told me she'd decided not to go to college. Not even Freed-Hardeman in McNairy

County. Said she wasn't ready to be away from home. I begged her to think about coming to Virginia.

"If you live here and I go to school in Virginia, we'll never see each other. Why don't we just get married and then you could live with me there?"

"Is that a proposal?"

She looked so beautiful that night, dressed in a blue satin dress the color of her eyes and her hair swept up, leaving the nape of her neck exposed. I'd been longing to kiss that spot since I picked her up.

"You bet that was a proposal."

She threw back her head and laughed. The happy sound went straight to my heart. The world felt like it might be tipping right side up again.

"That was not a proposal," she said.

Jackie drew me out to the dance floor as the band played "Are You Lonesome Tonight?" I held her close and tried to breathe in the scent of her, to bury it in my memory so that months from now, I'd be able to close my eyes and conjure the sweetness of the White Shoulders perfume and the warmth of her skin, which always smelled as if she'd just come in from the sun. Her head rested against my shoulder and my palm pressed into the curve of her back. The months of being apart fell away. The dance seemed to last forever and when the music stopped, Jackie kept swaying.

"Don't stop," she whispered. "Everything will be different when we stop. Just keep moving."

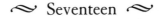 Seventeen

1985

The noise is a roaring, howling scream punctuated by claps of thunder. Nothing can survive this.

Tucker claws his way into my lap, panting so fast a heart attack may take him before the storm. His panicked scratches on my arms dot the floor with small, dark circles of blood. A buzzing noise comes from the radio cradled in Elle's lap. Her face is thrown into the closet's shadows by the flashlight beam, revealing nothing of how she is feeling. The words *hang on, hang on, hang on* whirl through my head. I whisper them into Tucker's ear. *Hang on, boy, hang on.* The warmth of another hand closes around mine. Elle and I are now both holding on to the dog.

A vibrating throb pulses through the house. Elle grips my hand tighter. I lie like a son of a bitch and tell her we're going to be fine.

"Yep. No problem," she says, yelling the words above the chaos.

One minute passes. Then another. The rattling will not stop.

Jackie was not a grace-under-pressure kind of person. When the girls were little, I would get semihysterical calls at work from her. *Louisa stuck an M&M up her nose and I can't get it out; get home NOW. Honora fell off the porch and her arm hurts and is bleeding and it might be broken, for Christ's sake. Did I tell you she's BLEEDING?*

"Go out with me."

Tucker stops panting for a second.

"What?" Elle yells.

The wind lessens. "When this is over, let's go on a date like regular people do."

Elle aims the flashlight at me, its brightness forcing me to shield my eyes. "Are you crazy?"

Tucker licks her hand. *Traitor.* Before I can figure out what to say, the dog eases himself up. Elle and I lean on the closet door, listening. The steady fall of rain drums on the roof. Thunder echoes again but from a distance now. The tornado is gone.

We make a quick tour of the house and the only damage we find is a few blown-out windows on the back side. The glass crunches beneath our boots like egg shells cracking. I try to call Georgia and Osborne but the phone lines are down. When I suggest that Elle should spend the night at Lacey Farms, she says she has horses to mind.

"Let me help you, then."

"I can handle it."

"But you don't know what it's going to be like over there. It could be a lot worse."

The raincoat is zipped, the hood pulled back over the short dark hair. The movements are efficient, swift. I do not want to let her go. Neither does the dog. She gives him a pat.

"Look," she says. It's not clear if she's talking to the dog or to me. "I won't go out with you but I'll give you riding lessons. Assuming we both still have horses to ride. I've got to go."

Before I can respond, she slams the door shut behind her. I collapse on the bench in the front hallway, my pulse still crazy from adrenaline. The rain pings against the windows now as if it is only a normal thunderstorm. The flashlight guides me into the kitchen to a lone Budweiser in the fridge. Elle's applesauce sits next to a tub of margarine. Still standing, I make my way through a whole jar of the sweet fruit, giving Tucker the last spoonful. There is little left to do except drink the beer and fall asleep on the sofa. Tucker throws himself on the floor in front of me, unwilling to let me out of his sight.

The power comes back on at five o'clock in the morning, flooding the living room with stark light. The wind and rain have stopped. In the predawn, the front window reveals shadows of the mess left behind. Branches cover the driveway. One oak tree is upended, the tentacles of its roots exposed. The morning's silence is uneasy; not one bird is singing. The front porch light guides the dog and me around the branches as we walk down the front steps. Pale gray roof shingles lie on the ground in groups of twos and threes. The phone jangles from inside the house. At least we've got electricity and BellSouth.

"Didn't wake you, did I?" Elle sounds hoarse, as if she hasn't made it to sleep yet.

"I'm awake."

"I can see the Laceys' driveway from my top floor and it looks a mess. The dog and you doing okay?"

"How's your place?"

"Storm went right around me. The horses nearly broke out of their stalls but settled down after I forced tranquilizers down their throats."

This conjures an image of a horse rearing up over Elle, powerful hooves inches from her head. "You could've been hurt. You should have let me help you."

No response.

"You should check on the horses over there," she says. "Heard from Georgia and Osborne?"

"Not yet. Wait a minute."

A white Cadillac drives slowly up to the house, making wide loops to avoid branches along the way.

"Listen, they're coming home right now. I should go."

There is a pause and both of us seem uncertain how to end the conversation. Tucker lets out a bark announcing the car's imminent arrival.

"Call me when you're ready for a riding lesson," she says before hanging up.

My hand lingers over the phone. I'm itching to call back and tell her to keep talking; it doesn't matter what she says. I like the feel of her voice next to my ear.

The last time a woman besides Jackie seemed worth the trouble was right after the divorce. Leona Price worked at the plant as a secretary. I walked by her desk every day on the way to the floor. Soon as word got around about Jackie and me splitting up, Leona took it upon herself to say hello. It didn't take long to notice how the top two buttons of her blouse always seemed to be undone. The divorce might have sent me crawling into a hole, but I wasn't dead.

Leona and I lasted two months. The sex was good; she had a beautiful body and always seemed in the mood. But I got tired of having to tell her how pretty she looked and listen to her go on about how she hated her job, her house, her mother. Jackie found out about the two of us, which wasn't hard to do in a town the size of Clayton. It was probably one of my sisters who told her, Daisy most likely. When Leona and I had been seeing each other for a few weeks, I ran into Jackie and the girls at the Mabry Piggly Wiggly. Honora and Lou hugged me until Jackie told them to go pick out something for dinner. The custody agreement called for them to spend every other weekend with me but the shed was cramped, so it ended up being more like once a month.

Jackie leaned over to me and said, "And how is Leona the Loose?"

She was jealous and had no right to be. So I said I was glad, after all these years, to be with a woman who didn't need to be talked into fooling around. It wasn't true. Not all the way true at least. But enough true to hit home, making Jackie turn and storm off.

"Thank God you're all right, Ezekiel!" Cousin Georgia hugs the breath out of me before turning to the house. "Look at it! I told you, Oz, it would stand up to that storm. And it did! Just a few roof shingles!"

Osborne climbs out of the car with neither relief nor happiness on his face. He plants his feet wide and puts his hands on his hips, looking out toward the lake.

"Tornado didn't touch down here. Or we would've lost everything. What do you say, Zeke? Did it pass over the house?"

The Cummins's place, where they spent the night, lay three miles to the west and only suffered high winds and rain. The three of us make our way around the house, surveying the property as we go. Tucker trails behind, sniffing at every branch. When we reach the north side of the house, Osborne stops short. Georgia gasps and grabs his hand, hides her face in his shoulder. Where yesterday stood neat rows of apple trees, today stands nothing. The orchard is gone. Not a single tree remains, only an empty dirt plot.

The path of the tornado becomes clear in the morning light. It touched down at the western edge of the orchard, churning up everything between it and the lake. The loblolly pines I had admired only the day before are broken in half like matchsticks. I close my eyes at the sight, wishing I had been able to prepare them to view this.

A black and white barn cat speeds across the dirt. Tucker makes a halfhearted lunge for it. The sun breaks over the Blue Ridge, spilling amber light through the fog and illuminating the strange emptiness of the orchard. The wind carries the sound of a car starting somewhere. Surrounding farm owners must be making the same inventory as the Laceys, waking to worlds altered.

Osborne lets go of Georgia's hand. He turns and walks back to the house, shoulders hunched and head down. Standing next to me, Georgia shakes her head.

"Lord have mercy," she says softly.

∽ PART II ∽

LILLIAN
1985

Blessed is he whose transgression is forgiven, whose sin is covered . . . When I kept silence, my bones waxed old through my roaring all the day long . . . Thou art my hiding place; thou shalt preserve me from trouble; thou shalt compass me about with songs of deliverance.

Psalm 32:1-3

∼ Eighteen ∼

I am not dead. Yet. My body is wearing out, too tired to bother much anymore. Violet drove me to Tolliver yesterday to hear the results of the chest X-ray. Dr. Trent said there's a spot on one of my lungs. Isn't it amazing when you think about it— that a machine can see right through your skin, through your blood, and see what's wrong inside?

I'm not going to stop smoking. What for? So I can live a bit longer? No, thank you.

The twenty-seven-mile trip back to Clayton felt like it took hours. The green branches of pine tree after pine tree blurred past. I was jealous of their tallness, their view down on all of us humans, shuffling around at ground level, never sure of where we're going or why we're going there. Violet sniffled away in the driver's seat, crying enough tears for both of us.

"We'll fight this, Momma," she said. "You're too young for us to lose you."

I told her to wipe her eyes and concentrate on not getting us killed on the way home.

This town is about as near dead as I feel. Nobody but old people lives in Clayton anymore. And there's not many of us left. Carter Sr.'s been gone almost five years now. Heart attack at sixty-three. My Violet still lives in Clayton but only because she and Louis can't afford anything else. It all started with the school. In 1968 they closed it and bused the kids over to Mabry. Now what family is going to move to a town without a school? Way before that the lumber mill shut down. Then the number 35 and 36 trains stopped running every day. The Main Street Hotel went out of business in 1960, and on and on until what's left is a bunch of empty, falling-down buildings and town folk who are dying more than they're living.

The phone rang off and on the whole night. I didn't pick up. Nothing to say, really. Daisy probably called first. Then Violet. I imagine my oldest daughter spent most of the evening watching my house out her kitchen window, trying to make sure I didn't stick my head in the oven. Not that I would. But it's good to know what your options are.

Ezekiel ran away from home today. Threw a duffel bag and that stinky dog into his truck. Wouldn't tell me where he's going. I wonder if Violet told him my news. If she did, he didn't say a word about it. Of course, that's not unusual. It's been twenty-five years since the child said more than "Good dinner, Mother" or "I'll fix your roof on Sunday" or "Hello, Mother." Still.

Summer is almost gone again. It's been Mississippi hot around here. Muggy. Thunderstorm every week. Nothing to do really when it's miserable like this. Nothing but lie about and think. Remembering is the only thing left to me. And it's not enough. If Dr. Trent's right, the cancer will eat through my lungs until there's nothing left. Unless he operates. Then I have a chance. Unless the surgery kills me.

We slip out of our mothers with a certain number of days for living already decided. Now it's like the doctor's waved one of those yellow NASCAR caution flags in front of me. My husband loved to watch NASCAR on TV. I didn't mind it. Going fast was something I could appreciate.

No one left to pay much attention to me. There's some telling left to do, though. If someone wants to listen, fine. If not, doesn't bother me. All I need do is tell.

The starting point is the middle, where everything fell into place and fell apart. In 1941 I was pregnant for the third time. I knew it would be a boy. A dream kept coming to me where two dark-headed boys sat perched on a limb, high up in a catalpa tree. Every time they called to me I would climb up, but as soon as my hand reached out to them, I'd fall to the ground.

Carter Sr. told me not to get his hopes up for a boy. After the girls were born, he figured I couldn't make a son. We didn't have any of the tests you get nowadays to tell you what it will be ahead of time. You got what you got.

Lord, did I get big—could barely walk, couldn't tie my own shoes for months, kept burping up every bite of food I managed to get down. My husband liked to die one night when I lifted up my gown and told him to watch the belly. Looked like there was an octopus inside me, poking through the skin of my stomach, with arms and legs here, there, and everywhere.

"Jesus, Lillian, what have you got in there?" he said.

About a week before the boys were born, I was out on the front porch swing with my feet up. The October air blew nice and cool against my skin. For once, Carter Sr. had told me to go sit while he gave Violet and Daisy their baths. The girls started wailing for me to come. Their Daddy never gave them a bath. Carter told them to hush up, and so they did. I was grateful Carter was around. His heart murmur kept him out of the war and home with us. We both knew birthing time was near. Had to be.

Coming down Five Hills Road were Pearlene Washington and her husband, Moses. They lived a quarter of a mile up the road. Moses made a living fixing anything that was broke, or near broke, and Pearlene knew more about delivering babies than all the doctors in Tolliver, as far as I could tell, having been taught by her grandmother, who used to deliver all the slave babies over at the Twineddy Plantation way back when.

They stopped in front of the house and I waved them up. Pearlene took one look at me and said, "Mrs. Cooper, that belly is surely big. Bigger than with your other babies. You been eating a lot?"

"Never mind," I said. "Listen to this name I picked out for the baby—Ezekiel." I said it again, loving the way it swam off my tongue.

Pearlene put her hands to my belly and pushed gently on it, this way and that, frowning the whole time. "You got a whole lot of baby in here, Mrs. Cooper. Whole lot."

I swatted her hands away. "'Course it's big. It's a boy. I heard 'Ezekiel' on *The Shadow* last week. It's from the Bible, you know, one of the prophets. Doesn't it sound important? Like a boy who'll have a lifetime of good things?"

Pearlene stood up, her arms crossed over her chest. "What's Mr. Cooper think about the first son not getting his daddy's name?"

Carter let me name Violet and Daisy. He said I would be better at picking out a girl's name. But a son. That would be different.

One of the boys kicked a foot beneath my ribs and I gasped. This was a favorite game of theirs in the last weeks. I used my hand to press the soft heel over to the other side of my belly.

The Washingtons stared down at me, trying not to smile too wide.

"I'll settle for naming him Carter Ezekiel if I have to," I said.

Six days later, the labor pains hit me so bad I dropped the iron skillet on my foot as I was pulling corn bread from the oven. I let out a howl, not sure which was worse—the vise strangling my belly or the smashed toe. Violet and Daisy, only four and two at the time, came running in asking what was wrong. I told them to get their father. Daisy burst into tears and Violet froze right up.

"Please, Violet. Get your father."

"Okay, Momma," she said, running off to the front yard, where Carter was working on his truck.

I put Daisy on my hip and grabbed a cool cloth for my toe. My husband barreled through the kitchen doorway, carrying Violet and breathing heavy.

"What the hell's going on in here?"

"I'm having a baby, goddamn you."

The girls' eyes got big. I never cursed in front of the children. At least not until they were older.

"Now?" Carter asked.

I started to cry, suddenly scared of what was before me. And it wasn't even the birthing so much as the caring for another baby. I was already so worn out.

The tears made Carter move. He told Violet to take herself and her sister over to their aunt Charlotte's, just a few doors down from our house. Then he scooped me up in his arms, not an easy thing to do when your wife weighs almost two hundred pounds, and began carrying me out to the car. Another contraction sliced me in half. When it passed, I told him to take me to our bed.

"We're not going to make it to the hospital. Go get Pearlene."

At ten minutes past midnight on a clear October night, our first son was born. While Pearlene washed the baby and swaddled him in a warm flannel blanket, I began squirming with pain again. Pearlene called Carter in from the living room to hold the baby so she could tend to me. After prodding my belly for a minute, she looked up, a small smile creasing her face.

"Mrs. Cooper, I don't believe we're finished here yet."

"I'm finished, Pearlene. Give me my son."

The contractions came again but I figured it was the afterbirth. Carter put the baby in my arms. He cried and cried but stopped as soon as I got him settled on my breast.

"Hey there, son," Carter said, stroking the dark, silky hair on the baby's head. "Hey there, Carter boy."

"Now, you know," I began, "I want to name him—"

Another pain hit me. Then another.

Pearlene came back in the room with a fresh stack of towels.

"Am I bleeding that much?"

She shook her head. "Not for you."

At twenty minutes past midnight, I got my second son. Ezekiel. A little smaller than his brother but twice as loud.

On their first night in the world, I made up a lullaby for my sweet boys:

Good night, my sons
The day is done
Wait only for angels
To carry your dreams
Let sleep begin
So we may meet again

I sang it to them at bedtime for years until one night, when he was eight, Ezekiel said, "Momma, I don't need a lullaby no more."

~ Nineteen ~

When Carter and Ezekiel were babies, I'd take them out in the back garden and sit them in the dirt while I weeded, talking the whole time about what I was doing—*See, Carter, Momma's pulling this weed up because it'll choke our little tomato plant. See, Ezekiel, this is going to be a great big cucumber in a few weeks, just right for you to munch on.*

They were always happiest when they were together. If I tried to give one a bath without the other, they'd cry so much I'd end up putting both of them in the kitchen sink at the same time, the two of them splashing water all over the floor with their chubby little arms, squealing like there wasn't anything better in the whole world.

My husband and I took up favorites pretty early with the boys. He seemed to like holding Carter more, maybe because the child had his name, and I couldn't get enough of Ezekiel, my surprise baby. The month before the boys turned two, another surprise came. A bad one this time. Clayton suffered a measles outbreak. All of the children got it but Carter caught the worst case. He got the rash and then a fever I couldn't bring down.

Back then there were only a few doctors left at the hospital in Tolliver. All the younger and able-bodied ones were over in France patching up the soldiers. A Dr. Kentfield, who must have been almost eighty years old, prepared us to lose our boy. He said a child as young as Carter couldn't last much longer with a fever over 104 degrees, and he suspected encephalitis, as well. Two days later my baby slipped into a coma. The ladies from First Baptist came to Tolliver and sat with us in the waiting room praying for little Carter. Praying. And praying. And praying.

On day twelve, Carter woke up and pointed at the water pitcher. It was the first sensible thing he'd done since falling sick. The whole family fussed over him when he got home, treating him like a king. I fixed him his favorite treat of corn bread crumbled in a glass of buttermilk; his father bought him and Ezekiel matching cowboy outfits with holsters and hats; Vi and Daisy drew pictures filled with rainbows and hearts.

It took a while to figure out how the fever changed Carter. He still played the same with Ezekiel, still laughed when I blew air on his tummy, still cried when the whip-poor-wills let out their squawks at night. But by their third birthday, I could tell something wasn't right. Ezekiel was already telling us tales—making up stories about the wild cats under the house and talking so much that sometimes I'd have to say, "Ezekiel Cooper, your momma's going to go crazy if you don't hush up that mouth of yours." He'd toddle off to find somebody else's ear to bend. Carter didn't speak until he was four going on five. I kept telling his daddy something was wrong, really wrong. We'd take the child to the doctor—have his hearing tested, his vision. And the answer was always the same. Normal.

My sister Charlotte's first child was a son the same age as my boys. She used to bring Charlie over to play with Ezekiel and Carter. One winter morning we sat drinking coffee at the kitchen table, watching the three boys pull all the pots out from the bottom cabinets. Ezekiel had been the instigator, pulling the first one out. Then Charlie. Then Carter. Charlie and Ezekiel began stacking the pots, one on top of another, until they had a tower. Carter sat there with his knees pulled into his chest, just watching.

"Go on, Carter," I said. "You put a pot on the tower."

Carter shook his head, smiling a little.

"It's all right, son," I said. "You go on."

"He don't know how, Momma," Ezekiel answered for his brother, stacking another pot.

"'Course he does," I said. "He's the same age as you. You go on, Carter. Go ahead."

But my boy came over to me instead and climbed up into my lap. Charlotte and I looked at each other. My eyes slid away before I had to answer the question in hers.

I taught Ezekiel his letters and numbers before he went to school. I'd read to him from one of my *Photoplay* magazines, pointing at each letter until he learned them all. When I tried to teach Carter, he'd just stare at the pictures of the movie stars, pointing and asking, *Who that, Momma?* not caring one bit for the letters on the page.

Baby Rose came along when the boys were four. Carter liked to smother that girl to death with all his kisses. He couldn't get enough of seeing her tiny fingers and toes. It was Carter who held Rosie's hand as she took her first steps. Carter who wiped her tears when she fell over. Ezekiel thought Rosie was sweet, but he didn't pay her much mind.

The year the boys started school even my husband, who could ignore a fire in his own house until it singed the bottom of his toes, had to face up to Carter being different. Lord, how I had to fight for that child. When they were in kindergarten, that mean old bitch Miss Ryder sent Carter home every week for this or that. Once, it was because he didn't know how to tie his shoes.

The summer before the boys started first grade, Dr. Grady told me about a Memphis doctor who worked with "special" children. Dr. Grady knew I was worried about Carter, and he thought this Memphis fellow could help us figure out what was wrong, if there was anything wrong. Carter Sr. and I argued about it for weeks. He thought it was a waste of money we didn't have.

Things were tight in 1948. My husband gave up trying to feed a family of seven by raising cotton. One of his cousins was a pipe fitter over in Germantown and told Carter it was good solid work. So he spent six months working for almost nothing as an apprentice in Memphis. By the end of summer he would be ready to get jobs on his own from the union.

He wouldn't budge about the doctor. "Our boy is fine, Lillian," he said. "He's just slow, is all. We don't need some city doctor telling us what we already know."

I gave up fighting about it. Instead, for the first time in my life, I asked a relative for money. My cousin Georgia Parker had married a boy from a rich Virginia family and I knew she would help me. Within a week, I had enough to pay for the visit fee, the train tickets, and a little spending money while we were in the city.

Carter Sr. got a call from the pipe fitters union about a three-month-long bridge construction job over in Alabama starting in early August. I scheduled the doctor's visit for the fifteenth. I'd have to tell Carter Sr. eventually—somebody from town was sure to say something when he came home about me taking the boys on the train—but I would deal with him later.

The morning of the trip was clear and hot. I had to get the three girls delivered to my sister's house and the boys dressed before the seven-o'clock train came through. When the two loud blasts of the whistle rang out, I was finishing up braiding Daisy's hair.

"Run on down to the crossroads, Ezekiel, and ask Mr. O'Leary real nice if he'll hold the train for us. Tell him your momma's running just a minute late."

Michael O'Leary was a saint and did as Ezekiel asked. The boys and I came running up at five minutes past seven.

"Lillian Cooper," Mr. O'Leary called out from the engine car, making a point of looking at his pocket watch, "it's a good thing you're easy on these old eyes. I wouldn't hold this train for just anybody now, you know."

I smiled and added the tiniest extra swish to my walk as I hurried the boys up the stairs of the passenger car. We made our way past a few people in the front rows toward the empty seats in the back. Carter sat closest to the window, then Ezekiel, then me. I opened my purse and took out a handkerchief, dabbing the sweat from the back of my neck. All of the windows were down in the car, but with the train standing still, no breeze came through.

The boys wore their best Sunday clothes—brown pants and checked shirts, ironed fresh that morning, and hair washed the night before. Two little princes they were.

~ Twenty ~

The towns along the Southern Railway line rolled by: Mabry,
Roger Springs, Saulsbury, Grand Junction, La Grange—where
all of the houses are painted white and trimmed in green—
Moscow (there's one of those in Russia, Ezekiel tells me, like
I don't know that already), Rossville, Collierville, Forest Hill,
and Germantown. As the train drew near Memphis, the boys
couldn't believe what they saw out the window.

The deep green of farmland gave way to the gray of
concrete and the muddy red of brick buildings. The boys put
their hands up to the window's glass like they were trying to
touch every office and shop and house that went past.

Carter tugged at my sleeve, speaking in a half whisper, "What happened to all the grass? Why are there so many
buildings? Where do people live?"

"A taxi! A real taxi!" Ezekiel said.

Passengers turned at the loudness of his voice, smiling
at us around their newspapers. The train sailed down South

Main, tall poplars lining the way, before coming to a stop in Central Station. As we stepped off the platform, I felt so scared I wanted to gather my boys up and head right back home. The noise of all those people—yelling, talking, spitting—and the trains, their engines idle but not quiet, was too much. I didn't know where to turn. People strode in front of us, behind us, jostling us.

"Look at all these people!" Ezekiel said as he whirled around, taking it all in.

"Too many people," I said, reaching into my purse for the cream-colored paper with the neatly printed directions the nurse had mailed me. We had to take two buses to the office. I managed to get us on the right ones. When we got off the second bus, Ezekiel kept stopping to look at things. "Momma, look at that building! How tall it is!" The throngs of people sharing the sidewalk caused Carter to walk so close to me that I could feel his leg brush mine with each step.

"It's all right, little man," I said. "I won't let anyone sweep you away."

We passed Audubon Park with its lawns like green velvet and its pure blue lake. The doctor's office was in a plain brick building with a sign on the door that read "Dr. Christopher Allen, please ring bell." Before ringing anything, I took my time straightening the seams on my stockings, smoothing my hair back into its bun, and wiping the boys' faces.

"I guess we'll do."

Ezekiel and Carter stood in front of me, hands in their pockets, eyes cast downward.

"I don't want to go, Momma," Carter said. The worry in his voice was heavy.

"Me either," Zeke said. "Let's go to the park and get milkshakes like you promised and ride the train again."

We had traveled so far, but I felt the same urge as the boys. Run. Now.

"What's this? The Cooper boys aren't feeling scared, are they?" I placed a hand under each of their chins, tilting them upward so they had to look at me. "Where is my Superman? Where is my Captain Marvel? Anybody gets scared in there, what word can we think of to say?"

The boys looked at each other. "Don't be scared?" offered Ezekiel.

"That's a sentence. I'm looking for one word. A magic word. SHAZAM."

This got a smile. Ezekiel seemed surprised that I knew the favorite saying of one of their heroes, a result of comic books being the only reading material in the outhouse.

I rang the bell. When the door opened, the three of us walked in, Carter tucked between his brother and me.

Dr. Allen was a tall, thin man. In a too loud voice, he told the boys to stay in the waiting room with the pale-faced nurse while he and I talked. The office smelled of leather, rubbing alcohol, and cigar smoke.

"Dr. Grady sent me your son's medical information, Mrs. Cooper. But I'd like you to tell me more about the case of rubeola he contracted as a small child."

I told him how Carter woke up in the middle of the night screaming, his little body burning to the touch. "He spent two weeks in the hospital. Before he went into the coma, all they did for him was put that poor baby in ice bath after ice bath. I never want to see ice anywhere near my boy again, Dr. Allen. I can tell you that much. I can still picture the way Carter looked at me when the ice water touched his baby skin."

The doctor folded his long, skinny fingers on the top of his desk. "I'd like to run some tests on Carter."

"What kind of tests?"

"I won't be using any instruments on him, if that's what you're worried about. I want to see how Carter's brain works. We'll get better results if you remain in the waiting room while I perform the tests."

I asked if his brother could be there. Dr. Allen shook his head.

"Carter's not going to like that."

He patted my hand, the pressure staying a second longer than necessary. "Don't worry, Mrs. Cooper. It'll be fine."

I drew my hand back as if he'd slapped it. I doubted that anything was going to be fine.

Carter must have been in that office for over an hour. Ezekiel kept asking me what the doctor was doing to his brother. I said he was giving him a special kind of test.

"What kind of test? I want to take it, too."

I shooed him over to the toy box and told him to play. Finally, the door opened and Carter came out. He ran straight into my arms and said, "Don't like tests." I kissed him and looked over at the doctor. He nodded for me to come back in the office. Before closing the door behind us, he asked the nurse to bring us some coffee.

I sat in a red leather chair across from Dr. Allen's desk. He ignored me while he finished writing notes in a file. The nurse brought coffee. She poured two cups, never looking at me or the doctor. The sweat began to drip behind the knees of my crossed legs. Dr. Allen put his thick black pen down and asked if I wanted cream or sugar. I shook my head.

He handed me the delicate china cup and saucer. It was his mother's china, he said. His wife hadn't taken a shine to it, so he brought it to the office.

"What do you think of it?"

"Beautiful." I took a sip, the coffee's bitter taste flowering against my tongue.

My hand shook just the slightest bit and I tried to quiet the scared inside me. I didn't know how much longer I could sit there before I tore out of the chair, grabbed him by the lapels of his white coat, and demanded to know what was wrong with my boy.

"Are your sons identical twins?"

Strangers asked the question at least once a week. From a distance, they looked identical. But up close, you saw Carter's eyes were brown like his daddy's and Ezekiel's were blue like mine. Their build was different, too. Broader through the chest than his brother, Carter had always been a good five to ten pounds heavier and a couple of inches taller than Ezekiel.

"No, sir. They're fraternal."

He took off his glasses, setting them on the desk. "Fascinating. I'm assuming your other son has exhibited normal brain function. He hasn't shown any of the signs that give you cause for concern about Carter?"

I tried to untangle his words. Normal brain function. Cause for concern. A question about Ezekiel. He asked it again. *Did Ezekiel appear normal?*

"Ezekiel didn't get that high fever with the rubeola like Carter. Zeke already knows how to read."

"Good, good. That's a blessing for you. In my experience, God rarely closes one door without opening another. Even if it's only a crack of light shining through."

Dr. Allen fancied himself a preacher as well.

"Please tell me what the tests showed."

He drained the last of the coffee from his cup before setting it back on the saucer, the sound of china meeting china a soft clink in the small room. The window behind him opened onto the street below. Footsteps pushing off the sidewalk and cars honking made me long to be outside again, to escape this room and this man.

"Mrs. Cooper, in my years of experience with dealing with children like Carter, there is no easy way to tell a parent of my diagnosis. In the early years of my practice, I tried to soften the blow with kind words and hope. But I've learned that I have never been wrong about a child's potential and that it serves neither the parent nor the child to paint the diagnosis with a gentle brush. So, I will be blunt. I believe the encephalitis Carter suffered as a result of the measles affected his brain, preventing it from developing in a normal fashion. Your son is what we call a retarded child. It is my belief that he will never be capable of learning to read or write or lead a life of his own without your supervision."

The thought of words damaging a person had never occurred to me before that day. Guns, knives, balled fists—those could hurt you. Words were only pieces of breath strung together.

I stared at the desk in front of me, noticing how the granite pen holder and nameplate, engraved with gold letters, were perfectly lined up beside each other. Not a speck of dust covered the blotter or any other part of the desktop. I imagined the rest of Dr. Allen's life must be just as orderly. No messy retarded children at home to deal with. No tired wife sweating over an old stove making dinner. The small photo on his desk showed a smiling wife wearing an evening gown with flowers in her upswept hair.

"Do you have children, Dr. Allen?"

A look of surprise crossed his face. "No, Mrs. Cooper, I don't."

"Let me ask you this," I said, the question forming on my lips as I spoke, "if you could choose between having no children or having a retarded child, Dr. Allen, which would you choose?"

He pushed his chair away from the desk and came around to my side, mumbling that he knew I must be very distressed. His arm snaked around my shoulders and landed near my right breast. I shook the arm off with enough force to slam it into the wall. He winced and retreated to his seat, though he didn't sit, just placed his hands on the back of the chair. "We do not get to choose these things, Mrs. Cooper. God decides. Our job is to accept his decisions."

Chicken, I thought. He could hide behind his God.

"You'll need to discuss the issue of institutionalization with your husband. Sooner rather than later. This will only get more difficult as your son grows older. I can recommend several in the state, if you'd like."

I walked out of that office without saying a word, grabbing my boys in the waiting room as I went. The nurse called to us in the hallway.

"Mrs. Cooper! Mrs. Cooper! There's the matter of the bill. And we need to schedule your next appointment." Her heavy white shoes squeaked across the wood floor behind us.

Carter looked up at me and shook his head. What choice did I have? He was my baby boy. I stopped, took the money out of my wallet, and gave it to her without a word. The boys and I walked fast to the front entrance. We were through the doors and then the outside rushed into my lungs, filling them with fresh, clean air. The sun shone down on us and I was grateful for its heat. This was the way things were supposed to be. The doctor's office almost disappeared into the summer haze rising from the sidewalk.

A pharmacy sat at the end of the block, and I took the boys inside for a real restaurant lunch. They sat at the counter and had chocolate shakes, cheeseburgers, and French fries. I watched them devour it all. Matching brown mustaches formed above their top lips. Ezekiel dripped ketchup down the front of his nice shirt and I didn't say a word. Carter kept stealing fries off of his brother's plate, laughing every time. It was the sweetest hymn.

∼ Twenty-One ∼

The doctors want to schedule the surgery soon. They say it'll only be a matter of months before I'm dead if I don't. Daisy and Violet want me to have it. And why not? It's not their ribs the doctors will break before they pry apart my chest to get the poor little tired lung out. Now, to be fair, if they had told me not to have the surgery, the girls would have always wondered whether I might have lived longer. The funny thing is I don't care. Either way I'm going to end up in the same place. Eventually.

My sister, Charlotte, visited this week. Kept telling me how good I look. What does she know? She looks so worn out it hurts my eyes. Six kids for her, one more than me. And all of hers still living. Half of them still living *with* her. A nice quiet evening for Charlotte is when none of her boys is drunk and the grandbabies she looks after aren't sick. When we were young mothers with unlined faces and babies balanced on still-slim hips, I asked her if this was all there was to our lives—taking care of the house, the kids, the cooking. *What else do you want, Lilly?* More, I said. *Like what?* Anything.

Back then nobody asked a woman what she wanted. Didn't matter. One day you were a little girl with dreams woven through your pigtails and the next day you were a wife and, if you weren't careful, a mother, too. I guess my girls didn't get asked what they wanted, either. But my granddaughters will. Those girls are our best hope for making something of the Cooper women. Especially that Honora. She's got magic dust in her. Just like her grandma.

Grandma. I glanced in the mirror the other day to see if I looked like a grandmother. The hair is a little gray on the account of me missing my last dye appointment. But if you look me in the eye, you'll see this isn't a grandmother in here. This is a fifteen-year-old girl. Prettier than all the other girls in town, and the best damn singer in the county, maybe even the state. That's who's I am, underneath the wrinkles that even Oil of Olay can't help now.

Every Sunday I'd step up to the front of First Baptist and sing, all the love I had to give rising up inside me, spilling through my voice in perfect round notes. I always closed my eyes when I sang, liking the way everything else fell away but the music. When I opened them one Sunday morning after singing "Tell Me the Story of Jesus," I saw Preacher Dawson wiping his eyes with the back of his hand.

After the service, he stopped me on the front steps, grabbing both my hands into his. "Child, your voice opened our hearts to the Lord today. God bless you. What a gift. Praise the Lord."

Momma nodded at him but pulled me along, her fingernails pressing into the soft flesh of my arm. She whispered in my ear, "Don't you start thinking too highly of yourself now. I don't want you singing anywhere but in this church."

Preacher Dawson's words had made me feel like I was holy and had something special to offer the world. As long as I was singing, I was happy. I just wanted to breathe music into the air.

What did I know? I liked to burn with this thing. I'd lie awake at night, my sister sleeping beside me, and dream of singing at the Grand Ole Opry. My daddy always played the radio while he was working in the yard, and I kept him company, singing along with "I Only Have Eyes for You" by the Flamingos or with Teddy Wilson and Billie Holiday on "Pennies from Heaven."

And then Carter Cooper showed up. At eighteen, he was all blue eyes and long legs. We met at church. The first time he heard me sing, he said it was so pretty it just about broke his heart. He knew right then, at that second, that he would marry me. That he *had* to marry me.

It took Carter a good two months of heavy pursuing before I finally broke down and let him walk me home from church. Another two months later, I was pregnant with Violet. Fifteen, pregnant, and still wanting to be a star. I didn't tell anybody about the baby. Not even Carter. And then one Sunday morning, when he came by to pick me up for church, I was gone. Nobody knew where.

I made it as far as Chattanooga. I almost threw up the minute the bus left the station over at the crossroads. My Violet has never enjoyed a road trip, not even when she was growing in my belly. But I bit the inside of my lip the whole way to distract myself from feeling sick. When I got off the bus to go to the bathroom, Carter was sitting in the station playing a game of solitaire while he waited for me to show up. The guy who sold me the bus ticket at the Mabry station knew my daddy's family and had called the house to tell them where I was headed. Somehow Carter convinced my parents to let him come get me. I didn't even put up a fight. Not really. I knew New York was done. But I knew this man loved me. And I thought it would be enough.

I haven't opened my mouth to sing in thirty years. The last time I remember was at Leroy's funeral. I know Carter thought it strange that I carried on like I did over Leroy's passing. But I still think my husband had no idea about Leroy and me.

Adultery is a sin. I won't argue that one. Particularly when you're sinning with your husband's brother. The apostle Peter was right about beseeching us to abstain from fleshly lusts, which "war against the soul."

It's a crime against the souls of your children. See, Ezekiel figured out what was going on with me and Leroy. I know that now. He never told me he knew but he did, kept it to himself all these years. Daisy told me Ezekiel knew, a few years back when she came to me about feelings she was having for a male friend of hers who was not her husband. I think she wanted me to tell her to go ahead and follow her feelings. Instead I told her to never speak to the man again. End of story.

I loved my husband. But if I'm being truthful, and I am trying to be truthful these days, at least with myself and the Lord, I never forgave Carter for getting me pregnant with Violet. I was only fifteen, for God's sake.

Momma never told me more about making babies than "just wait until you're married, Lillian." And I'd always ask, "Wait for what, Momma?" Well, I found out. I know it wasn't my husband's fault, not really. It's just—I had ideas. Good plans for my life and not a one of them ended up happening. And don't you just want to blame somebody?

For a long time, I tried to make my life work, to make our family work. I got tired, though. Five children wears you out until the only thing left inside of you, the only thing you've got to give, is a memory of what you thought you'd be.

And then Leroy looked at me funny one day. It was the Fourth of July picnic, the year I turned thirty. The whole family was over at our house, eating barbecue and potato salad and the kids climbing all over everything. I went into the kitchen to bring out more lemonade when Leroy stopped me in the doorway.

"Lillian," he said, "I reckon you could still look pretty even when the rest of us done wilted."

That was all it took. Doesn't sound like much, does it? Carter used to say stuff like that. But when your husband says it year after year, and your hips keep spreading after each child until you think they're going to end up over in Arkansas one day soon, you think he's lying. When Leroy said it, I believed him.

And I needed to believe someone still saw a spark in me, something that didn't have to do with Carter or the children. Maybe that's why most married people have affairs. Because the affair is separate from the family; it's just about you.

Of course, in the end, it winds up right back with the family.

∽ Twenty-Two ∽

Violet knows now. She knows where Leroy was headed that day, almost thirty years ago now, when he came down Five Hills Road too fast. Too drunk. Daisy told her. They were having a fight about the lung cancer. Daisy didn't tell me everything, but I imagine she said something like *The old woman deserves it*. Then Vi probably said, *Daisy, that's awful. How can you say something like that about our mother?* And Daisy, who has had enough of her big sister being the good daughter for decades, finally broke down and told her. Told her what only she and Ezekiel figured out years before.

Violet showed up on my doorstep not long after. Knocked loud and insistent. When I opened it, I knew what she was there for. I saw it on her face.

"Is it true, Momma?" She looked at me with more hurt in her eyes than I could stand.

"Is what true, honey?"

"Leroy, Momma. Is it true Leroy was on his way to see you that horrible day?"

Guilt can wrestle down a person's voice, her breath. They told me later I collapsed in the doorway, hit my head on the handle of the screen door as I went down. This was more proof for my daughters that even when confronted with my own unspeakable sin, I put the attention back on myself. Me. Look at me.

When I woke up in the hospital that night, I didn't know my own name. Recognized nobody. And it wasn't exactly a bad thing. In fact, it was a kind of relief. So when the memories flooded back—they came a few days later, in one solid whoosh like those pictures in the paper of the Des Plaines River surging over its banks and taking out whole towns—I decided to give myself a rest and pretend, just for a little while, that they hadn't.

My family and the doctors all think I've lost my mind. I haven't. The one child who still believed in me, still thought I was something like a good mother, is lost to me now. And it is too much. I would rather be alone with the cancer and surrounded by crazy old people than face my children.

It took a few weeks, but now all of my daughters come visit me at the Preserve Nursing Home and Care Facility in Mabry. What kind of name is the "Preserve"? Makes me think of those game preserves down in Florida that I've read about, where the rich guys go to pretend-hunt the pretend-wild animals. All of the workers here wear faded yellow smocks with "The Preserve—Your Loved Ones' Home Away From Home!" embroidered in blue thread across the front.

My girls think I don't know them but I do. Inside. I know them. Daisy comes every Monday and Wednesday morning.

Rosie comes on Saturdays. And even Violet comes by on the weekends. She always says, "Hi, Momma, you're looking well." Vi was my firstborn. Looks more like my mother than any of the kids. She tells me about Owen, her second child, born almost fifteen years to the day after his sister. On my dresser sits a school picture in a frame with baseballs and bats around it. I look at the photo and wonder about the boy now almost in college. Is he happy? What does he know about his big sister? Does his mother love him enough? Does she love him too much?

Nobody should have to go through what Violet did. It didn't just stop Vi's heart, but mine and her daddy's and Leroy's, too. He and I had been seeing each other, off and on, for a few months when it happened. I kept ending it and then he'd show up at my back door clutching a handful of daisies when the kids were in school and Carter Sr. was away working. And I'd open the door.

God bless my Carter for never having more than one beer a night and for not touching the hard stuff. But Leroy couldn't stay away from it. Their mother drank herself to death, so it's in their blood, and Carter knew enough to keep his distance. But not Leroy. No, sir. He never came to me drunk, except the day it happened. I told him I'd never be with him when he was drinking. I hated the smell of it on a man's breath. Now, that didn't mean I couldn't have a little vodka in my iced tea. That was different.

After Vi and Louis got married, they moved into the old Smith place around the corner from our house. It was so small it was more like a shack, but it was all they could afford, and Vi thought it was her own little palace. She thought they were going to live happily ever after and everything would be perfect from then on. Never mind that she was only sixteen and Louis nineteen. Cassie was born on July 6. Like half of my labors, Vi went too quick for us to get her to the hospital, so Pearlene and I delivered the baby at home. When I held Cassie in my arms for the first time, she looked up at me with blue eyes wider than the Gulf of Mexico, all seriouslike, until at last she blinked, as if she were saying, *All right, you're my grandma, you'll do.*

Took Cassie a long time to walk. Vi worried something might be wrong with her legs. I said the baby was so content in our arms, she didn't see any need to walk around. Cassie didn't spend more than two hours of her waking life not being held by her momma, her daddy, or me. The thing that finally got our girl to walk was the cows across the road. Pete McAllister kept four cows in his pasture, which faced Five Hills Road. Cassie could see those cows from her own front yard. I'd sit with her out on the porch and she'd point and make moo noises at them. About five months after her first birthday, she wiggled out of my lap, scooted off the porch, and stood up on wobbly legs, mooing as loud as she could. She took one step, then two. I yelled for Vi to come out.

We both watched as she took one more step before falling back on her bottom. She cried and cried, pointing at those cows. So we each took a hand and walked her across the street. You'd have thought those cows were Santa Claus and his flying reindeer the way Cassie carried on. She wanted to touch their soft brown ears and velvet chins. Vi and I just laughed and shook our heads. We'd been waiting for her to walk for so long and all it took was a sorry bunch of cows.

After that, Miss Cassie Louise took herself wherever she wanted. She about drove Vi crazy. Vi would be washing the dishes in the kitchen, hear the back door slam shut, and see Cassie taking off after a squirrel in the yard. Even though she hadn't figured out how to walk down the stairs, she'd just scoot that little behind down each step and then throw her chubby legs over the side of the last one. I kept telling Vi to put a hook-and-eye latch up high on the doors. Cassie looked to be tall, like her daddy, and I knew it wouldn't be long before she'd be able to reach all kinds of trouble. Vi paid me no mind.

"Momma, she's just a baby," she'd say. "You worry too much."

Now, why is it that a woman who raised five children of her own is all of a sudden a worrier? I wasn't a worrier. I knew. There are some children who don't care to pull the books off every shelf or run into the street or pour turpentine down their throats. But then there are children who do, children who would be safer if they were tied down from the ages of one to five, until they developed some sense. Walking showed Cassie what she'd been missing curled up on her momma's lap.

On a morning three weeks before Cassie's second birthday, Vi was out in her backyard hanging the clothes on the line. The sun shone the way it does on a perfect September day, the heat of summer past us. Cassie busied herself taking all of the wet clothes out of the basket before her momma could hang them up. Vi kept telling her to stop it and she'd give her some old clothes to play with, but just as soon as Vi would turn around to hang a pair of pants up, Cassie would be right back in that basket, giggling the whole time. I don't blame Vi for getting mad at her. Small children can drive you to drink more than a man can.

Carter Sr. was over in Tuscumbia again, working on the big bridge project. I knew Leroy would stop by. When Carter was away, Leroy would have lunch with me at the house while the children were in school. He'd park his car about a quarter of a mile up the road and then walk down. Small as Clayton was, we had to be careful.

Of course, lunch usually didn't get eaten. We fell into bed as soon as he set foot in the door. Our loving was always hurried, breathless, needy. There was something about the way we came together—rougher and faster than with Carter.

After Vi yelled at Cassie to stop pulling out the clothes, the baby started to cry and Vi had had enough. She took her back in the house and put her in the crib. Then Vi went back outside. What happened after that we've only guessed at. I imagine our Cassie cried for a bit before she calmed down enough to look out the bedroom window, the one facing the street. And there were the brown cows, probably all lined up in a row as if they were waiting for her. So she took it upon herself to climb out of the crib, something she'd never done before, and get to the front door. Nobody in Clayton locked the doors back then. They probably don't now, either. With Vi out back by the clothesline, there was no way she could have heard Cassie go out the door, no way at all.

I've thought about that day over and over again. If I'd gone to visit Cassie instead of waiting, less than a block away, for my husband's brother to come over and screw me silly, things would have been different. It only took me two minutes to walk to Vi's place. Two minutes from my front door to hers. Two minutes.

Leroy had planned to come see me. Told me he even picked fresh daisies from the field next to the mill that morning. Except when he got into work, Buddy Wright called him into the office. Said lumber prices were dropping and they needed to scale back on the day shift and let Leroy go. Just like that. Leroy had been working there for two years. Longest he'd ever held a job. And he knew that another job that paid as well as the saw mill would be hard to come by. This happened a little after nine in the morning. By ten o'clock, Leroy had finished off the fifth of Jack Daniels he kept stashed in the truck's glove box. He knew he wanted to see me. Said he felt like I would make things better. Going home to Annie and telling her he'd lost the best job he'd ever had could wait. So he drove down Five Hills Road to my house.

I can just see Cassie looking proud as she pushed the front door open. I'm sure she scooted her way down the front steps as the cows lowed to her the whole time. From Vi's front steps to the road was fifteen yards. Cassie probably started to run that crazy, shoulders-hunched, side-to-side run she'd just started doing. I bet she wrinkled her nose as the wind carried the scent of the cow poops her way.

Leroy knew how to drive drunk. He knew you went real slow and kept your eyes fixed on the road ahead. If he'd been in his right mind, he would have parked up the road away from my house and Vi's, like he usually did.

We've none of us figured out what happened next. Maybe Cassie ran out into the middle of the road just as Leroy came over the hill, which would have hid her from sight until it was too late. Maybe he took his eyes off the road reaching for a Lucky Strike. We'll never know.

As Violet hung up the last pair of Louis's work pants, she heard a car with a cranky muffler coming over the hill but thought nothing of it. It wasn't until the loud, shrill cry of squealing brakes broke the afternoon's quiet that Vi felt the first inkling of fear. I came out to see what the racket was about, thinking somebody hit a deer again. They were always dashing out of the woods and into the road, though usually in the early morning or at twilight. I stepped into the middle of the road and saw Leroy's truck, black marks slashing the road beneath it where he'd skidded to a stop.

He was out of the truck, looking around like he'd lost something. I walked toward him. Even from a distance I could see that he was drunk from the way he kept scratching his head and squinting like the sun hurt his eyes.

I called out to him. His head came up. "You all right?" No answer.

I met Violet in the road and we walked together to Leroy. "Everything okay?" she asked.

"Something in the road. Tried to stop. Big bump. Can't find it. Where is it?"

I don't know why but I turned to Violet and asked her where Cassie was.

"In her crib. She's fine." Vi caught the scent of my fear. "I'll check but I just put her there a minute ago."

Leroy and I began walking around the car, looking for what neither of us knew. At the fence, McAllister's cows stood all bunched together near the back of Leroy's truck, lowing and restless. The slap of Violet's screen door made me look over to her house. She was running and right then I figured it out. I knew.

My mind tumbled over itself trying to figure out who should find her first. Should it be me? Should it be Vi? I gave up and closed the distance between me and the truck's tailgate. Leroy followed behind me, almost stumbling into the ditch.

Violet's voice carried across the road. "Mother, did you hear me? Where are you going? Listen to me. Cassie's not in the—"

I saw her first. She lay in the road, directly behind the rear wheels of the truck. The pink of her shirt was muddied from the ground and her face was turned away from me. I said her name.

"Cassie?"

No movement.

Her left leg was at a strange, right angle to her body, and the pavement beneath her head gleamed with a dark wetness in the sunlight. I placed my hand on her back and felt the sharp curve of her ribs through the thin shirt, her favorite one with the three kittens on the front. It had been a first birthday present from my sister, Charlotte, who had done the embroidery herself. I left my hand there, waiting to feel her ribs rise with a breath. Waiting. Waiting. Waiting.

Leroy came up behind me. When he saw Cassie he stopped.

"Get in the truck." I snapped the words, my mind spinning crazy.

He stood there.

"Now."

I gathered my grandbaby up in my arms, holding her against my chest. My hand cradled the back of her head and longed for its usual feel of downy silk, not the roughness of hair matted with blood and dirt.

Violet's steps drew closer. I closed my eyes and prayed, just for a second, that I would find the words to tell my daughter. When only a few feet remained between us, I stood up.

"I found her."

Violet stared at the silent, unmoving child. She took two steps forward and wrenched Cassie from me.

"What are you standing there for?" She began running toward the house. "We've got to get her to the hospital."

I followed behind, listening to her croon to Cassie, telling her baby it would be all right, the doctors would fix her, she would be safe soon. When Violet stopped in the driveway, confused because Louis had their only vehicle at work, I finally spoke.

"Violet, honey, our baby doesn't need the hospital."

She shook her head at me, insistent, and clutched Cassie tighter to her body. "She does, Mama. She does."

I went to her carefully, placing my arms around them both. Violet looked down at Cassie until the awful recognition dawned on my daughter's face. She sank to the ground, rocking our baby back and forth, back and forth. I knelt behind Violet and my body found the same motion. Back and forth. Back and forth. The gravel beneath us bit into our knees, tiny pieces embedding themselves beneath the skin.

~ Twenty-Three ~

Nothing much was the same after that. Not for any of us. It sounds strange but I believe Leroy suffered the most. Violet and Louis—they were devastated but would go on to have another child. I knew they would. What I hadn't known then was it would take fifteen years, long past the point when they had given up hope.

Leroy's grief bottomed out deeper and deeper every day. Louis wanted to prosecute but Violet knew it wouldn't bring back their little girl. Carter Sr. talked to Louis and asked him what he thought putting Leroy away would do for him and his family. Louis said it would keep him from killing somebody else's kid. Hardeman County district attorney Harlow Simms saw an opportunity to get his name in the paper and planned to go for the death penalty.

In the dark hours of the night, while my children slept in their beds, I stayed awake wondering why I hadn't stopped seeing Leroy. If I had, he wouldn't have been coming down that road to see me. Mistakes can be forgiven but not that kind of sin. It does not deserve forgiveness. Instead, it sits in the bottom of your soul, twisting and turning over the years, so you never forget it's there.

Two days before Christmas Eve, Leroy left me a note on the back door asking me to meet him behind First Baptist at nine o'clock that night. I told my husband I had to get out of the house and take a walk. I walked down Five Hills Road and turned right at Main. The temperature was due to drop below freezing and I wrapped my coat around me tighter. The possibility of snow by Christmas had the children beside themselves at home, and I welcomed escaping outside, though my stomach felt all turned around about seeing Leroy.

A small triangle of light from inside the church's front window glimmered out into the darkness. I picked my way around to the back. The orange glow of Leroy's cigarette led me to him. He sat on the ground next to the creek, flicking the ashes from the cigarette into the grass, whose tops shined a frosty white. We hadn't spoken alone since the day of the accident. I didn't know what he needed to say to me. I just knew I needed to hear it.

"Too cold to be sitting on the ground, Leroy."

He didn't turn to look at me. "Doesn't really matter, now does it, Lillian?"

His voice turned me colder than the wind. It was all hollowed out, like there was nothing left inside of him. When we were seeing each other, Leroy's voice could make me melt as fast as his hands could. The sound of it would make its way down through my ears and through my chest before landing right in that secret spot between my legs, making the sap run sweet and sure.

The wind swayed the oaks above us. Leroy kept smoking. The nine-thirty train rattled by. I crouched down next to him, my bottom resting against the backs of my calves.

He stubbed out the cigarette, heat hissing against the cold grass. "I needed to see you is all."

I took my hand out of its glove and reached for his. His fingers were freezing. I blew on them gently, trying to warm them. I could feel the cracked skin of his knuckles.

"I won't cry on your shoulder, Lil. Don't deserve to do it. I took your grandbaby away from you. I killed that little girl. I swear I never saw her on the road, I swear it. I told my Cathy what happened, and you know what she told me? She threw her arms around my neck and said, 'God forgives you, Daddy. He knows you didn't mean to hurt Cassie.'"

He grabbed his hand away from mine and stood up. "Louis Rydell will never have his baby girl speak to him, never know the feel of her in his arms again. I can't take it, Lillian. I can't live with it."

"You don't have a choice, Leroy. You've got to live with it. I know you didn't see her. I know it was an accident."

He turned his face to mine. I hoped he could see the forgiveness, because I really did forgive him, but I know the hurt shone more brightly. It was hard to look at him and see the face of my Cassie's killer. I just saw Leroy, my Leroy. He kissed me then. The pressure of his lips came down hard on my own. I could feel the air from his lungs mingle with mine, warming us, until he pulled away.

"I'm sorry, Lilly." And he was gone.

Leroy took it upon himself to spare us going through a trial. On Christmas Eve, he put a shotgun to his head in the barn behind his house.

∾ Twenty-Four ∾

Ezekiel tells me I never admit when I'm wrong. Says he never heard me once, his whole growing up, apologize for being wrong about anything. And, according to him, I was wrong about a lot of things. But see, my boy doesn't understand. As soon as I admitted one wrong, the rest of them would all come tumbling down, and then where would I be? Collapsed in the middle of the living room floor with five kids and a husband to take care of?

Things got better slowly after we lost Cassie. Carter Sr. finally saved up enough money to run indoor plumbing through the whole house. Might sound odd to say that that cheered me up after losing a granddaughter, but it did. Cheered the whole family up. Violet and Daisy had been so embarrassed about not having it they never had any of their friends over. "What if someone has to pee, Momma?" Daisy would say. "I can't tell them to go out back and do it in a hole in the ground. I won't." We'd never heard a sound sweeter than a toilet flush. When we tore down the outhouse, we made a party out of it—using the wood for a bonfire—and the kids, Carter Sr., and I danced around it like we were drunk.

Of course, not a week after the plumbing went in, I started nagging my husband about getting one of those new automatic washing machines we heard about on the radio.

"Lillian, haven't you learned to be grateful for anything?" he said.

I had. I had learned to be grateful. For a few years I was grateful every day my children walked out the door for school, leaving the house quiet. Daisy led my brood, that sweet blonde hair of hers swinging in a ponytail down her back, the boys kicking rocks and tripping their way behind her, Rosie bringing up the rear trying to keep up with everybody. When they disappeared around the corner, I went back in the house and sat in the front room, not doing a thing, for a whole half hour. If the phone rang, I didn't answer it. When one of the kids took sick, I nearly cried for losing my morning time. It was mine. More than once I bundled up an ailing child, got some cough syrup down her throat, and sent her off to school when she should have been kept at home. Was it wrong to do that? Probably.

When Ezekiel headed off to Mabry High School for ninth grade, my morning time came to an end. Carter couldn't go to the high school. He was doing work at fourth-grade level. That angel of a teacher Miss Weaver went and got married, leaving Clayton for Jackson. She told the new teacher at the Clayton School about Carter, but Mrs. Lake didn't think much of having a boy like Carter in class.

"He'll be too much trouble, Mrs. Cooper," she said. "And besides, what kind of example is he setting for the younger children? Why, there are eight-year-olds reading better than him!"

I didn't think much of Mrs. Lake. So, Carter and I stayed home together. Part of me felt better with him at home. I knew he was safe. The past few years at school, he and Ezekiel started getting in fights with some of the other boys, who got meaner as they got older. Boys like Earl Smith, who called Carter "Dumbo" every day at school. Carter usually ignored him and anybody else who called him a name—that's what I told him to do. But Ezekiel wouldn't tolerate it. He launched himself on anybody who so much as looked cross-eyed at Carter. And then, when he did, Carter would have to jump in, too. They came home at least once a month covered in bruises, shirts ripped, a note from the teacher folded in a back pocket.

When the rest of the children went off to school, Carter cleaned up the breakfast dishes, swept out the house, and did whatever special job needed doing. He took after his daddy and was good with a hammer, so for those few years, he fixed our house more than Carter Sr. did. Miss Weaver had told me to keep up Carter's reading and writing, so in the afternoon we'd have "school." I'd make him read me a story and write letters to relatives who needed writing. Sometimes he'd start to rub his eyes and get a headache.

"Momma," he'd say, "let's rest. Let's go swing a while."

I needed a rest as much as he did. My son was a good head taller than me by then. Occasionally I'd rest my head in his lap, and the motion of the swing swayed me to sleep. Carter Sr. found us like that one Friday. We weren't expecting him home since he was working in Memphis on an office building.

"Momma, wake up," Carter said, touching my arm. "It's Daddy. Daddy's home."

Clouds bumped one another in the blue sky beyond the porch. Rain was on the way; I could smell it. We would have to bring the laundry in from the line. We had time, though. At least an hour.

Carter Sr. strode up the steps, looking as handsome in his coveralls and work boots as any man I've seen, and stopped when he saw us. A smile lit his face. "What have we got here? My girl and my boy having a rest? Am I the only one who works in this family?"

He stood in front of the swing, arms crossed over his wide chest.

"Sit, Daddy. Come sit with us."

"You think it'll hold all of us? They've been feeding me good in Memphis."

"Sure it will," Carter said.

The swing groaned with the weight of him, but it held. He sat between us, one arm resting across my shoulder and the other around our son's. The strong smell of cigarettes and the city clung to him. We all sat together, pushing the swing every so often, until the rain clouds became too dark to ignore. When I left to pull in the wash, Carter leaned on his father, telling him the story of Jitterbug—the rabbit he and Rosie found under the house the week before. The sound of my husband's laughter reached me in the backyard, its deep rumble traveling through my bones and making me smile.

As Carter grew older, he liked to wander off. Sometimes I got busy cooking or listening to one of my radio programs and wouldn't notice that he had slipped out the back door and gone for a walk in the woods. But about once a month he'd get lost and end up at the Culvers' house on Highway 57, confused and crying because he couldn't find his way back home. Then the call from Ann Marie Culver would come.

"Your boy's here again," she'd say. "You need to watch him better, Lillian."

But I couldn't watch him all the time. He was growing up. He was fifteen. He was sixteen. Seventeen. We all understood things would be different at home when Ezekiel went off to college. Since high school, Carter and Ezekiel had the same daily routine—the minute Ezekiel walked in the front door after school, he'd yell for Carter and the two of them would take off fishing or to play basketball in the yard or any old thing boys liked to do. Carter knew those days would be finished with his brother in Virginia.

I knew I'd miss Zeke, but my boy was getting out. It was the beginning for him. The next right step. Then law school. Or maybe medical school. Dr. Ezekiel Cooper. I liked the sound of that.

The day before Ezekiel left for school his daddy and I threw him a party. All of Clayton came over to the house. Carter Sr. barbecued thirty pounds of hot dogs and hamburgers. The girls helped me bake pies all week and clean the house, Daisy grumbling the whole time about making such a big fuss. We put the dining room table under the eaves of the back porch and covered it in plate after plate of baked beans, potato salad, corn bread, apple pie, peach pie, and the tallest hummingbird cake I ever made.

All of Ezekiel's friends came, and he talked with Tommy Jackson and Bud Trent until Jacklynn showed up. Then the two of them put their heads together, talking real low, telling secrets, making promises I knew my boy wouldn't keep. When Jackie lost their baby, I thanked God. If things had gone differently, Ezekiel would have been tied to her, to Clayton, forever.

"There's a lot of people here to see you, son," I said.

"You should be talking to everybody." I looked at Jacklynn. "You understand?"

Ezekiel kissed her on the cheek and let me lead him away. *They'll be finished soon enough,* I thought. I dreamed about him meeting a girl from a good Virginia family, a wealthy family. Grandbabies sleeping in lace-covered bassinets. It never crossed my mind he might end up marrying Jackie anyway.

The longest face at that party was Carter's. He stayed on the front porch away from everybody. I took him a glass of lemonade and a plate of food. Didn't even give me a smile when I handed them to him.

"You all right?" I asked, already knowing the answer.

He kept his head down, stayed silent. I sat next to him, putting an arm around him. Carter sank into my side and scooted himself down so his head could rest on my shoulder. His long legs stretched out across the peeling paint of the porch steps. The sheer size of Carter puzzled me. The boy was gone.

"Your brother promises to write you every day, sweetheart. He keeps his promises. You know that."

"Yes, ma'am."

"You want to go with him, don't you?"

"Yes, ma'am."

I stroked the hair back from his forehead. "Ezekiel needs to go by himself this time. You understand?"

Noises from the backyard drifted toward us. Everybody talking at once. The bang of Carter Sr.'s new shotgun. Showing it off, I'm sure. Squeals from the kids shooting marbles in the driveway.

Carter pulled away from me. "It's not right. I can read, Momma. I can learn like Zeke. Cousin Georgia needs help on the farm. I can do it. Let me go, Momma. Let me go, too. It's not right for him to be there and me here."

But it was right. It was exactly right.

"Son, you'll be okay. You'll see."

Rosie came barreling around the corner and grabbed ahold of the railing. "Come play basketball, Carter. Zeke's playing."

Carter shook his head.

"Come on. Tommy Jackson's on Zeke's team. I need you."

She hoisted herself up onto the porch and stood behind us, hands on her hips. "Time's wasting."

"Your brother's a little sad today," I said. "Maybe he'll come later."

Carter stared at his hands in his lap, lacing the fingers together like I taught him when he was a boy. *Here's the church, Carter, here's the steeple, open the door and see all the people.*

Rosie grabbed one of his hands and tugged on him. "We're all sad," she said. "That's why we need to play now. While Zeke's still here."

Carter lifted his head then. "You'll play when he's gone, right? I'll still have somebody to play basketball with, right?"

"'Course."

This got him up. I watched as they swung down from the porch, Rosie reminding Carter about Tommy Jackson's killer jump shot and telling him how to block it as they walked to the backyard, the sea of friends and relatives swallowing them up.

∼ Twenty-Five ∼

In the days after Ezekiel left for Virginia, Carter moped around the house. On the first Saturday without his brother, I decided to take Rosie and Carter in to Mabry to see a movie. *Please Don't Eat the Daisies* was playing at the Downtown Theater, and Carter loved Doris Day.

Saturdays were my hair days. Wash and set at Ruby's at two o'clock. Kept that appointment for over thirty years. Until she up and died on us the year Reagan became president.

I dropped the kids off a little before two for the matinee. They grinned when I pressed an extra quarter into each of their hands for popcorn and Raisinets.

"Wait for me outside after the movie. By the box office," I yelled out the window.

I started to pull away from the curb, then stopped. Carter had never been in town without his brother before. "Rosie, come here."

Dressed in the rolled-up jeans I hated and sneakers, she jogged over to the car.

"What is it, Momma?"

Carter stood by the movie poster studying the picture of Doris Day and David Niven. *She's almost as pretty as you, Momma,* he'd told me once.

"You look after your brother."

Rosie gave me a soldier's salute.

"I mean it," I said.

"Yes, ma'am." The words were tossed over her shoulder as she ran back to the faded yellow awning.

Ruby was running thirty minutes behind schedule. The mayor's wife had shown up without an appointment first thing in the morning and thrown everything off.

"I'm sorry, Lillian," Ruby said. "You have a seat and read a magazine. I'm giving everybody a free Coke today."

I didn't mind waiting. Thirty more minutes to myself sounded good. The movie would get out around 4:30, making me a few minutes late to pick up the kids, but they could behave themselves.

Ruby talked me into putting my hair up that day. It took a little longer to fix but it was worth it. We both agreed it was a real shame I didn't have anywhere but home to go, looking as fancy as I did. When I pulled up to the theater, I daydreamed I was driving a red Studebaker Lark convertible instead of the old Ford Deluxe.

I turned off the engine and sat for a few minutes thinking about what to cook for dinner—not beans and corn bread again, I couldn't stand it—when movement near the side of the theater caught my eye.

A half circle of people stood watching something, their backs to me. The theater manager, Bob Dunlap, hurried out of the box office toward them. A white sneaker flew over the shoulder of a kid standing in the crowd, landing a few feet from the curb with a thunk. It looked like Rosie's. I got out of the car.

Rosie was screaming. I couldn't make out the words until I got closer.

"Get off my brother! You're killing him!"

I couldn't see yet who she was screaming at. Running now, I broke through the circle to find Jed Smith holding Rosie up off the ground as she thrashed around, landing scratches and kicks wherever she could, and Bob Dunlap pulling a bloodied Earl Smith off of my boy.

"Go inside and call an ambulance," Bob yelled. "Police, too."

One of the older kids ran off to the theater. At the mention of the police, Earl broke free from Bob's grip and started running down the street, knocking people out of his way as he went. Jed stared after him, still holding Rosie, who kicked backward, landing the heel of her foot in his crotch.

Carter lay still on the sidewalk. A dark stain flowered onto the cement beneath his head. It was my turn to scream. I knelt beside him. Blood ran from a deep gash across his forehead and down his right cheek. I tore off the scarf from my neck and pressed it to his head. Within seconds, it was soaked through.

"The son of a bitch used this. Goddamned cracker kid." Bob held the bottom of a broken Coke bottle in his hand, splatters of crimson dotting the jagged edges.

"Earl wouldn't stop hitting him, Momma. We were waiting out here and then Earl came up to Carter and said, 'Didn't you and your brother get my dad in trouble with the revenuers a few years back?' Carter told him no. Earl said,

'You're not Ezekiel. You're the dumb brother, aren't you?' And then he started hitting. I tried to get him off. I tried. He kept slamming Carter's head into the pavement. I yelled for somebody to help us. Carter fought back. He did. Oh, God, Momma, look at him."

Rosie fell to the ground beside me, reaching for Carter. The world stopped, leaving only the boy in my arms and the girl holding on to him. Both of us talking love words to him. Both of us whispering apologies. Both of us praying. Begging.

～ Twenty-Six ～

For the first time since the rubeola when he was little, Carter stayed at Tolliver Hospital. The days dragged into weeks and the wind began to blow the leaves off the oak trees lining the front entrance, each leaf wider than my own palm. The nurses brought a cot into his room for me. Coffee and cigarettes were the only things I could manage after Carter fell into a coma. To have a child dance so close to death a second time filled me with a kind of anger I hadn't felt before—it spread to every part of my insides until sometimes, at night, I would have to go down the hall to the toilet and throw up awful yellow bile.

My husband got called for a big job in Mississippi and left a month after our boy got hurt. With the bills piling up, he had to go. I'd never felt more lonely in my whole life.

Carter's body slowly began to heal itself on the outside. The bruises along his broken jaw faded. The stitches on his face came out the second month, leaving a deep scar that ran from his forehead over his right eye to his jawbone. He would never see the same out of that eye again. Spiky brown fuzz sprouted from his scalp, shaved by the nurses that first night for the emergency surgery. Scars formed a map across the back of his head, their lines intersecting at points, like a tic-tac-toe board. Every day I touched his feet, his legs, his right arm, his hands, his chest. Every place those Smith brothers hadn't. And I prayed over him. *Thank you, God, for these strong legs. These beautiful fingers. Thank you for these lungs breathing in and out.*

My son woke up two months and three days after the beating. He didn't recognize me. Didn't remember a thing, not even his own name. The doctors had warned me this might happen, given the swelling around his brain, but nothing prepared me for those first days after the coma. Carter just sat in bed with his hands folded in his lap, staring out the window. Wouldn't even get up to go to the bathroom, though his legs worked fine. He didn't speak a word. When I talked to him, I knew he didn't hear me. This ghost boy was almost harder to bear than the comatose one. I wanted my son, my Carter, back. All of him.

Violet brought me dinner and drove her sisters over to the hospital every other day. I found out later that Rosie spent the night in the McNairy County jail after setting fire to the Smith boys' house. They were out on bail (one of their cousins was a bail bondsman) and sleeping in their beds when she did it. Their mother smelled the smoke and called the fire department. Most of the house burned. Violet's husband, Louis, had played high school basketball with Sheriff Duffy and was able to sweet-talk him into letting Rosie go.

The Smith family knew we would nail their boys to the cross if given half a chance, so they offered us a deal. They wouldn't cooperate with the police about the arson if we wouldn't press assault charges. I called Carter Sr. in Jackson and he yelled curse words I hadn't even heard before. My husband had been making calls of his own and found out why Earl thought our boys had said something to the revenuers about the Smith family still—they were known for making the best moonshine in McNairy County. Carter and Zeke used to swim in a pond near their still, and Earl caught sight of them once. Revenuers showed up a week later and destroyed the still, so Earl figured it was our boys that told. When Earl saw Carter without Zeke at the movie, he saw a chance for payback. Mr. Smith said Earl didn't mean to really hurt Carter. Just "rough him up a little."

Of course we agreed to the deal with the Smiths. I didn't want Rosie anywhere near a jail, juvenile or not. But no one felt like justice was served. Preacher Dawson told me God would reckon with those boys in ways we couldn't imagine, and I said that was fine for the hereafter but I had to live in the here-now.

By November, Carter's memory began to return. He recognized me. His sisters. The first words he spoke were *Where's Zeke?* And this is where I messed up. I know that now. But at the time, I did what I thought was best.

After the attack, I refused to let anyone in the family write to Zeke or call him about it. It would only have taken him away from schoolwork. The thought of my boy studying in some grand library was the only happy thought I had during those hospital days. Carter Sr. wanted to send a telegram, but I said, *No, we'll wait and see.* If Carter's not better by the first of the year, we'll send the telegram.

Ezekiel's stream of letters to his brother went unread and unanswered. I wrote when I could and told of things like the weather and how much we all missed him and how proud we were of him. It was too expensive for Zeke to call us on the phone back then, even though Cousin Georgia wouldn't have minded, so it had been pretty easy to stop the word from spreading.

When Carter asked for his brother, I reminded him Ezekiel was in Virginia.

"Get him," Carter said. He talked funny, garbled, like his mouth was full of rocks.

If my son had asked me to get him Bob Pettit from the St. Louis Hawks, his favorite basketball player, I would have. If he had asked me to get him the moon, I would have called NASA and done my best. But I would not give him Ezekiel. His brother was where he needed to be. If he came home now, he might never return to school.

The only other thing Carter kept mumbling about sounded something like *Where's my yo-yo?* When I mentioned this to Rosie, she closed her eyes for a second before telling me one last detail of that afternoon at the theater. Every Saturday and Sunday matinee show, Bob Dunlap held an audience contest during intermission—silly games like how fast can you drink a Coke or sing a famous song backward. That Saturday it had been the yo-yo contest. Carter loved yo-yos, so Rosie urged him to go up on the stage. He beat out everybody else by keeping the yo-yo going the longest and won a brand-new glittery red Fli-Back wooden. Rosie figured it must have gotten knocked out of his pocket during the attack, so I called up Bob Dunlap and asked him about getting Carter another one. *Sure thing, Mrs. Cooper,* he said. I gave it to Carter the very next day, assuring him that it was, in fact, the exact same one he had won.

As Christmastime grew closer and Carter continued to get better, however slowly, the hospital began pestering me to take him home. The circumstances of Carter's injuries led the staff to be kind to us in the beginning, to give us the benefit of the doubt about our ability to pay for the room, the medicines, the tests. The third week of December, the doctor took me aside. Bone skinny with a tendency to stutter when he had difficult news to deliver, Dr. Sidwell spoke in a tone meant to ease my mind.

"Institutionalize him, Mrs. Cooper," he said. "Or care for him the rest of his life. Th-these are your choices. We've done all-all we can for him here."

"I'll discuss it with my husband."

"Soon, Mrs. Cooper."

As I watched him walk down the hallway, I reached inside my purse for a cigarette, my hand groping among the lipstick I hadn't used in months and the scraps of paper with notes I'd scribbled. *Call Charlotte to pick up Rosie. Remind Violet to get mail. Tell Carter stories from when he was little. So he'll remember.* My hand found the pack. Empty.

I went home that night. Got dinner ready for poor Rosie, who had barely seen me or her daddy since the beating. It was the first time I had cooked. The sizzle of the corn bread batter as it hit the hot skillet made me happy. This meant the bread would have the crispy bottom and soft top Rosie liked. She sat at the kitchen table working on algebra homework.

"You're going to like this, baby girl."

She smiled without looking up from the math problems. Carter Sr.'s truck wheezed to a stop in the driveway.

"Daddy's home."

"You go on and finish your homework in the living room, okay? Your father and I need to talk."

Rosie stared right back at me with the look she'd been

giving me since she was two, the look that said, *I'll be damned if I'll do anything you tell me.*

"Just go. Please."

"Fine," she said, picking the paper and books up from the table. "Go ahead and fight. It was better when you stayed at the hospital."

If she'd been closer, I'd have slapped her. But Rosie was smart. She was already halfway to the living room and out of reach. The sound of Carter's heavy footsteps came up the back stairs. I busied myself at the stove, pushing hamburger around in another pan. I could hear him taking off his work boots, one, then the other, dropping into the dirt with a solid weight. The slap of the screen door shutting made me jump.

My husband filled the doorway. The smell of the cold outside air clung to him. He was not a tall man. I could wear one-inch heels but no higher during the forty-two years of our marriage. His shoulders and arms were the biggest thing about him, built up from years of welding together pieces of pipe. There was a space within those arms where I felt safe and treasured. He came up behind me and rested his hands on my hips.

"Nice to see you cooking, Lillian." He kissed the back of my neck, letting his mouth trail down inside my blouse.

I kept stirring the hamburger, steeling myself against the kisses, focusing instead on the faint smell of sweat on him.

"Where are the girls?" he asked.

The question came as his hands reached the roundness of my bottom. He kneaded the flesh gently.

"Daisy's over at Charlotte's helping with the kids." My mind skittered toward the bedroom, and I tried to put space between our bodies.

"Rosie's in the living room, Carter."

He mumbled something into my neck, his teeth nibbling at my skin.

"The living room," I said again, louder.

"Nothing wrong with a man loving his wife, Lillian."

There had been nothing of man and wife between us
since Carter went into the hospital. Rosie walked in.

"Hey, Daddy." She kissed him on the cheek. "Finished
my homework. I'm going to Aunt Charlotte's for dinner."

She spoke this to her father, not me, knowing that I
would object.

Carter's hand squeezed my waist. "Sounds fine."

I shook my head. "I made your favorite meal, Rosie.
You'll stay."

My husband whispered, "Don't," into my ear. He
peered over my shoulder into the pan. "Looks great. I'll eat
Rosie's, too."

My daughter knew the battle was won and she left.
When the front door shut, announcing that we were alone,
Carter walked over and turned the lock. He came back to the
kitchen and put the latch on the back door.

"Never mind about dinner," he said, pulling me to him.
"We'll eat later."

I let him lead me into the living room, wanting to feel
close to my husband again. To forget the weight of the hospital and what was to come.

We left a trail of clothes behind us. My blouse. His
shirt. My bra. His belt. In the living room, Carter took the
wedding-ring quilt draped over the couch and laid it out on
the floor. We kissed standing up. On and on we kissed, the
silence of our never silent house wrapping around us. His
hands found my breasts and we lowered ourselves to the floor.

The old fabric of the quilt was soft and smooth against my back. Carter slipped into me quickly and easily. We moved together and let ourselves cry out. Loud. Without fear of a teenager stumbling upon us.

The chill of evening dropped down on us. Carter pulled another quilt from the couch on top of us. We lay there, arms entangled around each other, for a long time. Not talking. I wanted to stay like that for another hour. Another day. Forever.

I broke the silence first. "We need to talk about Carter." On our backs, we faced the ceiling. I didn't turn to look at my husband, just kept talking.

"The hospital's done all it can for him. They want us to take him home or put him in the state institution."

He went still beside me. I could feel his rib cage push against my own as he took a breath.

"We'll bring him home, then, Lillian Grace."

The use of my first and middle names meant he would not argue the subject. It was the response I had expected. It was the answer I wanted to give. But couldn't.

"Who's going to take care of him? You're gone most of the time, Carter. I've taken care of that child and four others for the past twenty years. We don't know what's going to happen to our son. He could get worse."

"He could get better."

I got up and found my blouse, stood with my back to him, buttoning it.

"You're his mother, for God's sake." He came up behind me, put his hands roughly on my shoulders to turn me around. "You'd rather see our boy in a crazy hospital. Are you sure about that, Lillian?"

Of course I wasn't. But all I had been thinking about on the drive home from the hospital was how tired I was. How Ezekiel was gone. How Carter would never get better than he was. All I could see were days stretching ahead of me that looked the same—get up, cook breakfast for Carter, help him bathe, help him put on clothes, do housework, keep him out of trouble, fix lunch, take him shopping, where everyone would stare at him, fix dinner, get him ready for bed. On and on until my hair turned gray and so did my son's.

"I can't."

The words came out so quiet I didn't know if Carter Sr. heard me. He placed a finger beneath my chin and tilted it upward, the wetness on my face visible. In our years of marriage, I had never said those words to him. Not when he left for a whole year to look for work, leaving me with the kids and ten dollars. Not when his mother took sick and I invited her into our home and turned the dining room into a sick room, caring for her until the day she died. I had done what needed to be done for our family. And more.

"Lilly." He breathed a thousand questions into the word. "Our boy will die in there. You know that. He's barely held on in the regular hospital."

I brushed my cheeks with the back of my hand. "We can go see him every week. They'll take care of him. Don't you understand? They'll do better than me. I can't. He'll be okay, Carter. He'll be okay."

The house had gone dark. Only the light from the kitchen could be seen, slicing the space between us. My husband looked at me for the longest time before dropping his face in his hands. I couldn't tell if he was crying or praying or both.

The burned stench of the forgotten corn bread filtered into the living room, replacing the warm smells of our bodies. He raised his eyes to mine.

"We'll do what you want for a little while. You just need a rest, Lillian. That's all. You're tired."

He opened the circle of his arms, and I stepped in, not realizing that nothing would ever be the same again.

∽ Twenty-Seven ∽

Last week I quit playing dumb at the old folk's home. The game wasn't fun anymore and it was too hard pretending in front of my daughters. And I wanted to go home. But instead of letting me go, the doctors just moved me over to Tolliver Hospital. The surgery is tomorrow. Dr. Trent started to tell me about the operation this morning—*So, Mrs. Cooper, we'll begin with an incision along the rib*—I told him to shut the hell up. Why does the man think I would want to know what he's going to cut on me? Really. Men are just stupid sometimes. But not as dumb as women can be. I made a list today, nothing else to do, on the back of my breakfast napkin. "Lillian's Life Lessons," that's what I'll call it:

1. You can be pretty until the cows come home but it doesn't get you a life you want.
2. (which is related to 1.) Eventually everybody gets old, and being pretty, no matter how much Mary Kay you put on, is not an option anymore.

3. Your children will suck the life out of your bones and then be mad at you for not baking their favorite chocolate cake for their tenth birthday (Daisy is still mad at me over this one).

4. For women, our children are all we've got and if we screw them up, it's all over.

5. (which is related to 4.) Once a woman falls in love, she can't get anything done after that.

That's it. Nothing earth-shattering, I guess. But can I tell you how much I messed up? The whole damned thing, I think. Maybe if I'd been able to keep my knees tight against the persistent pressing of one Carter Cooper, I'd be in Manhattan right now. Living in my penthouse apartment with my younger live-in lover, managing quite nicely on my occasional guest appearance in a Broadway show—*Come and hear the legendary voice of Lillian Grace Parker in a limited engagement.*

At night over at the Preserve, when all the crazy people were sleeping their hazy-dazy dreams, I would think about my boys, Ezekiel and Carter, and my girls—Violet, Daisy, and Rosie. If New York had worked out, what about them? Those children wouldn't have walked the earth. And while some, namely my own children, might think I'd get up and do a dance about that, I wouldn't. Not hardly.

Carter was the hardest for me. Would have been for any mother. I wanted my kids to get more from life than I had been able to grab. And because of that rubeola, Carter wasn't ever going to get two miles past Clayton. Not two miles. Just like me. Just *like* me.

I tried to make Ezekiel understand why I put Carter in the state hospital all those years ago. But he wouldn't listen, thought I was some kind of monster for putting his brother away. *Throwing* Carter away, that's what Ezekiel said. That's what it looked like. I know. I didn't want to throw Carter away. Forget, maybe. For just a little while. Until I got some rest. Until Carter got better.

The boy I thought I wanted to lose was never lost to me. His brother, on the other hand, never came back. Ezekiel hasn't hugged me the same since he came home from Virginia. When he puts his arms around me, he doesn't pull me close. He just holds me out so I can barely catch the scent of warmth and little boy that was like air to me.

Part of me hoped that if Zeke found a way to forgive himself for not saving his brother from drowning, maybe he could figure out how to forgive me. I know he blames himself for Carter's death. When the police investigated the drowning, they asked me if I had any reason to think Ezekiel would want to cause Carter harm. None, I said. Those boys loved each other the way most families can only hope for. No, it was a terrible accident. Nobody knows what happened.

After Carter moved in with Zeke, he brought me wildflowers every day until the day he died. If I wasn't home, he'd leave a note: *Where are you? Here's the flowers. Love, your son.*

I'm ready to see Carter again. It's not going to be long now. And when we meet up, I'm going to love that boy to pieces.

∼ PART III ∼

EZEKIEL

I will seek that which was lost, and bring again
that which was driven away, and will bind up that
which was broken . . .

Ezekiel 34:16

～ Twenty-Eight ～

1985

The day after the tornado, the phone rings nonstop. And every time it's answered, a Cooper woman is on the end of the line worrying about me getting blown to bits. My sisters call, one after the other. The phone hardly rests in the cradle before jangling again. Osborne emerges from his room to grab coffee in the kitchen. He wears a large, brown bathrobe and navy socks with frayed holes at the heel. We manage to say hello before being interrupted. He looks at me, then looks at the phone. All I can do is shrug. But I will not pick it up. With a snort, Osborne crosses to the phone and answers it. He holds it out to me.

"Your ex-wife."

Technically, Jackie doesn't qualify as a Cooper but she still acts like one.

"Are you okay? Are the Laceys okay? I put the TV on this morning and there was Bailey, front and center. 'Killer tornado,' they said. God, Zeke."

Louisa gets on the phone next, telling me she has been praying all morning I'd be okay. "Come home, Dad. Please."

Honora refuses to speak to me directly, choosing instead to shout in the background. "Way to pick a place to go, Dad. *Nice* choice."

Jackie gets back on and says pretty much the same thing. When she lowers her voice so the girls can't hear, I brace myself.

"You need to know that your daughter is getting very serious with this guy, Zeke. This senior guy. I just wanted her to go to homecoming with him, but now they're studying together every day after school and going to the movies on Fridays."

Our daughter has sworn up, down, and sideways that boys are "the stupidest dorks on the planet" and she will have nothing to do with them. And though I'm no fan of her weekly hair-dye jobs, they serve the purpose of making her look "weird," something I know most Mabry teenage boys are not interested in exploring.

"Who is this boy? Does he play sports?"

"He plays drums in the school marching band."

"Are you kidding? You're letting her go out with a musician? Is she smoking and drinking now, too? Goddamn it, Jacklynn. Just tell her no."

Curtis bellows in the background that they are going to be late for dinner at his parents' house. Jackie lowers her voice again.

"I'm not going to tell her no. She'll just do it anyway behind my back. At least I know where she is. She needs a father right now. You picked a bad time to have a midlife crisis, you asshole."

When the word *asshole* enters the conversation, there is nowhere to go but down, so I get off the phone, though not before promising to come back soon. I *know* Honora needs me. But I can't go back. Not yet.

Mother makes it through next. She is worried sick and wants me to come home. Calls me crazy for preferring to stay in a state where entire cows get lifted off their hooves and thrown onto a different farm. Her voice sounds weak and I ask if she is all right.

"Nothing a little death couldn't fix," she says.

It is another moment when I should say something about the lung cancer. But two decades worth of not caring, or attempting not to care, get in the way.

"It's a mess here, Mother. I should go."

Being outside, away from the pull of BellSouth, feels like the only safe place, tornado or no tornado. I find a pair of work gloves in the barn and start dragging piles of branches. There are so many of them, spread over every inch of the property, it will take months to clear it all. The tornado did $250 million worth of damage over three counties and killed two people in a neighboring town. Cousin Georgia wants to replant the apple orchard, but Osborne refuses to talk about it beyond saying, *Don't be stupid, Georgia, it's gone—one hundred years and a wind took it all away.*

The roar of a chain saw interrupts the meadowlark's morning song and the chatter from the radio in the barn, where talk of the tornado has been replaced by breaking news of the passengers' release from the hijacked Italian cruise ship *Achille Lauro*. Georgia and Osborne's handyman/groundskeeper/farming expert, Jimmy Trotter, calls me over to help him cut a large branch from a downed tree.

Jimmy and his family live in a small house on the eastern edge of the property. Georgia says he saved the orchard several years ago when fire blight threatened to destroy the trees.

It takes the two of us to drag the cut branch to the pile. I ask if he thinks the orchard should be replanted.

"Who knows? This is good growing ground. Maybe not apples."

When Jimmy leans over the chain saw and it jumps to life again, I motion for him to wait.

"What, Mr. Cooper? I need to work."

The jarring loudness of the saw requires me to yell my question twice.

"Miss Chambers?" he says. "She's the best riding teacher around here."

"She's giving me a lesson later this week. Says she'll have me riding by the end of it."

"Miss Chambers doesn't fool around. You'll see."

Elle had called earlier and said she'd be happy to give me a lesson. It would provide a welcome break from clearing branches on her farm. Best riding teacher around, is she? Probably never taught a forty-two-year-old out-of-shape guy before.

When Friday finally arrives, I take longer than usual with showering and dressing. A dusty, half-empty bottle of Old Spice sits on the dresser in my room. It smells close to how it should, so I slap some on my face and neck before heading up to the stables with a cup of coffee. "Peanut Farmers Get the Shell Out" is written on the mug.

Getting acquainted with the horses before Elle shows up seems like a good idea. They hear me coming and neigh in a friendly way. I fill each of their feed buckets and hang them over the stalls. After reassuring myself that the horses are too busy eating to be worried about me, I grab the shovel off the wall and set to work. Darcy throws me a backward glance when I get to hers. I tell her she can either leave me alone or step in crap the rest of the day, and after stamping her back foot once, she returns to breakfast.

By the time Diamond's stall is cleaned out, patches of sweat have formed under my arms. I take off my heavy flannel shirt and work in my undershirt. Whitey finishes her oats first and keeps looking over at me, so I stand by the stall and scratch behind her long, hairy ears. Darcy finishes next and begins nickering at me, too. Which one will Elle suggest I ride? Diamond looks like the safest bet. He's much bigger than Darcy and Whitey and possesses a reassuring calmness. I pat him on the forelock and bribe him with the promise of fresh apples tomorrow if he makes me look like Travolta in *Urban Cowboy*.

"Diamond's everybody's favorite."

The voice comes from the stable doors. Elle stands between them. Her legs are encased in tight riding pants, knee-high boots hug the roundness of her calves, and she wears a long-sleeved shirt with "Chambers Riding School" in faded letters on it. I begin not to care if I fall off.

"Good morning," I say.

"Don't bet on it."

"Trying to scare me?"

"No," she says, laughing, then adds, "well, maybe a little."

Elle looks me up and down, stopping at my feet. "No cowboy boots?"

"Nope." Never owned a pair of them. The old, brown lace-up work boots are the closest thing I have.

"You're not wearing them," I point out.

"That's because I teach English riding, not Western."

I wonder if this means we'll have tea instead of a beer after the lesson. She disappears into the tack room. All three of the horses hang their heads over the stalls, nostrils flaring. Darcy keeps tossing her head. Whitey watches me out of the corner of her eye. Diamond's ears prick up and he does a little dance back and forth in his stall.

Elle explains each step as she tacks him up—how to insert the bit gently into his mouth, to always remember to put a blanket beneath the saddle to prevent its chafing the horse's skin, how to cinch the saddle properly so you won't fall off. She pulls a few sugar cubes from her pocket.

"And this is the final piece. Give them a treat before and after you ride and then they'll love to see you walk in the door."

There is a soft, lilting quality to her voice that suggests the South but isn't deep enough to make me believe she grew up here.

"Where are you from?"

She rolls her eyes. "People ask me that all the time. I think you Southern folks are obsessed with accents. It's like you want to tell the exact county a person is from by the way they talk."

She's right.

"The drawl, if you can call it that, is from living here for almost five years and going to college out here. I'm from California originally."

California transplants are a scarce breed in the South. Most of the visiting Californians I've run into talk about how quaint the South is and how slow the pace, but you can tell they'd go crazy with all this slowness if they lived here.

"What made you stay out here?"

She shakes a finger. "Quit stalling. We're getting you up on this horse. And the answer to your question is I fell in love with this part of the world when I went to college at UVA, and even a nasty divorce from a Virginia gentleman couldn't keep me from settling down here. No place like it, really. "

"I went to UVA, too."

"What year? I graduated in seventy-four."

I turn away from her and pat Diamond's neck. The tendons are pronounced and thick. "I was there a little before your time."

If I say more, she'll know what an old geezer I am and that I never graduated. "How long have you been divorced?"

"We are curious this morning, aren't we?" she says, leading Diamond out of the stables.

"I'm divorced, too. It's been about two years. Since it was legal. We were separated for a few years before that. My ex-wife remarried last month."

I tell myself to shut up; she doesn't want to know any of this.

Elle stops next to a tree stump. "Let's focus on the horse now, okay? Hop up on the stump."

"How come?"

"Trust me, okay?"

We face each other and our eyes meet. Today hers are the color of slick river rocks, darker than I recall. In them I glimpse guardedness. The confidence falls away for a moment and I see her, really see her, for the first time. She has been hurt. Deeply, I suspect.

"Are you ready or not?" The tone is all business again.

The saddle is a tiny scrap of leather that looks big enough for a small child, not a grown man. There is no saddle horn. When I mention this fact Elle nods.

"That's right. English saddles don't have horns. Sorry."

She looks far from sorry. As I climb on top of the stump, getting a leg over the saddle without having anything to grab becomes a big problem. Mounting a horse consists of two motions—putting the foot nearest the horse into the stirrup and then, in one fluid motion, hiking the other leg up and over the horse. She notices my scowl.

"Mounting is the hardest part of learning to ride English-style. Don't worry. We won't get it down perfectly today. We just need to get you up there. Ready?"

"No, but I don't think that's going to stop you."

"Give it a go, old boy."

She stands next to me and places my hands in the right spots on the saddle. I can feel the rough calluses on the plump underside of her fingers against mine. Elle taps my left leg and motions for it to go in the stirrup. After almost losing my balance twice, I manage it.

"Now, on the count of three, I want you to push off with that back leg and swing it with everything you've got over to the other side of Diamond. Got it?"

I glance at the horse, who is busy nibbling at a fly on his chest.

"He's not going anywhere. Diamond would wait patiently for a week for you to get on him."

I mutter a curse before attempting to throw my leg over. Somehow it gets stuck halfway and my body begins sliding in the opposite direction. Elle quickly shores me up, allowing the leg to make it around Diamond's ample side. It takes a minute to situate my feet properly in the stirrups.

The ground looks far away and I grip my legs tighter. The high vantage point offers a view of the farm all the way to the towering sycamore grove to the east, untouched by the storm, and the symmetrical lines of the peach orchard to the west. Diamond stands stock-still like the champion he is. I feel no need to set the horse in motion.

"You did it!" Elle claps. I grin.

"Now, I want you to hold the reins lightly, don't exert any pressure, while I lead him into the ring."

"I'm pretty happy just sitting up here. No need to do anything else."

"Don't be a wuss."

The rest of the lesson passes without catastrophe. Diamond pretends to let me tell him what to do. Toward the end, Elle asks if I want to take it up to a trot. When "trot" is defined as going faster, I shake my head.

"I agree," she says. "We've got to have something for you to look forward to."

Walking suits me fine. I have never been one of those guys who are hooked on speed. The world turns too fast as it is without me trying to keep up.

After taking off Diamond's saddle, blanket, and bridle, we let him loose in the ring. Elle suggests letting Darcy and Whitey out to join him for a little exercise. As I lead Darcy out to the ring, she nicks me on the shoulder, not hard enough to break the skin but with enough force to make me jump.

"She's mad at you. She's jealous because you rode Diamond instead of her. Got to look out for that one."

"So I hear."

We lean against the ring's wooden railing and watch. Darcy and Diamond chase each other while Whitey stands in the middle, his tail flicking every so often to ward off a fly. The sun has burned off the morning mist. Next to me, Elle lets her head fall back, closing her eyes.

"I love this time of the year. The sun still warms you but doesn't make you break out in a sweat and the air smells like apples and leaves."

Without thinking, I turn to her and lean in, unsure of what to do next but certain of the desire to be closer to her. I want to taste the sweetness of her mouth. The wind blows a dark curl across her face and I reach up to grasp it, tucking it behind her ear. I hear the soft intake of breath when my hand makes contact with her skin.

Her eyes fly open. She looks ready to run. "Zeke."

There is a warning in the word but the sound of my name in her mouth does me in.

The warmth of her breath against my cheek is hot and moist. Strangely hot and moist.

We are not alone.

Darcy has sidled up and put her large nostrils inches from my face.

Elle giggles, a relaxed and girlish sound. "See, I told you she was a jealous one." She steps away from the railing, putting distance between us.

We both pretend I had not been trying to kiss her. It is not my style to bear down on a woman with a kiss. I was raised to ask a girl first.

"What's your schedule like tomorrow?" She will not look at me, focusing instead on brushing dirt off the tops of her pants.

"I don't imagine I have much of a schedule."

"A man of leisure these days. I forgot. How about another lesson after lunch? I've got a couple in the morning over at my place."

"Why don't I meet you there?" I want to see her in her own surroundings.

She says no, it's better for me to keep riding Diamond. "See you tomorrow then."

"At least let me walk you home."

"Why do all Southern men think women are helpless?"

Her tone rings with a surprising bitterness. Most likely her ex is responsible for putting it there.

"See you tomorrow," I say.

Elle turns and gives me a wave, causing a lift in my chest that can only be described as dangerous.

∾ Twenty-Nine ∾

Letters to Home
1960

September 2, 1960
Lacey Farms
Bailey, Virginia

Dear Carter,

I made it to Virginia. Remember I showed you on the map where I'd be going to school? Right in the middle of Virginia? The train ride took fifteen hours. I wish you'd been with me. It went through the Appalachian Mountains, and those mountains stretching up toward the sky, touching the clouds—it was one of the prettiest things I've ever seen.

You caught anything worth eating lately? Remember to get some of those worms from up in the catalpa tree. The bluegills can't resist those.

Cousin Georgia and her husband's family have the biggest house and farm I've ever seen. Georgia and Osborne live on just one floor of the main house. Her in-laws live on the second and third floors. My room's on the back of the house, overlooking the apple orchard. I'm going to box up some of the apples once they get ripe and send them back to you and Rosie.

Things sure are different here. Every night I have to wear a tie to dinner. Cousin Georgia and Osborne and I eat with his mom and dad in the formal dining room (*formal* means fancy). They have candles lit and these special dinner plates from England. We eat a lot of food I've never had before, like parsnips (they taste a little like carrots but not really) and aspic, which is pretty disgusting stuff—you don't even want to know what's in it. And they mainly talk about their real-estate business during dinner—which property needs work, which property needs to be sold, which property they should develop next. I don't say much.

Compared to our house, Lacey Farms is pretty quiet. They have lots of animals, but they live down in the barn, and there aren't any kids running around crazy like at our house. Cousin Georgia and Osborne couldn't have kids, so it's just them and his parents, who are really old—they must be fifty. After dinner Georgia plays the piano. She asked me what kind of music I like. I told her rock and roll and she and Osborne laughed. She plays classical music, which is nice to listen to while I'm studying or reading. I don't know how to tell you what it sounds like except it's kind of like church music.

Classes started yesterday at the university. White columns seem to hold up every building. The library looks like a church. You walk up the steps, pass columns so wide I can't reach my arms around them, and inside it's quiet enough to hear the scratch of someone's pencil against paper. There are so many books, Carter. I want to live there and go floor by floor, row by row, and read every book in the place.

Speaking of reading, are you reading at night like you promised? I left *The Adventures of Huckleberry Finn* at home for you. You like that story better than Tom Sawyer. I know it's hard to read without me there, but you can. I know you can.

Guess I'll say good-bye for now. Remember I'm coming home at summertime, okay? That's only nine months away.

Love from your brother,
Zeke

September 15, 1960
Lacey Farms
Bailey, Virginia

Dear Jackie,

See, I told you I'd write and here I am. It seems so long since I've seen you but it's only been five weeks. Virginia is beautiful. I wish you were here and we could go and see everything together. Next week Cousin Georgia's taking me to see Monticello, Thomas Jefferson's home. I know you'd like to see it, too. Sure you don't want to come out to Virginia? There's a good girls' school nearby. I've met a couple of girls from there and they say it's a real nice school.

How's the dress shop? There are a lot of little shops like Abigail's in Charlottesville in a place called the Corner. I pass by it going to class and think about you every time there's a salesgirl in the window putting an outfit on a mannequin.

I miss you. You thought I'd get all the way out in Virginia and forget about you, but I think about you all the time. I have the picture of you from the junior social, with the gardenia in your hair, on my nightstand. Do you miss me? Are you still sad about the baby? I think about the baby sometimes. How it would've been born by now and you'd both be at Lacey Farms with me. I get a little sad then.

You'd like Cousin Georgia. She's real sweet. I've told her a lot about you.

Classes are tough. I'm taking biology, Greek and Roman mythology, American history (since before the Revolution), algebra, and basketball. My favorite professor is Dr. Fitzpatrick. He teaches the ancient myth class. He's from Scotland, and it's hard to understand him when he speaks fast, which he does all the time because he gets so worked up about what we're reading. This week we discussed the *Iliad,* and when this basketball player said it was the most boring, longest poem he'd ever read, I thought Dr. Fitz might punch him, he got so riled.

There are a lot of rich kids. When people find out I live with the Laceys, they think I'm rich, too. Makes you laugh, doesn't it? I've made friends with a guy named Frank Chancellor. He's from Richmond. He knew all about the Laceys. His daddy works for one of Osborne's brothers. Frank said I was lucky to come from a family like the Laceys. I told him I was lucky to come from a family where five kids slept in one room in a house that didn't have indoor plumbing until 1957.

He laughed and said, "No shit?" And I said, "Only in the outhouse." We have biology class and play basketball together. I'm not good enough to be on the team, but there's a group of us that play intramural. Frank lives on campus in one of the dorms. I have one night class, biology lab, on Tuesday nights, and I sleep on Frank's floor those nights. It's kind of nice to stay where all the other students are.

Will you come visit me soon? Homecoming is next month and I would love to take you to the dance. Think about it, will you? Promise?

Love,
Zeke.

October 12, 1960
Library
University of Virginia
Charlottesville, Virginia

Dear Carter,

Hey brother of mine. Why haven't you written back? Too busy to write a few lines about what you've been doing? You're going to be in trouble when I come home in June.

Cousin Georgia took me to the Appalachian Trail last weekend. I wish you could've seen it, Carter. The trees and the colors—dark fiery red to pumpkin orange to gold spread over the mountains like quilts. It reminded me of how Lavice Valley looks when we climb up the steps of the Tipton Trail tower.

Daddy taking you fishing much? I know he's gone mostly, but you ask him nicely next time he's home for a bit and he'll take you.

Sometimes I miss home so much. Don't get me wrong, I'm thankful for Cousin Georgia and Osborne and all they've done for me. But I don't fit quite right here. Everybody's so different. I'm keeping up with the schoolwork and have made a friend or two.

Should be studying for my biology midterm, so I'd better get to it. Miss you, buddy.

Love your brother,
Zeke

November 1, 1960
Lacey Farms
Bailey, Virginia

Dear Jackie,
    I sure am sorry you couldn't come up for homecoming weekend. Train tickets cost a lot, I know. I guess I was just dreaming. We won the football game—27:21. Frank and I went. He's gone to military school since he was six and says the university is like being set free. Frank has a girlfriend over at Raintree Academy. Her name is Brenda and she's real sweet. I showed her your picture and she said you were pretty. Frank took her to the homecoming dance, and she had a friend named Shelly who really wanted to go, so I took her. We had a good time but she's not nearly as good a dancer as you.
    I have a big favor to ask. Carter hasn't written me since I've been gone. Could you check on him? I know he's fine but it's strange not hearing one word from him. I promise to bring you the best darned peaches in the state of Virginia as a thank-you next June. (That's a joke, unless you want me to.)
    It's strange being away from Carter. Our whole lives, from the very beginning, we've been together. Here, almost no one knows I have a twin brother. And sometimes it's nice. I get to just be Zeke. Not Ezekiel, Carter's brother. The other day I figured out that I hate pork rinds. Can't stand them. But

I've eaten them all these years because Carter likes them. When you're a twin, you feel like everything you do is connected to this other person. That you really can't exist without him. Truth is, you can.

Biology is my hardest class. I got a C– on the midterm. I don't think I'm going to be a bio major. Dr. Fitzpatrick is still my favorite professor. He gave us an extracredit assignment of writing an epic poem about our own life. I gave it a try and Dr. Fitzpatrick gave me an A. He said my writing showed "great promise." What do you think about that? I wrote Momma about it and she said that was just fine but not to forget I was meant for greater things than writing.

She wants me to be a doctor or a lawyer. And you want to know the truth? I don't want to be anything close to a doctor or a lawyer. My mind doesn't work that way. I don't know what I want to be but I think a writer doesn't sound too bad. Cousin Georgia said it's a fine profession. Osborne said being a farmer is a shade better but, all in all, I could do worse.

I hope you're doing okay. I miss you every day. Write me. I miss holding you. I love you, Jackie.

Love,
Zeke

November 30, 1960
Lacey Farms
Bailey, Virginia

Dear Mother,

I had my first Thanksgiving away from home last week. Laceys from all over descended on the farm. Folks started arriving on Wednesday afternoon. I swear that Cousin Georgia, Sallie (she helps cook sometimes), and Alice (Sallie's sister) cleaned and cooked for two weeks straight before the actual holiday. Every room was aired out, since most of the relatives stayed over Wednesday and Thursday night, some even Friday and Saturday.

On Thanksgiving morning, Georgia, Osborne, his parents, and I went to church at St. Timothy's. It was the "Blessing of the Hounds" service—you remember how there are a bunch of rich folks here who ride around on their horses trying to catch a little old fox? Every Thanksgiving morning all of the foxhunters, their horses, and their dogs gather outside the church to be "blessed."

When we got there, the bagpipers in their plaid skirts were just starting. The fog wrapped around the gravestones in the cemetery. The sound of those lonely pipes and the quiet of everyone—five hundred people came but no one said a word—was like nothing you've ever heard. I felt filled up somehow.

All the foxhunters were dressed in scarlet coats and shiny black boots with their dogs sitting at their sides. And the horses! These great big beasts—their coats gleaming in the sun, stamping and snuffling, itching to get on with things and start the hunt.

Osborne told me the Blessing of the Hounds comes from St. Hubert, patron saint of hunters, who lived in eighth-century France. The prayers said are to protect the hunters and offer thanksgiving for the harvest. A little different from Thanksgiving service at First Baptist, isn't it? When Georgia and I had a minute to ourselves, she said the folks who go to St. Timothy's are the descendents of the first English people to settle this area and they take their traditions a little too seriously for her liking.

When one of the horses took a poop right in the middle of the service—you could see the steam coming off it in the cold air—Georgia rolled her eyes and whispered, "Good grief."

I hope you and the family spent a good holiday together. I sure missed being with everybody. Did Daddy let Carter help carve the turkey this year? I did it last year, so this year was Carter's turn. I didn't help carve the turkey here. That's old Mr. Lacey's job. Thirty-five people came for Thanksgiving dinner. And all of them relatives. I always thought five kids around a table was a lot but the Laceys beat us.

Cousin Georgia says she misses seeing the Parker family. She told me the last time she saw most of the Parkers was at her wedding and that was a good fifteen years ago. She says the Laceys are pretty much the only family she has now, with her parents dead and her sister living all the way out in Wyoming.

We're getting ready for final exams. The only class I'm a little worried about is biology. My friend Frank and I have a whole study plan worked out—we'll meet every day for an hour and a half until exam day to go over the material. Dr. Fitzpatrick told me I should write for the school newspaper, so I'm going to check that out for next semester. You write about campus life, sports, stuff like that. He said it would be good experience for me. I know you don't think much about me writing but I know I can do it and still keep up with my studies. Don't worry. I know you already have your graduation dress picked out.

Would you please tell Carter to write me a letter? The lazy guy hasn't written me one word since I've been here. What have you got him doing that he's too busy to write his brother?

Love to everyone,
Ezekiel

December 7, 1960
University of Virginia Library
Charlottesville, Virginia

Dear Jackie,

You're never going to believe this. Cousin Georgia knocked on my door last night and asked if she could speak with me. She's never done that before, so I got worried I'd done something wrong like eaten steak with the salad fork again or left my muddy shoes by the front door. But that wasn't it at all.

She came in and sat on my bed and said she and Osborne had been talking about what to give me as a Christmas present. They'd been thinking really hard about what I needed most, and they thought about books for school and clothes and things like that, but then she said they both looked at each other and they knew—what I needed most was to go home and be with my family. So they're giving me a round-trip train ticket and some spending money for the trip and a little extra to buy presents for the family.

Can you believe it? I've got two more finals, and now I feel like I can survive them knowing I'll see you in only a week. I went to the train station this morning before my history final and got the ticket. I'll be home on December 21. The train gets into Corinth at five minutes after seven o'clock that night. Will you meet me in Corinth, Jackie? Please?

Got my bio final tomorrow, so I've got to study now, but I love you so much and will see you in two weeks. Fourteen days.

Love,
Zeke

PS: Don't tell my family about me coming home, will you? I want it to be a big surprise.

∾ Thirty ∾

1985

"Death does funny things to people, Ezekiel."

Georgia sets her purse on the kitchen table, looking up as Osborne walks upstairs. They attended Joe Cummins's funeral this morning. I offered to go but she told me not to be silly. Why attend a funeral for someone you don't know?

"Most people walk around thinking it will never happen to them—they'll never die, no one they love will ever die, things will stay just as they are forever. And then when it happens, and it always happens, people are shocked."

I lower the heat on the stove's burner and flip over a sandwich. She peers into the pan.

"Smells good."

"Let me fix you one. It's my specialty."

My father taught me how to make fried ham-and-cheese sandwiches the summer Mother spent three days in Memphis with Aunt Charlotte. Mother cooked a whole ham and left it in the fridge for us. Ham for breakfast, ham for lunch, ham for dinner. When she came home, Carter ran up to her and said, *Momma, I don't want to eat ham ever again.*

"Eliza is beside herself." Cousin Georgia selects a bottle from the pill-filled lazy Susan in the middle of the table and holds out a tablet. "Take this. It's vitamin C. I feel like I'm getting a cold. Don't want you to get it."

"I'm not much of a vitamin taker."

She waits until I pop the sour thing into my mouth. Only then does she turn back to the sandwich and milk I set before her.

"This is good, Ezekiel. Did you put Miracle Whip on before you fried it?" She takes another bite and chews appreciatively. "Eliza keeps asking me why. Why would God take her Joe home now, when they were just beginning to enjoy life?"

Noise comes from the second floor, the sound of furniture being dragged. Georgia rolls her eyes. "Oz is moving the chair over to the window so he can see the lake. He'll sit there for the next four hours looking at the damn lake."

I finish frying my sandwich and take a seat. Osborne hollers from upstairs for a cup of coffee. Cousin Georgia slides out her chair but I motion for her to stay put. I put the kettle on and search for the Folgers jar in the cabinet.

"Left-hand side," she says. "Osborne said his good-byes to Joe at the funeral home yesterday. He came out of the viewing room sobbing like a baby. I was afraid he might collapse. I've never understood the point of talking to the dead shell of a person. Joe's spirit is with God now. If we want to talk to him, we should be praying."

"Does Osborne like it strong or weak?"

"Weak. Two sugars and a splash of milk. Just like his father."

Georgia feeds Tucker a crust of bread underneath the table. When I ask her to stop because he'll turn into a scraps beggar, she says the dog is old enough to do whatever he wants.

"You know what makes Joe's death hard? It's that Osborne and I both know we've reached the age where this is only the beginning. Our friends will begin to die off in ones, twos, and threes. And, of course, Osborne's own illness . . ."

She joins me at the sink, still chewing on the sandwich, and we stand side by side looking out the window. Stray branches still lie here and there on the rear lawn. Both our gazes are drawn to the empty rectangle of land directly in front of us. The orchard. Georgia sighs. I notice the faint tinge of a yellow bruise on her temple.

"What's this?" I gently touch the bruise and she flinches.

The kettle lets out a high-pitched whistle.

"Last week I reminded Oz to take his blood-pressure medicine and he refused." She moves to the stove and takes the kettle off the burner. "We got into an argument. And he hit me."

She prepares Osborne's coffee, stirring in the sugar slowly. "Don't worry. It's normal."

"Normal?"

"It's the disease. I've started going to a support group at the hospital. And when this happened, they said it's one of the symptoms. Bursts of violence. Oz didn't mean it."

The coffee spoon clatters against the stainless-steel sink where Georgia tosses it.

"Show me pictures of those beautiful girls of yours. I haven't seen any since they were babies."

I want to ask if she feels safe but am not sure what to say. She puts her hand to my face.

"Ezekiel, having you here makes me feel like I might get through this."

Her expression reveals a grief already beginning for the husband she knows.

"Enough of this," she says, pressing her fingertips to the inside corner of her eyes. "Show me your girls."

I dig out last year's school pictures from my wallet. Louisa's shy smile is covered in braces, a recent development since Curtis could pay the $2,500 to put them there. She hovers somewhere between child and young girl. Honora's hair is dyed dark black, with one side cut longer than the other, and dark lipstick covers her mouth. The dark hair makes her wide blue eyes stand out even more. She could be a budding vampire.

"They're darling," Georgia says. "Honora must be the spunky one."

"You could say that."

"I've always loved your daughters' names. Such beautiful old names."

Jackie and I had argued for hours about Honora's name when she was born. I hadn't liked it. Said it sounded too fancy and people wouldn't say it right. Her whole life she would have to tell people, *No, it's Ahn-or-ah not Hahn-or-ah.*

Osborne yells down the stairs again for coffee.

When I take the coffee up to his room, Oz is sitting in the leather chair next to the bed. *Anglers Monthly* magazine lies open in his lap.

"Just set it on the table there."

"Need anything else?" I ask.

"Make Georgia lie down, will you? She was up all night with Eliza and only worries about me. I'll be fine."

He closes the magazine, running a hand along the front cover, which features a sixty-something guy in a boat reeling

in a large-mouth bass. Standing over Osborne's shoulder, I can
see shiny pink patches of his scalp where the hair has thinned.

"Every time a new issue came in the mail, Joe and I
called each other. We talked about the new lures or planned a
fishing trip to one of the places in the magazine. We both knew
we'd never actually go there but it didn't matter. It was more
fun to talk about going than going could ever have been."

He stares down at his hands as if they don't belong to
him. It is hard to tell if he wants to be alone or if it's better to
stay. The gentle step of Cousin Georgia on the stairs echoes in
the hallway. When she enters the room, she goes straight to
her husband, kneeling next to him and taking his hands in her
own. Oz looks down at her and his mouth lifts.

I step out of the room, closing the door as quietly as possible. Their devotion is almost painful to watch. In the beginning, my own marriage seemed similarly destined. We felt so
much love for each other. And then, we didn't. Jackie says I
withdrew from her and the girls when Carter died.

But things between us were changing even before then.
Jackie herself became distant. I would ask her what was wrong
and she would shake her head and say, "Don't borrow trouble,
Zeke." After hearing this answer a few times, I asked what the
hell did that mean? She started to cry. Never being able to stand
tears, I gathered her in my arms and made love to her, trying to
bridge whatever trouble lay in her heart. A month later Carter
died, throwing marital concerns far from my mind.

Five more years passed before she asked for the divorce.
We fought a lot. Jackie said she should've listened to her mother
when she said she'd spend the rest of her life in Clayton if she
married me. When I said I thought she liked living where we
grew up, Jackie screamed that there had to be something more,
there just had to be. I guess Curtis Baxter was something more.

He's got more stuff, that's for sure. Jackie will get a brand-new car every year, whatever she wants off Curtis's Ford lot. Ford trucks have been my chosen vehicle my whole life, but when this one gives out, I'm switching to a Chevy. No way am I putting money in Curtis's pocket.

Despite the divorce, I'm pretty sure Jackie still loves me. It's just different now—all twisted and knotted up. The four times we made love after the divorce it was like two strangers meeting up in a hotel room instead of two people who'd been sleeping together since they were sixteen.

The image of Elle Chambers lifting her face to the sun replays itself in my mind. I am intrigued enough to want to learn her quirks and the feel of her body, not necessarily in that order. Tomorrow I will ask Cousin Georgia about her. For now, Georgia and Osborne have their own talking to do.

Daisy calls after dinner. My sisters have called me more in the past month than in the past year. She is in the middle of cooking dinner for her three boys and her husband. The sound of balls hitting the floor and meat frying in the background comes through the phone.

"Vi found out about Leroy being on the way to go screw Momma when the drunk bastard killed Cassie, and she asked Momma about it and Momma just keeled over. Right there on the front porch. Had to get stitches on her head from hitting the door handle as she went down. That along with the lung cancer has done Momma in."

The oldest boy, Sean, yells in the background and Daisy tells him to shut up; she is on the phone. No one has talked about Leroy Cooper in a long time.

"How did Vi find out about Leroy?"

A pause.

"Dais? Who told her?"

"I did. All right? It was me. She was going on and on about how horrible it was that Momma got lung cancer at such a young age and how she'd never done anything, *really,* to deserve this, and I couldn't take it, Zeke."

"God, Daisy." I drop my head in my hands. Why couldn't she keep her mouth shut? "Vi didn't need to hear that. That's history. It's done."

A door slams shut. "Dave's home, Zeke. I've got to finish dinner. Call me later, okay?"

The insistent pull of Clayton grabs at me, trying to get its claws in me. But I'm only just beginning at Lacey Farms again.

My sisters and my mother are going to do whatever craziness comes next whether I'm around or not. That's clear. I'm not going anywhere.

I'm not.

∾ Thirty-One ∾

December 1960

The wind blew hard through the Corinth station platform and I turned up the collar of my new corduroy jacket, a gift from Cousin Georgia. During the fifteen-hour trip from Charlottesville, I had envisioned the scene of my homecoming over and over again—how I'd step off the train and Jackie would run into my arms, the soft feel of her body against my own. On this cold night four days before Christmas, a station filled with strangers looked out at me. Hoping Jackie was only running late, I bought a cup of coffee and sat on a bench near the front entrance, where she'd be sure to see me. Fifteen minutes passed. Then thirty. When the hands of the black clock in the waiting area read seven thirty, I knew she wasn't coming.

There was nothing to do except call home. My father said he'd be right over. I asked him not to tell Mother where he was going so some surprise could still be pulled off. This part I had imagined, as well. The conquering son returns home from college—smarter, more debonair, and laden with gifts. Thanks to Georgia's and Osborne's generosity, I had a suitcase full of presents. The one I most wanted to give was the new basketball for Carter. Each member of the UVA team had signed it.

Something made me call Jackie's house, just to see if she was home. She answered on the first ring.

"Jackie?"

"Is that you, Zeke?"

Why would she be home if she knew I was coming to the train station?

"You didn't come."

"What do you mean? Where are you?"

If Jackie was pretending to be surprised about my arrival, she was doing a good job. I had, in fact, never received a letter from her, not the whole time I was away. Doubt crept into my mind. She was seeing someone else now. Of course.

"Where *are* you, Zeke? Are you home?"

"Why didn't you write back?" The call for the eight o'clock train to Memphis came over the loudspeaker. "Say that again, please," I asked. "I couldn't hear."

She let out a long breath. "Ezekiel, I haven't heard anything from you since you left. No letters. Nothing."

"Not one letter?"

"Why would I lie about that?" An angry tone crept into her voice. "Did you get any letters from me?"

"No."

"Of course you didn't. I would've written you right back. I don't know what happened. It's probably got something to do with my mother. She's still pretty mad at you over the baby and everything. She gets the mail every afternoon when I'm at work."

Her mother would later deny meddling. But when she died unexpectedly in 1980, Jackie found the letters. Mrs.

Chatham had kept them hidden in a shoe box buried in a back bedroom closet for more than twenty years.

My father's easy lope crossed the station's front entrance. The amount of gray in his hair now surpassed the amount of dark brown. He was not a tall man, but he carried himself tall, straight backed. I caught his eye with a wave.

"Listen, my dad's here. I don't understand what's happened. Will you be home tomorrow morning?"

"I figured you'd be coming home, what with everything that's happened. But part of me wished you wouldn't, too. Call me at the shop tomorrow. I'll be there ten to six."

Before I could ask her what she meant, she hung up. An arm clasped my shoulder from behind.

"Son." There was real comfort in the word. At least this made sense.

He shook my hand and said I looked good, real good— taller and smarter. I laughed. More tired, maybe, I said. We walked out together, my shoulders now several inches past his.

"University life agrees with you?" The old Ford took several starts before it finally caught.

"It's different. Real different. But I like it."

He ruffled the hair spilling over my shirt collar. There had been no time for the barber shop before coming home.

"We'll have to get this cut tomorrow morning, won't we?" The idea seemed to please him. "You hungry?"

I nodded. Georgia had packed fried chicken and rolls and a piece of pie but I'd eaten it all long before the train rolled into Corinth.

"We'll stop at Calloway's on the outside of town. Bet those Virginians can't make decent barbecue."

"They can make the best ham in the world, though," I said.

The dark streets of Corinth passed by on the way to Highway 45. My breath formed small circles against the window. The heat in the truck didn't work, probably never worked.

"First snow fell on the Blue Ridge right before I left," I said. "The mountains look pretty dusted up in white. When's the last time it snowed in Clayton?"

He tapped his fingers on the steering wheel. "Must have been about ten years ago when that ice storm hit Memphis and shut the whole city down for a week. We didn't get the ice but we got the snow. You and your brother about killed yourselves sledding down Big Hill on your mother's baking sheets."

I remembered. Carter and I nearly ran smack into a station wagon. Turned out it was Tommy Jackson's mom. She nearly had a heart attack watching the two of us slide closer and closer to the front bumper. When she swerved to miss us, the car ended up skidding into the ditch. We tried to keep our faces straight while we pushed out the car, Mrs. Jackson yelling the whole time what fools we were.

At the restaurant we both ordered pulled-pork sandwiches, French fries, and RC Colas. We sat on the side with mostly white customers. Run by a black family, Calloway's was the only restaurant for three counties where whites and blacks got served at the same counter. Business was always hopping because everybody knew James Calloway made the best barbeque. Rumor had it that even some of the Klan patronized the place.

I was halfway through my sandwich when my father said there were things we needed to talk about. Questions tumbled through my mind—Was someone sick? Mother? Did he need me to come home and work to earn money for the family?

"It's your brother. He won't be waiting for you at home tonight." The bright light of the restaurant exposed dark circles beneath his eyes. He picked up the sandwich, then put it down without taking a bite, fingering the red and white checked paper lining the basket. My throat went dry.

"He's living at the state hospital in Tolliver now. The Smith brothers attacked your brother one Saturday when he and Rosie were over seeing a movie at the Downtown. They beat him up pretty bad and ended up hurting Carter's brain even more."

He stopped, looked down at his hands, the fingers tightly clasped. "He's not the same, Zeke. Won't hardly talk to anybody. His face didn't heal quite right, so he looks different, too."

Chairs scraped the sawdust-covered floor as they were pulled away from the tables. Voices rose and fell around us. Potatoes sizzled in the deep fryer. My stomach churned. I gripped the sides of the table, trying to hold on, trying not to let my father's words sink in.

"When?" It was the only word I could breathe out.

"About a week after you left for Virginia."

I counted off the months. Four. My brother lying in a hospital for four months.

"Why didn't somebody tell me?"

He fell silent. It took a minute but one by one the pieces fell into place in my brain. Mother. She knew that if they told me, I would come back, leaving UVA. And Dad went along with it, as he had with many things over the years. He did not fight for my brother. For me.

He reached for my hand across the table. I wrenched it away. "Do you have any idea what you've done? Why isn't he home, Dad? Why isn't Carter home where he belongs?"

My entire life I had been impressed by this man's strength—physical and otherwise. I'd seen him lift the front end of the truck off the ground with his bare hands. When he realized there was no promise in raising cotton, he sold every piece of farm equipment he had and worked for free to learn pipe fitting, despite loving the feel of being outside under the sun, hands in the earth. I recalled seeing him cry only once before, the morning after his brother put a shotgun to his head. Now, he covered his face with his hands.

The mistake had been trusting Mother to know best. He assumed she understood what was better for their children. In the end, that she birthed us and did most of the raising complicated her own judgment.

"I love Carter. You've got to know that," he said.

I pushed away from the table, knocking my glass to the floor. The dark liquid disappeared into the sawdust.

"Take me to the hospital."

The brother I knew was nowhere to be found in that hospital room. At least twenty-five pounds had been shed from his large frame. A scar eight inches long ran down his face. The right eye was swollen half-shut and its iris was clouded over. A sling cradled his left arm. I lowered myself onto the bed, careful not to jostle him.

"Who's there?" he said, waking up. When our eyes met, he turned his face away, his expression going still.

"Get out."

"Carter, I'm sorry. I didn't—"

"Get out." His voice grew louder. "Nurse. Nurse!" The words echoed out into the hallway.

A woman appeared at the door. "Now, Carter, what's going on?" She put her hands on her wide hips.

I backed away from the bed. My brother kept his face turned away.

"Tell him to get out."

There had been many times during childhood when my brother got mad at me. His temper could flare unexpectedly over little things like a lost marble or a questionable foul during a basketball game. The longest he had stayed mad was two weeks, after my scheme to put a radio antenna on the top of the roof went bad and nearly killed him when the chimney toppled off. It took a promise of as many MoonPies as he could eat and playing basketball whenever he asked to make him happy again. Standing in the corner of the room, a deep ache washed through me.

The nurse assessed me. "Who might this be? A nice visitor come to see you?"

"Get him out."

The words sounded garbled, as if his mouth had been damaged, as well. The nurse shrugged and suggested I leave.

Outside the room, she put a hand on my arm. "He's just starting to have better days. I wouldn't push him."

"I'm his brother."

Her hand dropped away.

"Boy, where have you been?"

∼ Thirty-Two ∼

1985

During the next riding lesson, I trot around the ring for the first time, almost making it up to a canter.

"Not bad," Elle says.

Diamond snorts loudly, offering his own praise.

Feeling full of myself, I invite Elle to dinner.

"With you?"

"Yeah," I say, as surprised as she is. Elle thinks for a minute, holding on to Diamond's bridle and patting the soft space between the horse's eyes.

"Where?"

This is a level of detail I haven't considered. I stall by dismounting from the horse.

"Where would you like?"

She leads Diamond back to his stall. "Michael's. Best restaurant in town. Pick me up at seven o'clock tomorrow night. Don't be late."

How it went from me asking her out to her asking me out I don't get. But I don't care.

Cousin Georgia's face lights up when I tell her about dinner. Michael's is nice but not fancy, she says. Slacks, shirt with tie, no jacket. Given my lack of funds, I should ask my cousin if the place takes Visa, but I'm too embarrassed, so instead I fold my last fifty dollars into my wallet and pray that plastic will work. I wear the black pants I got for my father's funeral and a white shirt with a blue tie that Cousin Georgia picks out from Osborne's closet. The truck gets a bath with the hose by the stables. As I ease out of the driveway, Cousin Georgia says she doesn't know who sparkles more—me or the truck. Tucker sits at her feet, watching me go with only mild interest. He has become Georgia's shadow, an arrangement they both seem to enjoy.

Fall descended on Bailey earlier in the week, dropping the temperature down to the midsixties during the day, high forties at night. Driving over to Elle's, the sky is a midnight blue backdrop against the dark green of the foothills. Her property is smaller than the Laceys' but still rolls on for acres. A large barn and riding ring can be seen beyond the small, white house. When I ring the doorbell, Elle calls from inside to come on in. She pokes her head around the hallway corner, the collar of a pink bathrobe visible, and says she'll be ready in five minutes.

I make a show of looking at my watch. "I thought you hated late."

"Other people. I hate other people being late."

I take a seat on the leather couch, not liking the slick feel of it beneath my hands. Four different horse magazines are strewn across the coffee table. I leaf through one, putting my feet up on the table before thinking better of it. Five minutes pass. Then five more. It is now ten minutes past seven. I rest my head against the back of the couch, closing my eyes for just a second.

"Don't fall asleep at the start of the evening, Zeke. It's rude."

Elle appears in the living room, dressed in pants the color of a well-oiled saddle and a light green blouse that matches her eyes. Red lipstick colors her mouth. The feeling of weariness falls off me. I stand up.

"You look great."

She cocks her head. "Is that so?"

I nod, shoving my hands into my pants pockets to restrain their urge to touch her mouth, to feel the fullness of her lips beneath my fingers.

She reaches up to straighten my tie. There is only about a four-inch difference between our heights. Jackie is a good foot shorter than me and always had to stand on tiptoe to kiss standing up.

"You clean up nice, too."

I'm not quite sure how it happens, who leans into whom first. But it does. We are kissing, her mouth opening beneath mine in the sweetest way. I put my hands around her waist and let them travel downward, running along the sides of her hips. She moves closer, the softness of her body pressing the length of mine. It has been a while, a very long while. After this goes on for a few minutes, I push away.

Elle's eyes are large and open in a way I haven't seen them before. "Are you hungry?" she asks.

I smile a little.

"For food?"

"I could wait."

She nods. "Me, too."

We both stand there, facing each other, unsure. Who moves first will be the one we blame afterward. *If you hadn't started, we would have gone to dinner*, she or I will say. The two-step distance between us feels canyonlike. We are at the edge of an action we will not be able to take back or forget. It occurs to me that she, too, is weighing what will happen next, deciding if the inevitable complications are worth the risk.

Elle turns and begins walking away from the front door, toward the hallway. I watch her go, uncertain if she means for me to follow. She stops, looks back.

"What are you waiting for, Ezekiel?"

I consider the question. Waiting is all I've done for years. For what? To die? To see Carter again? To feel something besides hurt?

Elle is real. Right now.

My fingers work at the small buttons on her shirt. She pushes my hands away and does it herself. As we walk down the hall, pieces of clothing flutter to the ground behind her. We reach the bedroom. I scoop up her naked body and gently set her on the bed. She is more fine boned than I imagined—the sharp edges of collar and hip bone balanced by the roundness of small breasts and hips.

My mouth follows the arch of her foot, up along the inside of her thigh to the spot where her legs meet. The tangle of hair is smooth against my lips and my tongue explores deeper, within the soft folds of her labia. When Elle puts her hands on my shoulders I think she wants me to keep going but instead she pushes me away.

"Stop. Before I come."

Her hips flex upward to meet my mouth. She goes still—her whole body suspended, breath quiet, and then small shudders overtake her.

I run my hands along the long muscles in her thighs—strong from the years of riding.

"You don't listen very well," she says.

"I wasn't listening to your words."

She pulls me up so we can kiss properly. As I guide myself into Elle, she eases her legs open. And just as I'm about to forget everything but the feel of her beneath me and around me, something within me is dislodged, making way for the pure joy of the feel of us together.

Elle gets up, despite my attempts to pull her back down, and lights two candles on the dresser. She pauses at the window. Stars press against the inky darkness of the night sky.

"It's going to get cold. Not a cloud up there to keep the day's heat in."

The light over the garage filters through the window framing Elle. A quilt is wrapped around her shoulders. The glow from the candles warms her face, highlighting the heat on her cheeks and the swollen roundness of her mouth. When she catches me staring, she smiles.

"Guess we're not making it to Michael's tonight," I say.

"Next time."

I nod, grateful that there will be a next time.

"Look at that." She taps lightly on a glass pane. "Northeast of Orion, you can see Gemini up there. First time I've been able to find it this year. Come check it out."

The comfort of bed does not invite leaving but she waves me over. The motion drops the quilt from her shoulder and reveals a curve of breast before she covers it again. Standing behind her, I find that she fits neatly within the circle of my arms, and I breathe in her scent—she smells of soap, a touch of jasmine perfume, and loving.

"Gemini makes me think of you and your brother."

"What do you know about my brother?"

She turns around, peering up. The house is quiet; only the soft ticking of a clock on the nightstand can be heard.

"Georgia told me he drowned about ten years ago. That you were twins. See, that's the story of Gemini. The two brothers in the sky—Castor and Pollux. They were twins, too. Castor was mortal and Pollux was immortal. When Castor died, Pollux was so devastated that Zeus placed the two in the heavens, side by side, for all eternity."

The notion of Carter's and my story having played out thousands of years ago, written by an ancient Greek guy, does not sit well.

"Why are you telling me this?"

She shrugs. "Just thought you might like to know you're not the only one to feel the way you feel."

Coldness creeps into the room. I turn away from her to throw on my clothes.

"Look, everybody's got a closet full of hurt tucked away somewhere," she says. "I didn't mean to upset you."

"If I wanted to talk about this, I've got three sisters just waiting for me to call." One boot is missing. The heel sticks out from underneath the bed. "Tonight was about us."

"Where are you going?" She follows me down the hallway. "Stop, Zeke. Please? Just stop."

I keep walking. The front door is a few steps away when she grabs my arm.

"Look at me."

There is nothing Elle could say that I want to hear.

What she doesn't know is that tomorrow is our birthday. Forty-third. I avoid calendars in the month of October. The day is no longer one worth celebrating. Being with Elle tonight was the one chance I had at forgetting about tomorrow.

The smack of the screen door ruptures the night's silence outside. The truck is too cold to start but finally catches after I pump the gas. Elle's shadow can be seen in the doorway. I glance in the rearview mirror and see her walk back into the house. The glow from the living room lights disappears, throwing the house into darkness.

~ Thirty-Three ~

December 1960

The memory of life in Virginia faded to black that night at the state hospital. Obeying my brother's wishes not to have me in his room, I wandered through the woods next to the parking lot. The temperature had dropped steadily, and each breath exhaled a fine smoke into the air. The hospital's outdoor lighting threw shadows at the trees, creating a skeleton forest. I should have known something was wrong with Carter. I should have known my brother needed me. I should have asked Georgia for permission to call home and find out why he hadn't written. The truth was that I had been too selfish to care enough.

The cold became unbearable and I headed back inside. Carter's nurse passed me in the main entryway and let me know the sleeping pills had worked their magic.

"Visitors aren't allowed to stay in a patient's room past visiting hours. But," she said, gathering her sweater closer around her shoulders, "we're short staffed tonight, so we won't have time to be checking on everybody."

She waved off my thanks but I could feel her watching me as I walked back to my brother's room.

In the circle of light from the small lamp on the night-stand, I watched Carter. Several times he stirred, twitching, a look of pain creasing his face. I would cross to the bed and hold his good hand in mine until he relaxed again. The privacy of a single room was a luxury. Most of the patients were housed in large, dormitory-style rooms. The time from evening until dawn was filled with the muffled opening and closing of doors and the occasional cry from a patient, the noise filled with enough despair to leave me chilled despite the steaming radiator.

It would be nice to pretend that I didn't hesitate about doing what needed to be done for my brother. But in the darkness of the long night, hope about my own life wrestled with Carter's needs. The shimmering image of the university library—its wide steps, columns, and miles of books meant to teach everything there was to know—hovered in my mind. The wind picked up outside, scraping brittle leaves against the room's high window. I did not sleep, not even for a few minutes. There was only one thing I was sure of—a desire to reset the clock. To turn it back to August and somehow stop Mother from taking Carter to the theater, leaving my brother unharmed, my future intact.

When the morning nurses arrived for work, fresh and chattering, Carter woke up. He turned his head toward my chair, searching as though he sensed someone was in the room. I met his gaze, fearful he would send me away again.

Before he could say anything, I spoke. "I'm so sorry I didn't come sooner. Nobody told me what happened, Carter. I'm sorry."

His gaze danced away from mine and he looked down at the blankets.

"I been missing you," he said, his voice barely above a whisper.

Carter placed his hand across his face. Great gulps of air escaped like he'd been holding his breath since the day I left for Virginia. I crossed to the bed and put my arms around him, hanging on to him as tightly as I could.

I ran my fingers across the spiky top of his head, making a bad joke about the haircut.

"Ready to get out of here, buddy?"

Learning everything there was to know would have to wait.

The nurses said Carter couldn't be released until one of our parents signed the papers. Mother appeared as I was packing Carter's clothes.

"Zeke, it's so good to see you."

Like my brother, she, too, seemed to have diminished during my absence. The blouse and skirt swallowed her small frame. The clothes were not perfectly pressed, a sign that she must have hurried over. She moved to hug me and I turned away, tucking a pair of my brother's pants into an old duffel bag.

Still bent over the bag, I said, "Carter is going home today. You need to sign the papers."

"Ezekiel, please."

A nurse walked in with another cup of pills. The tiredness and the mad swept through me. "Get those away from him."

The nurse looked to Mother. "He's scheduled to receive a dose."

"He's going home today," I said.

"I don't have those orders in front of me. I only have the orders that tell me it's time for him to get his next dose."

Without thinking, I walked around the bed and grabbed the small cup from her hand, throwing it against the wall. Two shiny pink pills fell to the floor with a soft click, spinning like tops on the linoleum. The nurse moved to pick them up. Mother put her hand on the woman's back and asked her to give us a minute.

"I'm not staying here, Momma," Carter said.

Her face softened. "You look good today, son. Your brother and I need to talk outside a minute. You rest, okay?"

Carter reached for my hand, grasping it tightly. "I'm going home, right? Today?"

"Yep," I said.

Orderlies in white uniforms filled the hallway, each one glancing at Mother as they walked by, her beauty still obvious enough to garner attention. A nurse pushed a wheelchair with a man in a straitjacket toward the elevators. He spit on my shoe as they went by.

"Jesus," I said, shaking off the spit.

Mother opened her mouth to speak and I held up my hand.

"I can understand how you thought you were doing the right thing by not telling me. It makes an awful kind of sense. But this?" I threw my arms out. "How in the hell did you convince yourself this was the right thing for Carter?"

She stared through me for a moment, looking off into a place I could not see. "Your brother was very, very sick. I couldn't take care of him, Ezekiel."

"You didn't want to. He needs to go home. He'll get better there. I'll take care of him." The fuzzy edges of a plan emerged, one that would require my father's help. "We'll make the shed behind the house into a place where the two of us can live. I'll find a job in town and Violet can keep an eye on him during the day."

She shook her head. "Sweetheart, I won't let you sacrifice your life for your brother's."

"You should've thought of that before you put him in an insane asylum."

The determination on her face was familiar. I'd watched it manifest itself over the years—the absolute, unshakable faith that her will could make things she did not want to happen go away. When black storm clouds gathered in the distance and thunder cracked not two miles away, she would stand out on the front porch, the first drops of rain beginning to fall, and face off against the storm, daring it to touch her house, her children, her town. Daddy would call out, *Lilly, get the hell in this house.* Peering out through the screen door one stormy afternoon, I asked what she was doing. *Reckoning with God,* she said. Half the time the storm would pass us by and she'd come in the house and say, *I told that storm to go away and it did. Sometimes things are just that simple.*

She put a hand to her throat. "You cannot give up UVA. You know that. I won't let you."

"Did you ask me if I would *let* you commit my brother? Better yet, did you ask Carter? What did you tell him, Mother? That this would be a nice place? All sorts of kind nurses and big orderlies to take care of him? And you'd come see him on Saturdays after you got your hair done? You found him a swell place."

Nurses began to look our way, and I knew I was losing control but couldn't stop myself. Didn't, in fact, want to.

"You should be in here, Mother. Not Carter."

Her hand slammed across my face.

My cheekbone hummed with the blow. It was the first time she had slapped me. Slaps were a rare disciplinary action, reserved for the worst displays of disrespect. Daisy caught more than a few of them. But not me. Never me.

She looked at her hand as if surprised by it then lowered it to her side.

An orderly no older than eighteen approached us. "Folks, let's move this outside." He tried to take my mother by the elbow but she shook him off. Carter was visible through the room's doorway. He had fallen asleep sitting up. His head slumped forward, a thin line of drool easing down one side of his mouth. The nurse must have gone ahead and given him the pills.

I faced my mother and the orderly, "Bob," according to his name tag. "Bob, my mother is not herself. She's *very* upset about my brother in there. I'm sure you understand?"

He glanced at both of us and then shrugged, drawn away by the more immediate need of a guy down the hall swinging punches. Mother snapped open her purse and lit a Lucky, blowing the smoke by the side of my head. This was new territory for the two of us. In many ways I had been like my father over the years, choosing not to fight instead of going to war with her. All of those concessions, inconsequential on their own, now piled on top of one another to form a small mountain.

"You ungrateful child," she said. The words came out in a low, controlled tone. "Do you have any idea what the past months have been like? Any idea how many nights I've sat at your brother's side? How many bandages I've changed? How many bed pans? The tears I've cried over those bastard Smith boys doing this to my boy? Who do you think fought to get him this room all by himself so he wouldn't have to deal with the crazies? I didn't want to put him here, Ezekiel. I *had* to. I didn't have anything left to give. Can you even begin to understand what that feels like?"

Her eyes were wide and desperate. I was eighteen at the time. How could I possibly have understood what she had been through? The only thing I could see was that she had made the wrong choice. Two wrong choices—not telling me what happened and commiting him. Now, with children of my own, I have a certain empathy for her. But not forgiveness. Because I know I would never do to my girls what she did to Carter.

"I only want what's best for you. I'll take care of Carter. I'll bring him home. I'll figure it out. All right? And then you can go back to school? What do you say?"

She smiled at me then, a sweet, oh-don't-you-want-to-forgive-me smile, and I dug my hands deeper into the pockets of my jeans to stifle the urge to choke her.

"Do you really think I'd leave again and let you put him right back here when you've had a hard day? You're not his mother anymore. No decent mother would have done this."

Tears gathered in the corners of her eyes and began to spill over. They fueled my anger instead of dampening it. She turned her head away.

"You don't understand," she said. "I love Carter."

I lowered my voice, conscious of the people around us, listening. "The way you love is like sucking all the air out of a person's lungs and then telling him you'll breathe for him."

She stood there, dressed in the too-big Sunday skirt and blouse. Something lit in her eyes and then died. She opened her mouth to speak but no sound came out. You could almost hear the chasm split open between us, the childhood years of love and affection tumbling inside. We were now on opposite sides, she and I. She stepped around me to enter the room. I watched her place a kiss on Carter's forehead, then whisper in his ear. She sat next to him on the bed for a moment before leaving.

"I'll sign the papers."

When she brushed past me, the air between our bodies went still.

The Smith boys spent four nights in Hardeman County jail for what they did to Carter. My father and Mr. Smith worked out a gentleman's agreement that neither family would cooperate with the police investigations in the hopes that nobody's children would end up in jail. Daddy wanted nothing more than to see Jed and Earl locked up, but not if it meant sending his baby girl off to juvenile hall. The McNairy County district attorney gave up on the arson case pretty quick, since the only person to see Rosie near the house the night of the fire was Jed Smith, and his mouth was firmly shut.

Bob Little, the DA of Hardeman County, took up Carter's case like a crusade. He interviewed everybody who was within a mile of the Downtown the night of the assault. But word got around that the Smith family would take it pretty personal if people spoke unkindly about their sons. To some, this meant no more deals on Mr. Smith's famous Midnight Special moonshine, and to others, it meant nighttime visits on their front porch from Mr. Smith with a shotgun thrown over his shoulder. Nobody talked, so finally Bob Little let the case go.

The desire to make Jed and Earl Smith feel some portion of Carter's pain began to fester. In school, I'd only fought if directly attacked or if somebody messed with Carter or Rosie. The next step here was clear.

A few days after we brought Carter home, Preacher Dawson came by to check on us all. He asked me to step outside for a minute, and we stood in the front yard, away from the commotion of present wrapping and Christmas cookie baking.

"Ezekiel, I am surely sorry for what happened to Carter."

Rosie had given Carter an early present—the new Johnny Cash album, *Ride This Train*. "Going to Memphis" was his favorite, and it played over and over again at top volume. The muffled sound of the song carried out to the porch, even through the shut windows.

I nodded, unsure about why he wanted to see me. Preacher Dawson pulled a handkerchief from his coat pocket and pressed it to his mouth. Years of leading Clayton's small congregation had worn him down and he looked ten years older than he was.

The man who had poured the holy baptismal water over Carter's and my head looked up at me without speaking. He knew what was on my mind. From inside the house Mother yelled, "Dinner." I pulled a Lucky Strike from the pack in my back pocket and lit it. I had never liked the taste of cigarettes before, but now they seemed to calm me down. As I inhaled, the smoke warmed my lungs before disappearing into the cold evening air, tendrils curling around the bare branches of the oak tree.

"The souls of Earl and Jed Smith are marked now," he said. "Marked with the stain of your brother's blood. God will not let that go unpunished."

"Sir, with respect, I won't let that go unpunished. Would you? If it was your brother? Would you walk away like nothing had happened?"

"Son, I would like to think I would leave it in the hands of the Lord. But to be truthful, I don't know."

The preacher pulled gloves over his hands. "You go on inside and enjoy dinner with your family. I'll be praying for you. You do the same."

When I left the house the next morning, Mother told me not to do anything stupid. I walked right past her without a word. Daddy followed me outside and reminded me of the agreement he had worked out with Mr. Smith.

"Don't be foolish, Zeke. Think of your sister. There's more than just you and Carter in all this."

I kept walking. Tommy Jackson was home from UT on Christmas break and I headed up the road to his house. He stood on the porch, glancing back into the house every so often. Keeping an eye out for his dad, who was probably still sleeping off last night's whiskey.

"Heard about your brother," Tommy said. "You're not going back to Virginia, are you?"

It was a relief to not have to explain it to him.

"How's UT? Heard you had a good season," I said.

"Zeke, cut the crap. What are we going to do about those boys?"

Tommy looked at me for a long moment before walking back into the house. When he came out, a baseball bat rested over his shoulder. In high school I had had little reason to fight after Carter stayed home, but not Tommy. In the yearbook he was voted Most Likely to Win a Fight. His temper flared in a heartbeat, the result of his father beating the breath out of him on a regular basis.

"Come on," he said, stepping off the porch with a smile. "This could be fun."

• • •

We found the Smith boys minding their father's still up in the hills past Chickasaw Lake. Earl said he'd been waiting for me, figured I'd come back. The sight of UT's starting linebacker next to me unnerved them a bit. Nobody messed with Tommy.

Earl kept right on smoking a cigarette, watching us. I knew he was the one to start something with Carter. Jed went along with whatever Earl did.

"Tommy and I need to have a talk with you two."

Rosie had told me the whole story the night before. How Earl thought Carter was me at first and started saying things like *What's the college boy doing home?* When Jed told him it wasn't Ezekiel, it was the dumb one, Earl got a look on his face like he'd won the Publisher's Clearing House Sweepstakes. And then he started swinging.

Tommy and I had a plan—he'd take Jed and I'd take Earl. Jed looked all scared, his eyes darting back and forth between me and Tommy and Earl. Everything was going the way it was supposed to until Jed reached behind the still and pulled out a shotgun. Pointed it right at me, his eyes settled all of sudden. We didn't think about either of them having a gun, which, in retrospect, was not good planning. The blood pumping through my heart stopped in that moment, waiting.

Tommy dropped the bat and pulled a switchblade from his back pocket, grabbing Earl around the throat before Jed knew what was happening, before I knew what was happening. The bright winter sun danced off the blade.

"Go ahead, Jed. Shoot me," I said. "But old Tommy here is going to have to slit your brother's throat if you do. Why don't you put the gun down?"

Jed hesitated, looking from his brother to me, his finger still wrapped around the trigger.

"Do it!" Earl yelled. A trickle of blood appeared below the blade at his throat as Tommy exerted pressure.

Jed put the gun on the ground in front of him, stepping back. I picked it up and heaved it into the lake. The splash echoed up to us.

No one moved until Earl jammed his elbow into Tommy's stomach, making him drop the knife. Tommy lunged for it, sending the knife skidding across the ground. Jed made a move for it, and I threw myself at him. I gave every punch I had. Out of the corner of my eye Tommy and Earl wrestled on the ground.

Jed clocked me across the face with a fierce right hook, laying me flat. Things went dark for a second. My hand felt something round beneath it. The bat. Nothing felt as good as swinging at Jed, seeing his skin break open, and hearing his breath stop when I landed a hit in his gut. Each time the wood connected, I said a different kind of prayer. *That one is for Carter's eye. This one is for Carter's arm. This for Carter's head. This is for taking Virginia away from me.* The anger spilled through me and it was hard to tell what I was angrier about. What had been done to my brother. Or what had been done to me.

Earl called out for his brother. Jed and I both looked over to see Tommy holding a flailing Earl over the side of the hill. Tommy wore a big grin. Then he let go. Earl screamed the whole thirty feet down to the water.

"Come on, Zeke. Let's go before he finds the shotgun and comes after us."

"Not yet."

Jed was on his knees before us, blood pouring down his face from a smashed nose. Fear clouded his eyes. I raised the bat.

"Please," he whispered.

My brother must have said the same word to him; my sister begged them to stop. They didn't.

It would be so easy to bring the bat down against Jed's head and feel the splitting of bones reverberate up the handle. Tommy caught my eye.

"Not worth it, Zeke."

My hands gripped the bat tighter. The knowledge that it would feel good to kill Jed surprised me. The world would not miss Jed Smith. Living provided more opportunities to hurt others the way he had hurt Carter.

My brother's words pumped through my mind. "I been missing you," he had said. Through the blaze of adrenaline, the prospect of leaving Carter behind again, for jail this time, loomed.

The bat dropped from my hands, falling to the ground with a final muffled noise.

There were weeks after the fight when memories of it would intrude, reminding me that whatever violence lurked in the Smith brothers also lay somewhere inside me. It was not a thought I wanted to take out in the light of day and examine, so instead I threw myself into preparing the shed for Carter and me. Despite the cold, my father and I spent the month of January getting it ready, stopping only when forced by the winter rains. We ran plumbing, then electricity. Made a bedroom and a kitchen, though you could barely turn around in it. When he was having a good day, Carter would come out back and help, too. By February, we finished. Carter and I moved into the shed on February 15, 1961. I wrote the date on the wall behind the stove. My brother wrote "me and Zeke's house" next to it.

In March I sent a letter to Cousin Georgia. Mother must have phoned her so they would know not to expect me back for spring semester. Putting down in words all that had happened wasn't possible, so I gave her the short version. Georgia wrote back and suggested that I go to Freed-Hardeman for a while, just to keep up my studies until I could come back to UVA.

Maybe Carter would get better and be able to be on his own eventually, but it seemed unlikely. His face would never look right again—the long gash down the right side became a thick ropy cord of scar tissue and his eye remained clouded over.

It was dumb, but I felt that if I couldn't go to UVA, I didn't want to go to any college.

Aunt Charlotte's husband got me a job at the Dover elevator plant in Mabry. I worked forty, fifty, sometimes sixty hours a week. Life fell into a routine. Work. Come home and be with Carter. Sleep. Get up and do it again. There was no time to remember Lacey Farms and the university.

Jackie started dropping by the shed at night. At first she brought over hamburgers from Gillbey's in Mabry or a basket of fried chicken, saying she was worried we would never eat anything but pork and beans. Then she'd call me at work and ask me what I'd like to eat that night and come over and cook it on the tiny one-burner stove. Mother fed us, too, leaving cakes of corn bread and plates of ham on the workbench that served as our dining table. Carter ate dinner at the house sometimes. But I didn't. I still couldn't be in the same room as Mother.

I saved almost every penny I made. The plan was to buy a house someday. And a ring for Jackie.

My brother got better. His body healed, though he never remembered what happened the day of the attack. But he was changed. He didn't like to go beyond the house much. If we went to the store, little kids would stare at him, their eyes wide looking at the big scar on his face and his funny eye. The lake was as far as Carter would go.

While I worked, he stayed in the shed playing cards or visited Mother or wandered over to Violet's house across the street. On the weekends, we went fishing. Carter would pack us breakfast and lunch. We sat on the shady side of the lake and cast our lines, watching the wind play over the water, not saying much of anything. I got him to laugh by doing stupid stuff like pretending to swallow a bait worm.

One afternoon after catching three dinners' worth of fish, Carter put his arm around my shoulder. This surprised me. Since the attack, he didn't like to touch people or be touched. He seemed afraid that everybody might hurt him, even the ones who loved him.

"Zeke," he said, "you're the best brother."

The only sound around us was the lapping of water against the shoreline.

~ Thirty-Four ~

1985

"Ezekiel Cooper, you have been keeping a few too many things to yourself."

Cousin Georgia finds me by the lake stacking downed branches. A week has passed since the date with Elle, and Georgia wants details. Not much to tell. We've both maintained radio silence.

"Your sister Daisy just phoned. You didn't tell me it was your birthday last week, and you also forgot to tell me your mother has cancer. Daisy said the surgery's been moved up to tomorrow."

The growing pile of branches feels like an accomplishment. By next week, most of them should be cleared. The wet smell of the rotting wood has become comforting. All I want to do is keep stacking, keep working, keep pushing thoughts of Carter, Mother, and Elle away.

I set the last branch to the side, pulling off my work gloves. The cold bites at my fingers. A covey of quail flashes through the pine trees—five or six babies speed off after their mother, forming a wide triangle formation as they trail across the grass.

"Surgery's tomorrow?"

She nods.

Tomorrow I was planning to go over to Elle's and apologize. In an act of pure optimism a few days ago, Tucker and I took a ride over to the Feed and Fuel and used a credit card to purchase a pair of black Durango cowboy boots. The sales girl talked me into buying boot polish, and I shined up the boots with an old washcloth, leaving my room smelling like a Memphis shoe-shine stand. The idea was to wear them over to Elle's house, admit what an ass I had been, and give her flowers. Since our "date," loneliness had found me again, accompanied by a stronger feeling of seriously missing Elle. She made me nervous and on edge in a good sort of way. Whenever she and I had any physical contact, even if it was just her arm accidentally brushing against my own, my body reacted like a thousand nerve endings had been stripped down and laid bare.

"I've got things to do here, Georgia. I should probably stick around. Mother will be all right. She's tough."

Georgia's expression clouds. "You can leave and come back, you know." She wears a white blouse, and the bony part of her shoulder socket is a round knob pressing against the thin material. The morning chill doesn't seem to bother her.

"Now, I'll not tell you what to do, Ezekiel. It's not my place," she says.

I brace myself, knowing she isn't finished. In and out of the oak trees above us, a scrub jay squawks and chases a cardinal, whose feathers shine like garnets.

"Your mother and your sisters, not to mention your children, are probably out of their minds with worry about this surgery, son. Lillian is a strong woman. You're right about that. But she needs her family around her. *All* of you."

I recall Mother as she looked the last time I saw her, seated on top of the stairs in the flowered housedress that hung too big on her, watching me leave Clayton, not knowing where I was headed or why. She had looked old, a word I'd never used to describe her before. In family pictures she could pass for Violet's and Daisy's older sister. Growing up, shopkeepers would say things like *Mrs. Cooper, you must have had those babies when you weren't even a teenager!* But that leaving day, she appeared old and defeated, as if she suspected the empty space between us would never be bridged.

"I'll think about it, Georgia. I promise."

The response is a cross between a throat clearing and a snort. She turns to go, then stops.

"Elle called." Georgia says. "She'll be over at ten this morning for a lesson. That's in fifteen minutes, so you'd better get a move on."

The boots crunch my toes all up, but they look good. At six minutes after ten, I make it to the stables. Elle says nothing, only points at her watch.

"Sorry."

"I've got another lesson at eleven-thirty."

She is dressed in jeans and a jacket. The jeans are just tight enough to outline the round curve of her ass. There is nothing and everything to say.

"Listen—" I begin.

"Listen—" she says.

I hold up a hand, certain I should go first. "I'm sorry, Elle. I shouldn't have left like that. I don't talk about my brother much."

"Maybe you should."

Now she sounds like Jackie.

Elle busies herself with tacking up Diamond, an indication that she is either nervous or can't stand the sight of me. Does she regret the other night? Maybe it was too much too soon. It didn't feel too soon. I want to kiss her, but she leads Diamond into the ring.

After adjusting the stirrups, she slowly turns to face me. She pulls a silver wrapper from a jacket pocket, unwraps it, and pops a chocolate into her mouth, watching me while she chews. That is one lucky piece of candy.

A small gold horseshoe pendant rests in the dip between her collarbones. It occurs to me that it would give me pleasure to buy her a beautiful bracelet or necklace and see her wear it.

"I'm sorry, too," Elle says. "About everything."

I frown.

"Okay, not *everything*. The being together part I'm not sorry about. At least I think I'm not sorry about it. It always seems to get complicated, doesn't it? Maybe we could try again?"

Diamond stamps a hoof, anxious for the lesson to start. I haul myself into the saddle.

"Exactly which part should we try again?" The question comes from the relative safety of Diamond's back.

Elle doesn't answer, but she laughs and I know we're okay.

The lesson drill is familiar now—mount, circle around for a bit, get the feel of the horse again.

"Let the reins go and put your hands behind your back," Elle commands from the ring's center.

"Are you crazy?"

I do it anyway.

"You need to learn balance. Hang on with your legs. Squeeze him a little bit with your thighs. That's it."

I perform this feat for a few minutes, scared with every forward lope that I'll be kissing the dirt. Next Elle says to close my eyes.

"Close my eyes?"

"Just do it."

I shake my head. "You must think I'm a dumber redneck than I look if you think I'm going to be blind while sitting on top of a horse."

She gets Diamond to hold up and marches over, her cheeks flushed. When she asks for the reins, I oblige. Diamond doesn't put up a fight, either, when she begins to lead him around the ring.

"You want to know why I want you to close your eyes?"

"Doesn't matter," I shrug. "I'm not doing it."

The horse stops abruptly. Elle is no longer walking. "Look, Zeke, you've been riding for what? A week? I'm the teacher here. Let me teach."

When I don't move, she hands the reins back. "Suit yourself."

Diamond turns to watch her walk out of the ring.

"Wait," I say.

She keeps walking.

"Okay. I'll do it."

This will be the stupidest thing I have done to impress a girl, beating by a landslide the time in eighth grade when I was madly in love with Irene McNally. We had homeroom together, and every morning I hid her books in the classroom before the first bell rang so she would talk to me. We would laugh and I would give her back the books until one day she stepped out of the room before the bell to go to her locker. Before she got back in class, I was called to the school office and forgot to return her books. She couldn't find them or the homework and notes for a test she had folded into her textbook. That was the end of that.

Elle takes her time returning to the ring. "This is about learning to trust yourself and the horse. You shut your eyes so you can feel—the motion of the horse, your body's response to it. When your eyes are open, the visual overrides the intuitive. To be a good rider, you need to be able to feel the horse and anticipate his movements as much as you need to be scanning the road ahead for trouble spots."

This seems similar to fishing. After a day of not catching a thing, I'd take the line out, put on some fresh bait, close my eyes, say a little prayer, and then cast away. Half the time, a nibble would come in less than thirty minutes.

Elle waits with arms folded across her chest. Diamond paws the ground with his foreleg.

"What do I get if I do it?"

"I'll make you a deal," she says.

This sounds promising.

"I'll let you hold the reins."

"Not good enough."

"What do you want?"

"A kiss."

Pause.

"Agreed."

Off we go. Diamond walks along until Elle clicks him up to a light trot. It's not so bad. The horse is solid beneath me, taking us where we need to go.

"Good job," Elle says. "You look great up there."

If she keeps it up, I'll stand on the damn horse with my eyes closed.

"Just let him lead you, Zeke. He knows where to go. Now try to post with his trot. Up down up down up down. That's it!"

The world narrows to Diamond's smooth movements and the rich sound of Elle's voice. The terror of hurtling out of control settles. A little. Diamond knows what he's doing. Diamond's a pro.

"Pull back on the reins a little," she says. "Gently. Not too hard. He's itching to canter."

Her words don't register until too late. Diamond *is* itching to canter and so he does. My eyes fly open and I jerk hard on the reins. Too hard. The horse stops instantly but I don't. As much as I try to regain balance, the force of momentum sends me into a slow, gradual tumble that lands me in the dirt next to Diamond. He turns an elegant long nose toward me with a look that says, *What are you doing down there, partner?*

"Well, hell."

Elle puts a hand over her mouth to disguise the grin spreading across her face. I get up, brushing the dirt off my pants, flexing my legs and arms to see if all parts are intact.

"Good thing you had those new boots on."

The comment deserves ignoring.

"Didn't you know that the first time you ride in a new pair of boots you're supposed to fall? It's practically guaranteed. I've told them to put it on the sales slips over at the Feed and Fuel, but they won't do it."

"Do you make fun of all your students when they fall?"

"Of course not," she says. "It's very unprofessional."

It takes her a moment to compose herself. She walks over and brushes dirt from the back of my shirt. "Most falls only hurt your ego."

I focus on getting Diamond's saddle off. The buckle jams. I wrestle with it, muttering a few curse words.

"Haven't you ever heard of getting right back up on a horse after you fall off?"

With a final wrench, the buckle comes free and I haul the saddle into the tack room.

"Don't you think you should try? It'll make it a lot harder the next time you get up on him if you don't."

"Seeing as I'm going to be on a plane back to Tennessee today, I'll take a rain check."

So, I'm going.

"You're leaving?" She takes Diamond's brush from my hand. "Why?"

At the western boundary of the Lacey property, the Blue Ridge foothills look as if they are aflame, so intense are the trees' autumnal shades of orange and crimson. Before sunset, I will be up in the air over those hills. The vacation, it seems, is over.

"My mother is sick. Lung cancer. She's having surgery tomorrow. Everybody's pretty worried about her."

"Oh. That's terrible." She frowns. "I'm sorry."

She throws the brush into a bucket next to Diamond's stall. "I'll miss you."

I walk over and pull her around to face me. "I earned this."

The kiss lasts half a minute but contains a promise.

With my arms still wrapped around her, I say, "I don't know how long I'll be gone. But I'll miss you, too. I don't want you to forget the night we spent together."

She smiles.

"Okay. Forget the part where I walk out, but remember everything up until then. Can you do that? I'm not sure where you and I are headed, but I'd like to see how it turns out. You won't forget or disappear or something?"

The sound of desperation is beginning to creep in, so I stop.

"Diamond and I will be here, Zeke."

"It's not the horse I'm worried about."

She pulls me into the shadows of the stable and we make out like seventeen-year-old virgins, leading me to believe that she may be the last thing I need to be worrying over.

∾ Thirty-Five ∾

1985

By three o'clock in the afternoon, the plane lifts off from Charlottesville headed for Memphis. Cousin Georgia makes all the arrangements, even books a rental car at the Memphis airport so I can drive to the Tolliver hospital. She says not to worry about Tucker or the truck. They will be waiting for me when I get back.

Get back. This does not have to be a repeat performance of leaving and not returning for twenty-five years. The dog is there. Barring everything else, I will have to come back for the dog.

Before the plane takes off, I call Daisy at home and tell her I'm on the way. The surgery is scheduled for ten o'clock tomorrow morning. The chances of survival are good; the chances of dying are good, too. Mother had looked so tired the day I left Clayton. And I ignored it. Ignored her.

It's after seven before I am on the road in a white Ford Escort. Darkness has fallen, making it difficult to follow the road signs. Outside Memphis, Highway 64 beckons. The wind picks up, swaying the treetops and requiring two hands on the steering wheel.

In Somerville, Dairy Queen provides a burger to go. A Memphis country radio station keeps me company, the voices of Willie, Merle, and Reba filling the empty space in the car. The station starts breaking up when the highway heads south eleven miles outside of Tolliver.

Only a handful of cars, mainly the nightshift workers, occupy the hospital parking lot. The last time I was here was to watch Louisa be born. Jackie's pregnancy was much easier the second time, and labor took four hours from start to finish. We'd been eating lunch over at the Country Kitchen in Mabry when her water broke. By dinnertime, we had another daughter. The maternity ward is on the second floor. Several windows glow with light. Babies are probably being born right this second. Moses Washington always says people love the beginning parts of life; it's the middle and end parts that end up being more work than we bargain for.

The strong antiseptic smell of the place hits me as soon as the automatic entrance doors close shut. It is hard to imagine anyone getting well in a place that smells this bad. At the information desk an older woman with hair somewhere between lilac and orange is packing up a crossword-puzzle magazine into a purse shaped like a dog. A round button on the lapel of her sweater reads "Ask me! I care about Tolliver Hospital."

"Excuse me. I'm looking for Lillian Parker's room."

She glares at me over reading glasses before consulting papers on the desk. "Third floor. Room three ten. Visiting hours end in half an hour."

I thank her and stand by the elevator, waiting for it to come down. When the UP arrow lights and the doors open,

Rosie steps out. She throws herself at me, hanging on tight like she always does. Her hair is cut short and spiky, like the "Hit Me with Your Best Shot" singer. Of the five of us, Rosie got the looks. Mother called her "my little ugly duckling" when she was little and all legs and huge brown eyes. *Wait and see,* Mother would say, *she'll be a swan soon enough.* By the time she was fifteen, every boy for two counties was knocking on our door.

"You look good, Rosie."

She hits my shoulder. "Do not. Drove down from Nashville today and I look like hell. At least I got some work done on the way listening to band tapes. I've listened to enough bad music for a year. Might've been one good one in the bunch. Maybe. How's Virginia?"

I can feel her peering at me. We haven't seen each other since Pigeon Forge. Someday I will tell her about the final-exit attempt. But not now.

"You're staying with Cousin Georgia out there?"

I nod. "Where are you headed? Mother all right?"

"I need some air. You just missed Violet and Daisy. They went home for the night."

"And Mother?"

Rosie pulls a cigarette from the pocket of her jeans. "Go find out for yourself. I'll be on the walking track. Come see me afterward. And you should probably call Daisy and Vi to let them know you made it."

The elevator dings open again. Above the front desk, the clock reads 8:35. The pay phones are next to the bathrooms, both of which have yellow "closed for cleaning" cones blocking the doorway. The janitor and I are the only ones around. I step over a mop bucket and call Vi's house first. She's not home yet but Louis takes the message.

Daisy answers on the first ring. "Thank God," she says, "I've been praying all day you'd make it."

The fact that she admits to praying says how bad things must be. Daisy thinks praying is for folks who don't have the guts to take matters into their own hands.

"Have you seen Mother?"

"Headed up there now."

"Good. You and Rosie stay at my house, okay? Violet will want you over at hers, but you all don't need to be driving any more tonight. I've got to get Dave's dinner going here before he heads in for the late shift. Then I'll be over to the hospital to pick you up."

Noise comes from the front entrance. A very pregnant woman and a man barrel through the doors. The woman clutches her belly and stops walking for a moment, taking deep breaths. The man puts his hand on her back, speaking to her softly. We all get into the elevator together. Between the first and second floor the man asks if she's okay five times.

"I am not okay," she says through gritted teeth as they get off.

"Good luck!" I call. He gives me a nod before the doors close.

On the third floor, TVs hum out from open doors. Two small children sit on a bed with an older woman in one of the rooms. The girl sees me pass by and offers a wave. The door to room 310 is shut. No sound can be heard from inside. Maybe she's sleeping. I'm still trying to grasp that she has a life-threatening illness. Both she and Daddy were healthy their whole lives. I don't even remember my father being sick. Mother caught the occasional cold but not him. He was under the hood of his truck when the heart attack hit. Landed facedown in the engine he'd been trying to fix for the better part of a decade. Carter seemed to get sick a lot—bronchitis, ear and sinus infections. Stuck in bed, he'd want me to stay and dote on him. *Zeke, come on over and tell me a story, will you? Go on out and get me some ice cream, Brother, I'm feeling poorly.*

A nurse who looks younger than Honora asks if I need help.

"I'm here to see my mother."

"You must be Ezekiel. She's been talking about you today. Your brother, too. What's his name? Carson?"

"Carter."

"That's it. You go on in. I believe she's just resting." She returns to writing on a patient chart.

The metal door handle gives way with a solid click. The ceiling-mounted TV casts the only light in the room, bathing it in a flickering blueness. The volume is turned off. Mother rests in bed with her head turned toward the wall. She stirs at the sound of my footsteps.

It has only been a month since I last saw her but she is transformed. The extra weight gained over the years since Daddy's death has been shed, leaving only the angular lines of her body. The skin around her cheeks and mouth is slack. But mostly it is her eyes. There is a filmy softness in them I don't recall seeing before. When our eyes meet, I realize it is not softness but resignation.

"You came."

She motions to the one chair in the room. "Tired? Virginia is a long way away, isn't it?"

The TV above flashes images of two guys in Easter egg–colored jackets chasing crooks in Miami. We both watch for a moment, transfixed.

"You'd look good in a turquoise jacket, Ezekiel. Match the color of your eyes. My eyes, you know. You and me have the same eyes."

She looks down at the bed, smoothing the sheets with her hands. "I need to say a few things, son. And I know you're not much for listening to me, but this is probably the last time you'll have to, okay?"

"It's not going to be the last time, Mother."

The comment makes her laugh—a brittle, nervous sound. "And how do you know? If anyone knows, it's me. I've got a feeling about this surgery tomorrow and it's the kind of feeling I've never had before, so I'm taking it as the Lord letting me know I need to get ready." She glances at the TV. "Those boys are too pretty for their own good. Where's the thing to turn it off? I can't concentrate with them staring at me."

The remote control is buried beneath the covers. The effort of digging it out leaves her breathless, and she lies back on the pillows.

"Turn it off. Please."

The remote control also has a button for a light. She squints as the fluorescent bulb sputters to life behind the bed. *What if she's right? What if tonight is the last time I will see her? It is an impossible thought.*

"How's our Honora?" Her eyes don't meet mine; she runs a hand along the top of the bed's rails. "Have you seen her yet?"

I fold my arms across my chest, an itchy feeling crawling across my skin. "I'll see her tomorrow."

"Good thing. It's her first love, son. She doesn't know up from down. The whole thing takes you by surprise. The force of it. You remember, don't you?"

The notion of my eldest being in love has never occurred to me. Not really. She's never had a boyfriend before. How did you go from hating boys to being in love with one?

"She told you she was in love with this boy?"

Mother looks at me with something approaching pity. "Honey, she's over-the-moon in love. Now, I told her not do anything crazy, okay? She's a smart girl. I don't think she'll get in trouble like I did. Like your sister did. Like Jackie." She shakes her head, remembering. "Even if Honora does, things are different now. A girl has options we didn't have all those years ago. Not that I would've changed anything. Except maybe being older than fifteen."

My expression must have changed to one of complete shock, because she holds up a hand. "Now, wait a minute. Before you go thinking this and that, the last time I spoke to Honora they hadn't gone beyond heavy petting."

If this is supposed to make me feel better, it doesn't. I turn away from the bed and walk to the window, trying to gather myself to finish this conversation when what I want to do is tear out of the room and find my daughter. The wind parts the clouds, exposing a round, almost full moon. Is Honora with the boy right now, looking at the moon from the backseat of his car?

"Now I've gone and made you worried. I'm sorry. Come here." Mother pats the bed. "Where I can see you. There. That's better."

She reaches a hand out shyly and puts it to my face, curving her fingers along the jawline.

"Thank you."

"For what?"

"Letting me touch you. It's been a long time."

In the first year after Carter was attacked, her touch filled me with rage. Any attempt to hug or kiss was rebuffed.

Eventually the anger faded from all-consuming to an after-thought, but avoiding her became a habit.

"Son, I love you. I need you to hear that. Do you? I'm sorry for all that's gone wrong between us, Ezekiel. I've loved you every day of your life, loved you more than I probably should, I know. But you are right here." She pointed to her heart. "Right here always. I was never happier than the night you and your brother were born. You were gifts from God."

Regret mixed with the small embers of anger, glowing still, surfaces inside of me. I try to look away, but she brings up both hands to hold my face.

"Can you forgive me? Can you? Please?"

The metallic clanging sound of a cart being rolled down the hallway comes through the door, accompanied by a loud laugh from the nurse's station. A phone jangles in the next room. I think of the couple from the elevator. Is the baby born yet?

"It's all right, Mother. It's all going to be okay."

Her hands drop to her lap. "Don't bullshit me, Ezekiel Cooper. I am too old and too near dead. Forgive me or don't. Whatever you say, mean it."

Talking is not easy; her breath comes in short, raspy bits.

"I'm sorry, too," I say.

A knock comes at the door. Visiting hours are over.

Mother's gaze exposes more raw love than anyone else has ever offered me. I remember seeing that same look when Carter and I were six. We were sitting on stools at a pharmacy in Memphis eating the best burgers of our lives. It had been a reward for enduring the doctor's appointment where they performed tests on Carter and told Mother he would never learn to read and never be able to take care of himself. Ketchup slid off a French fry and spilled onto my new shirt. I looked up at

Mother, waiting for her inevitable scolding. Instead, she leaned over and wiped the ketchup away with a napkin. *What am I going to do with you? Come here and give me a messy hug and see if I don't forgive you right quick.* I put my arms around her, and my brother threw his arms around me, and we were all hanging on to each other.

The hospital gown swallows her small body. When I wrap my arms around her, she feels like nothing.

∼ Thirty-Six ∼

1985

The wind outside is bracing and cool after the hospital's stale, heated air. I swallow big gulps of it. Rosie waves me over to the exercise track adjacent to the parking lot. With headphones clamped over her ears, my sister walks faster than some people run.

She cups her hands around her mouth like a megaphone. "Get over here. I'll race you."

Carter, Rosie, and I used to race from our mailbox to old man Cartwright's house a quarter of a mile down Five Hills Road. She beat us nearly every time. And the few times when she knew she was going to lose, she'd do her best to knock over Carter or me before we reached the finish line.

"I'm too old to race. The body's gone." I pat the small hill of beer belly to prove it. My paunch is smaller than usual, most likely a result of my average weekly beer consumption having dropped to almost zero at Lacey Farms.

"Oh, please. You're barely over forty. And that makes me almost forty. If I can do it, so can you."

She catches sight of my footwear and stops walking, pointing at the boots. "And what are those?"

"I've been learning to ride out at Cousin Georgia's."

"Horses?"

I nod. The subject of Elle Chambers is too new to discuss. "Who would put an exercise track next to a hospital? Don't they know there's a bunch of sick people in there who would give anything to get out and go for a walk?"

We fall into an easy pace. She links her arm through mine. It's almost as if we are twelve and eight again, walking to the dairy bar for a quart of milk for dinner.

"She thinks she's going to die, you know," Rosie says.

"Mother thinks a lot of things."

The night wind gusts and we increase our pace to stay warm. Gold- and rust-colored leaves from the oak trees lining the track scatter across it, crackling beneath our shoes.

"The whole drive down I kept saying out loud, 'my mother has cancer, my mother has cancer.' Trying to make it seem real. When Vi called and told me Mother had to have surgery tomorrow I didn't feel anything. Nothing. Do you think that's strange?"

She pauses, blowing air into her hands. They are Mother's hands—long, delicate fingers, the wrists narrow and finely boned. We head for a wood bench near the track. Rosie asks for my help in turning the bench so that it faces the trees and not the hospital.

I pull out a pack of Marlboros from my shirt pocket, offering Rosie one. The wind blows out the match twice. When we get the cigarettes lit, we both lean back and take long drags before letting the smoke out in one long breath.

"Do you think Daddy still loved Momma?" she asks. "Even at the end?"

"He loved her more than anything else in the world. Anything. Made him do crazy things."

"Such as?" Rosie takes one more drag before throwing the cigarette on the ground, mashing it out with the toe of her shoe.

"Now that was a waste of a perfectly good cigarette. Why smoke if you're only going to take two hits?"

She says she only smokes when she's anxious, and she can never do it around her singers because they all worry about it ruining their vocal cords. Never mind that half of them are closet chain-smokers. The management isn't supposed to do it in their presence.

"Made anybody a star lately?"

"You heard of Bradley Jason?"

"He's got that song out about the little boy who dies, right?"

"It's about his brother. Died when he was six. Brad was nine. Damn good song."

She says she heard him singing in a dive bar in Austin when she was at a conference. Knew he could be big. Signed him the next week.

"Pretty good at your job, aren't you?"

She shrugs. Sometimes I think she feels funny back home, like she doesn't want the extra attention just because she has the kind of job most people dream about. Mother used to pump her for details when she came home for Christmas, ignoring the grandchildren, the ham, just wanting to hear about Nashville.

"You really think Daddy still loved her? Even after that whole mess with Uncle Leroy?"

I look sideways at her.

"Come on, Zeke. Daisy told me years ago. Said the two of you found Momma and Leroy kissing out behind the church on Violet's wedding day."

"Daisy shouldn't have told you that."

"Why not? So I'd think better of Mother? I don't blame her for having an affair. She should have picked somebody besides her husband's brother is all."

"You don't have a problem with adultery?"

"Nope. Not when you've got five kids and your husband's gone three weeks out of four. We drove Mother crazy."

"That was her job, Rosie. Taking care of us. *All* of us."

She unfolds her legs and hops up, cursing the cold. "Should have brought my down jacket." Pointing a finger at me, she says, "You've never forgiven her for Carter."

How good it would feel to let it all out, rid myself of the betrayal and hate I have harbored for Mother. They cling to my insides, with no place to go. I knock Rosie's finger away with more force than I intend.

"How does a person forgive a thing like that? Maybe you can forgive the affair. But putting one of your own children into a mental hospital when he was perfectly well enough to live at home? Can you even imagine doing that?"

She doesn't answer, and this tells me all I need to know. I take off back to the hospital. Rosie's footsteps pound behind me. She is breathing hard.

"Wait a minute."

I walk faster.

"Wait the hell up, Zeke!"

She catches my arm, forcing me to turn around. "I didn't mean it like that. I don't think what she did to Carter was right. I hope I would make a better choice if I were in the same situation."

"You hope?"

She jams her hands in her jeans pockets. "Look, none of us knows what we'd do. We may think we do. But the truth is, we don't know until we get there."

"Maybe *you* don't know."

I light another cigarette, leaving the pack almost empty. I should've stayed in Virginia. Elle will be getting ready for bed now. Is she thinking about me?

Rosie keeps talking. "She wasn't going to leave him in State to rot, you know. She needed a break. She was going to get him out after Christmas."

"Who says?"

"She did, Zeke. She told me. If you'd ever talked to her about it, she might have told you, too. What did she say to you tonight? She told me she was sorry about not loving me enough when I was little. Said she was so damn tired by the time I came around. She's saying good-bye to us, you know, Zeke. She's getting ready."

The truth of this silences us both. Honora will take it the hardest if Mother dies. Mother taught her to bake and to cook, had her over every Sunday since she was tiny. She would never say she favored Honora more than Louisa or any of the other grandkids, but I knew. Could see it on her face when she asked after Honora or watched her open a Christmas present, intently watching my daughter's face. When she would call our house, she always asked to speak to Honora. Jackie saw it, too. *We have two daughters, Zeke. Two. Your mother only sees one.*

"Did she ask you to forgive her?"

Rosie's voice draws me back. I nod.

"And? What did you say?"

THE LOST SAINTS OF TENNESSEE

The easy answer is clear. The words are on the tip of my tongue.

"You couldn't do it, could you?"

"I told her I was sorry, too."

"For what, Zeke? For hating her all these years? For blaming her for Carter's death? For being a loser stuck in his hometown at a shit job? Jesus fucking Christ. I can't even look at you right now."

She stomps off to her car, a sleek convertible, and slams the door shut.

"Screw you!" I yell, my voice bouncing off the trees and across the deserted parking lot.

Mother's words about Honora press at the back of my mind. It takes ten minutes to drive to Curtis and Jackie's house, which sits in the middle of a cul-de-sac in Mabry's only new home development. My ex-wife and her then-boyfriend bought it a year ago. At the time, Louisa told me how fun it was to pick out the carpet and paint colors for her room—the first she would not have to share with Honora.

No one in my family had ever owned a brand-new home. What was it like to be the first person to inhabit a place? To have pristine walls and floors without scuff marks? Never mind the five bedrooms and six bathrooms.

Curtis's shiny F150 XL Supercab with its chrome wheel rims sits in the driveway next to Jackie's brand-new Thunderbird. I park at the curb and turn off the engine. So far, I have managed never to set foot in the house. The girls always know when I'm coming over and a single horn blast summons them outside. Through the front picture window I glimpse Curtis. He must have seen the unfamiliar car and walks to the front door, throwing it open. The outdoor light mounted above the driveway clicks on, lighting up the interior of my car like daybreak.

Fuck.

"Is that you, Ezekiel?" Curtis stands in the walkway. He wears pressed chinos and an oxford shirt, his blond hair parted on the side and slicked back.

I climb out of the car, telling myself not to punch him just because he is sleeping with Jackie and providing for my children. It would feel so good, though. Quick uppercut. Nice and clean. Rattle the old boy a little.

"Hey, Curtis. I dropped by to see the girls. Are they still up?"

"Sure, sure. Come on in." He waves me in the front door with a smile. "Let me get Jackie for you."

Before I can stop him and say, *Please, just the girls,* he is gone, disappearing down the front hallway that looks as big as our old house. The house smells of cookies baking and I wonder if it's real or just some fancy upgrade option they chose—"have your house smell like chocolate chip cookies with the superscent ventilation system even when you're too busy to bake."

I take a seat in the living room. The new house must have come with new furniture, too. Five years younger than Jackie or me, Curtis has made more money at his Ford dealerships than my father made his entire life. This also feels like a good reason to hit him.

The slap of bare feet against the hallway's wood floor comes toward me.

"Dad!"

My youngest throws herself at me. I grab her up—pink nightgown and all—and hang on with all I've got. She tucks her head beneath my chin.

"I missed you," Lou says softly.

"Me, too."

Recalling how close I came to never seeing her again makes me hold her tighter. Pigeon Forge feels like a thousand years ago now. How did I imagine leaving behind this little creature with her spindly arms and legs?

She looks up at me with the large brown eyes that make it nearly impossible to deny her anything. I gently set her back on the ground.

"Something's wrong with Honora," she says, grabbing hold of my hand.

My heart catches. "What do you mean, sweetheart?"

"Yesterday she stopped talking. To anybody." She shrugs. "I mean, she doesn't really talk to me much anyway but she's not even talking to Mom. Or the boyfriend."

When she says *boyfriend,* she makes quotation marks in the air.

Jackie walks into the room and gives me a brief hug. The physical contact is suprising—hugs are not something she doles out to me on a regular basis anymore—but then I realize it must be sympathy inspired.

"Did you see Lillian?" she asks. "The girls and I stopped by yesterday."

Lou tugs on my hand. "Will MeeMee be okay?"

MeeMee is the name Honora came up with when she was a toddler and couldn't manage "MeeMaw." The name stuck, and Mother said she never minded since it sounded French.

Jackie and I share a look above our daughter's head.

"I hope so," I say.

"Hang on a second, Dad. I want to show you something." Louisa disappears out of the room.

Jackie pulls me into the farthest corner, where we sit on a couch covered in what appears to be Holstein cowhide. "I'm going to talk fast because Lou will be right back. Just listen, okay? It's Honora. She's been in the kitchen for two days baking cookies. Only stopping to pee and sleep for a couple of hours. It's crazy. I think it has to do with the boyfriend."

"Did you ask her?"

"Zeke, do you think I'm an idiot? She won't speak to me. She's not talking to anyone. She communicates by writing shopping lists of ingredients for me so she can keep baking. She's having some kind of breakdown here and I need your help."

I run my hands down my face. What does Jackie want me to do?

"Mother thinks Honora is in love with this guy," I say. "What do you think?"

She nods.

"Can't we get through one crisis at a time? Is that too much to ask?"

"Have you always whined this much, Zeke? Because I have a hard time believing I put up with it."

I'm too tired to fight. Louisa returns holding something behind her back.

"Ta-da!" she says, revealing a trophy that looks half as big as she is.

Jackie and I can't help but smile at our daughter's glowing face and the size of her prize.

"I won 'most-improved player' on the soccer team this year. Remember how last year I kept missing my shots and forgetting who I was supposed to be defending against? Not this year. I wish you could've seen me play, Dad." Her expression dims. "I kicked butt."

"She did, Zeke. I went hoarse at the games screaming for her." Curtis makes this helpful comment from the hallway, where he appears to be eavesdropping. "And Jackie—" He clears his throat. "Honora is throwing flour in the kitchen. Not that it's a problem." He smiles that car-salesman, everything's-great smile. "Just wanted to give you an update.

"Thanks, honey," Jackie says. "Why don't you go ahead and go to bed? I know you've got an early call in the morning."

I keep my eyes glued to Lou's trophy, admiring it from every angle, while they exchange a good-night kiss.

Louisa tells me I should go talk to Honora. "Maybe she'll listen to you," she says.

"Do you really think that?"

She raises her eyebrows. "You've got to try, Dad. It's, you know, your job."

Jackie watches us from the doorway, inclining her head just the slightest, so I know she is amused by Lou's comment.

"Well, in that case, boss," I say, "I'm going in. What kind of protective gear do you think I'll need? A helmet? Maybe a chef's hat?"

Lou giggles. Jackie even manages a smile.

The kitchen is twenty by twenty-four feet, at least. Every inch of the island running down the middle of it is covered in wire cooling racks holding cookies—chocolate chip, peanut butter, lemon. My daughter has the oven door open and is peering inside. In profile, the bones of her face reveal the changes of the past year—the cheek and brow finely defined, the round innocence of little-girldom gone. Despite the dyed black hair and ratty pajamas she wears, she is a stunning girl.

A bag of flour is ripped open on the floor. Honora closes the oven and looks up. Our eyes meet and she inhales sharply.

"Smells good, honey." I walk to the island, grabbing the closest cookie. "Tastes great. How are you?"

She folds her arms across her chest and leans against the counter facing me.

I tell myself not be afraid of my own kid.

"I missed you, sweetheart. You okay?"

Her gaze narrows. She shakes her head slowly.

"You're not okay?"

She points as if to say, *Bingo*.

I step closer and she holds up a hand. I step back.

"What can I do?"

Honora responds with an eye roll and then looks entirely disgusted. She stares so intently I have to break the eye contact. She stoops down to grab something off the floor.

We are standing two feet apart and all it takes is one quick motion for her to dump the remainder of the bag of flour on my head.

I wipe what I can off my face, quelling the desire to smash a stick of butter in her hair. The girl is pissed.

She points again, this time at the doorway. When I don't move, she scribbles on the shopping list and then holds it up.

"Get out now" it says.

"I love you," I say.

Honora ignores me and removes a fresh tray of cookies from the oven, shutting the door with a swift bump of her hip.

My daughter does not want my help.

I slip out the back door without saying good-bye to Lou or Jackie. The patio furniture trips me up as I make my way in the dark to the gate. A chair crashes to the ground.

"Everything okay out there?" Curtis calls out from the bedroom window.

"Fine," I say. "Just fine."

By eleven o'clock, I park in the carport of Daisy's house and drag myself through the side door.

"Hey, brother." Daisy stands at the sink washing dishes. When she looks up at me, she frowns. "What happened to your hair? Did you go gray between the hospital and here?"

"Don't ask. Honora's having a crisis. We don't know what it's about or why."

My sister dries her hands on a towel. "Is it something big, do you think?"

"I'm not sure."

She wants to ask more questions but stops herself. "You look awful. Go get settled on the couch in the living room."

Streetlights shine in through the big picture window. The house is in the older section of Mabry, the one Mother used to take us through on Sunday drives after church. While we stuffed ourselves with the pimento cheese sandwiches she always packed, wrapped in the crinkly wax paper, Mother drove down street after street. She would stop in front of a house every so often and let out a big sigh. *Isn't that just beautiful? Look at that green grass and the black shutters and the two-car garage!*

A switch on the wall next to the mantel catches my attention and I flip it on. Bright blue gas flames pop up in the fireplace.

Rosie throws herself down on the couch next to me. She has apparently gotten the honor of staying in the guest room.

"Hungry?" she asks.

This is the closest she will come to an apology. Daisy carries in a tray loaded with coffee and Little Debbie Oatmeal Creme Pies and Nutty Buddy Bars. Rosie and I look at each other.

"What?" Daisy asks.

I take the tray out of her hands. "You sit. Drink your coffee. We'll go fix a little something more in the kitchen."

"You both drove miles to get here today. I'll get it."

"You look like hammered shit, Daisy," Rosie says.

This is not something I could say to either of them, but it seems acceptable between sisters. "If you don't sit down, we're leaving and going to Vi's so you can get some rest."

Daisy throws up her hands. "Fine."

The light over the stove guides us into the kitchen. Rosie opens the fridge and we both let out a sigh when we spot the ham. I make sandwiches while Rosie pulls out Piggly Wiggly containers of potato and macaroni salad, core food groups in Daisy's house.

Daisy calls out not to fix her anything; she's not hungry. When Rosie hears this she says, "Oh, no, she needs to eat." So she heaps a plate with a sandwich, potato chips, and scoops of both salads.

"Grab that bottle of Dr. Pepper, Zeke. Better yet. Check to see if they've got any beer in there. With all those grown sons of hers, there's got to be."

The Budweiser is hidden behind a gallon of milk, and I take out the whole six-pack.

"Is there anything left?" Daisy asks. She clears off the coffee table.

I toss Rosie a beer and open my own.

"What about me?" Daisy asks.

"Sorry," I say. "Thought you didn't drink."

"I don't. Not on a regular basis." She pops a top and takes a long swig, after which she lets out a huge burp.

Rosie giggles. "Remember how Momma always told us ladies don't burp and don't fart and don't eat more than two bites in public? She was so crazy. Trying to raise us up like Scarlett O'Hara with an outhouse."

Boys didn't require the same rules. Mother would only tell me to sit up straight and keep out of fights. Daisy takes a small bite of the sandwich, chewing it delicately.

"It's good. Thanks."

Rosie eyes her. "You've lost more weight since the last time I saw you, which wasn't but two months ago."

"I'm almost fifty now, Rosie. Got to watch out for the middle-age spread."

"Bullshit."

"Easy for you to say. You're not even forty yet."

One of the things I appreciated about being married to Jackie was that she liked to eat. Was, in fact, one of the few women in my life who never talked about how fat she was, what diet she was on, and how much weight she wanted to lose.

Daisy stuffs a handful of potato chips into her mouth and glares at Rosie.

"That's better," Rosie says.

"If you'd grown up having Momma tell you every time you turned around that it was a shame you'd inherited the Cooper women's hips and thighs, you wouldn't eat much, either."

"When she's dead, there'll be nobody left to say that, so you can eat all you want."

Leave it to Rosie to speak the unspeakable. The clock on the mantel reads eleven thirty. It's twelve thirty back in Virginia. Is Elle asleep? Or maybe she's still up reading one of the many horse books on her nightstand. Until now I haven't had time to miss her, but it hits me, a longing to be back in her bedroom, tracing the constellation of freckles across her back.

"Why are you looking at me like that?" Rosie says. "We all know Mother thinks she's dying."

"You don't have to sound happy about it," Daisy says.

Rosie finishes her beer, letting out a burp to rival her sister's. "I'm not happy about it. I don't know what I am." She pulls an old quilt from the rack next to the sofa and wraps it around her.

Daisy finishes most of her sandwich before speaking again. "Mother is proud of you, Rosie. She talks about you night and day so that you'd think you were her only daughter, you know."

"She didn't give a goddamn about me until I got a job in Nashville. She ignored me my whole childhood, told me I was out of my mind to think I could waltz up to Nashville and get a job in the music business, then turns around and makes me her favorite when I do. That's fucked up."

"Watch your language," Daisy snaps.

"You sound like Momma."

I make a time-out signal with my hands. Both of them tell me to butt out. The plates need clearing, so I grab them up. I return with what's left of a chocolate Bundt cake from the counter. This shuts them up.

"Put another pot of coffee on, will you, Zeke?" Rosie asks.

After finishing off the cake and the coffee, we all spread out on the floor in front of the fireplace. The whistle of a freight train echoes through the night's quiet. A whip-poor-will responds with a high-pitched cry. Rosie shivers.

"Mother hates whip-poor-wills. Says she always feels like they're stepping over her grave when they cry out like that."

"Jesus, Rosie," I say.

"What?"

We plan to meet Vi at the hospital by eight o'clock in the morning. The surgery is scheduled for nine and it should take around three hours to remove the cancerous part of Mother's right lung.

Tonight is the first night in a long while when the three of us have slept under the same roof. It's comforting having them both down the hall. The fireplace timer clicks off and the blue flames vanish.

～ Thirty-Seven ～

1985

By nine o'clock the next morning our family occupies the third-floor waiting room. Jackie sits between Honora and Louisa on a couch. Honora passes around a tin of lemon cookies—Mother's favorite. I was unsure about the girls being here and told Jackie as much, but she said they refused to go to school, saying they should be with their grandmother. Daisy and I have already smoked a pack of Luckies between us. We saw Mother briefly before they took her in for surgery. The nurse had given her a Xanax, but she still looked anxious. She called each of us to the bed for a hug and an "I love you"—first Daisy, then Violet, then me, Rosie, Lou, and lastly Honora. Mother almost wouldn't let go of Honora. The nurse appeared in the doorway to take her down and Mother called each of us over again, either forgetting she'd already done it or needing to hold us one more time.

"Why don't we all join hands for a second and say a prayer for Mother?" Violet says. She wears a white blouse with flowers painted on it and a matching skirt. Her dark hair is pulled back in a ponytail, making the silver streaks more visible.

"You know what, Vi? I don't feel like holding anybody's goddamned hand right now," Daisy says. She takes the last cigarette from my pack and lights it, ignoring the stricken look on Violet's face.

Rosie gets up from her chair and moves next to Vi, taking her sister's hand in her own. "Go on, Vi. I'll say it with you."

"Me, too," Lou says, dragging Honora and Jackie over.

Daisy mutters about needing more cigarettes and walks out. This leaves me sitting across from Vi and Rosie, who is motioning her eyes toward the seat on the other side of Violet. Once the three of us are sitting together, Vi holds on to each of our hands and begins to pray.

I don't listen to the words. Instead I notice how the walls hold multiple framed prints of water—a lake, an ocean, waterfalls. Are you less likely to sue the hospital when you hear bad news if you're feeling blissed out by all the water images?

"Amen," Violet says, echoed by my daughters, Jackie, and Rosie.

They all look at me. The second hand of the clock mounted on the wall makes a solid click-click-click sound.

Lou scowls. "Dad."

I sigh. "Amen."

Five hours later, when all of us are eating the ham sandwiches Vi brought from home, Dr. Trent walks into the room. He wears green scrubs, and his surgical mask hangs loosely around his neck. His hands are clasped in front of his body as if he, too, might be saying a prayer.

Daisy walks right up to him. The rest of us are frozen in our seats.

"So, how did it go?" she asks.

Dr. Trent pauses. "As you know, we planned to do a lobectomy, which would have only removed one of the three lobes in her right lung. But when we got in there, we saw that the tumor was much larger than the tests had shown."

"So you had to remove the whole lung?" Rosie asks.

He looks at her and then at all of us, his eyes lingering on Louisa and Honora. Jackie places her arms around the girls' shoulders.

"We were attempting to remove the entire lung when Mrs. Cooper began hemorrhaging." He clears his throat. "We couldn't stop the internal bleeding. I'm sorry to tell you that she did not survive the surgery. Please accept my condolences."

He hangs his head in a kind of defeat, and I consider briefly what it must be like to deliver bad news to a family, knowing that your efforts had not been enough to save someone's life.

Vi puts her head on my shoulder and begins to cry. Daisy backs away from the doctor and lowers herself into a chair. Rosie grabs my hand. I cannot take in the words. Not yet.

I reach out a hand to my daughters, but only Lou comes to my side. Honora allows Jackie to enfold her in a hug.

I stroke Lou's hair and lie and say it will be all right.

Mother was only sixty-eight. My sisters and I spend the next five days trying to accept that the four of us are the surviving members of a family that once numbered seven.

At the funeral home in Mabry, Rosie and I do battle with Vi and Daisy over the particulars of mother's casket.

Despite Mother having left instructions for a simple pine casket, Vi and Daisy feel she deserves better. They want the oak one lined in pink satin. When Rosie and I point out that Mother is dead and deserves to have her wishes obeyed, our older sisters call us heartless and cheap. In the end, Mother's body is laid to rest in an oak casket lined in hot pink satin, the more demure pink having been on back order. "Looks like a goddamned hooker's casket," Rosie whispers to me during the viewing.

Cousin Georgia called to say she couldn't make the service. Osborne ran the car off the road, intentionally or unintentionally, she didn't know which, and broke his collarbone. After inquiring after Oz, I told her I planned to pack up my old house, the shed, on this trip.

"Moving into your mother's house?" she asked, her voice guarded.

"If it's okay with you, I'd like to come back to Lacey Farms for a while and help out."

"Ezekiel, you don't even have to ask," she said.

We bury Mother on a small hill in the Mabry cemetery, right next to Daddy and Carter. The four of us—Vi, Daisy, Rosie, and me—stand shoulder to shoulder at the gravesite. The weather report called for rain, but the sky is stubbornly clear, as if reminding us that we could go fishing or walk in the woods. The preacher rambles on about the afterlife. I can't help but think, *What does he know? What does anybody here know about the afterlife?* There is a large family plot near ours, and I watch as a short woman in her eighties shuffles over to it. She carries a bouquet of yellow mums. The flowers are placed in front of the smallest tombstone. Two cherubs are carved into the pale pink marble. She then walks over to the larger tombstone and stands before it. I wonder if it's her husband's grave and the smaller one her child's. Is she all alone now?

A hand slips into my own. When I look down, it's Honora's. Mother's coffin disappears into the earth and my daughter squeezes my hand tightly.

After the funeral, my sisters put food out at Mother's house. Funerals and weddings are Clayton's main social gatherings, so most of the town shows up. Violet and Pearlene Washington stand in a corner of the living room. Pearlene hugs my sister close while Vi cries. In the kitchen, Daisy smokes a cigarette with Aunt Charlotte. She looks even more worn down than usual and I turn away, heading for the back door.

I grab an RC Cola from the ice chest, wishing it were a beer, and head outside. In the backyard, Moses Washington catches a pitch from Vi's son, Owen, who always carries a ball in one of his pockets and has even been known to sleep with one in bed. This year he hopes to be the starting pitcher for Mabry High, even though he's only a sophomore.

"You just about broke my hand, boy," Moses says, shaking out his fingers.

"Sorry," Owen says, looking worried. "You all right?"

"I'll live."

"Let me run home and grab you a glove. I'll be right back." Owen takes off at a jog up the street.

"You need some ice for that hand?" I ask.

Moses and I haven't seen each other since the day at Gerald's Gas when the dog and I were leaving Clayton. Forever, I had thought. Dressed in a black suit one size too big, his face softens when he sees me.

I reach out a hand but he bats it away. When his long arms make their way around me, it is the first time since Mother's death that I feel as if all the emotions piled on top of one another may collapse. Maybe it's because the strength in his arms reminds me of my father's embrace—a rare occurrence but remembered all the more because of its scarcity. Moses and Pearlene knew Mother's story as well as any of us and loved her, deeply, I think. For a moment, I lean into Moses and bow my head.

"Your family has lost too many of its own. I know what that's like. You're going to be okay, though, you hear me?"

I should have told Mother I forgave her. Even if it was only partially true. Or not true at all. She deserved to pass on believing that her son harbored no ill will toward her. I should have said *I love you*. That would have been true, and not just partially. Wholly. I just never figured out how to love her and be so mad and disappointed at the same time. When was the last time I said those words to her? I can't even remember. The last time I wrote them was in a letter. Twenty-five years ago.

Owen reappears with a glove tucked under his arm. "Let's go throw out back, Moses. You can come, too, Uncle Zeke."

Moses releases me with a final firm pat on the back.

"Now we'll see who can really throw," Moses says, walking over to Owen. "You ain't seen nothing yet. Coming, Zeke?"

I shake my head. "Real men play basketball."

"Don't start," Moses says.

"Ignore him," Owen says, grinning. "He couldn't hit a ball to save his life."

Slats of wood are nailed to the old oak next to the shed. I peer up into the leafy middle and spy the tree house. My father built it for Owen when he was only three or four years old. Mother tried to stop its construction, arguing with Dad about how Owen was too small to get up in a tree house, that he could fall and break his neck, was that what his grandpa wanted to happen? I climb up to it, my head barely fitting through the opening in the floor. Old plastic swords, Superman comic books, and tiny soldiers are strewn everywhere.

"Still climbing trees in your old age, Zeke?"

I hit my head on the side of a branch as I turn toward the voice. Jackie stands below me.

"Listen, Honora's disappeared."

She wears a navy blue dress scooped low in the front. From the height advantage of the tree, the satin material of her bra is visible.

I climb down a few steps before leaping off, trying not to wince when I land funny.

Our daughter stopped baking long enough to come to the service. She had resumed the cookie marathon the same day Mother died, returning from the hospital to whatever safety she found in the kitchen. She still hadn't spoken to anyone for a week. The boyfriend has not called the house, confirming our suspicions that all of this must have something to do with him.

"Find her, Zeke. I need to stay with Louisa in the house."

Having a purpose energizes me. As a small girl, Honora loved exploring the neighboring woods, so I instinctively walk toward them. She would make up stories about fairies living beneath the mushrooms and gnomes colonizing hollowed-out oak trees. The forest floor is damp beneath my feet, releasing the smells of earth and decaying leaves. The afternoon has brought gray clouds and a light drizzle falls. I peer through the maze of pine trees. A flash of purple stands out against the darkness of a tree trunk. I call out. She pushes off the tree and begins running.

Even in fancy shoes she's fast. My breath comes harder as I wind through the trees, keeping an eye on the moving eggplant-colored target ahead. My leg muscles begin to cramp and I remember what it was like to run as a boy. How strong my legs felt, pushing off the ground with each step. Fast. So fast. Arms pumping. Heart easily expanding. The certainty of knowing my body could do whatever I asked of it.

I lose sight of her for a minute. Stop. A muffled crying comes from nearby. I walk toward the noise. Honora sits on the ground, her hand clutching her right ankle. Already there is a faint blue tinge to the skin. When I kneel next to her she turns her face away, flinching when I gently probe the ankle. No broken bones.

"Do you think you can walk, sweetheart?"

No response.

"Do you want me to carry you? I think your old man's got enough juice to do it. We might have to take a break every so often, though."

She does not object as I lift her into my arms. Her head rests beneath my chin and the scent of rain comes from her hair. We walk a few minutes before the strain on my back makes me gently set her on the ground.

"We'll just take a rest, okay? Are you cold? You look cold. Take my jacket."

I pull off my suit jacket and place it around her shoulders. She sits on a tree stump, the bad leg stretched out in front. A smile flickers across her face.

"You haven't carried me since I was nine. I must weigh a lot more now."

The week of silence is broken. *Don't make a big deal of it. Keep her talking. Play it cool.* By habit, I reach for a cigarette, then reconsider. I grab the pack of Doublemint instead, offering Honora a piece.

The loud sound of our chewing draws a scrub jay, investigating.

"This was Mee-Mee's favorite gum. She always let me dig in her purse to find the pack she kept in the bottom."

The ankle is now easily twice its normal size. We need to get back to the house and put ice on it. I move to pick her up again but she shakes her head.

"Let's sit a little while longer. It's not hurting as much now."

This can't be true. But we stay. The branches of a nearby pine keep the rain off us. She picks at a stray thread from an embroidered flower on her dress.

"Brian and I slept together. A couple of times. Then he said he didn't want to go out anymore. Stupid, huh? I actually thought I loved the loser. And now—"

She stops, pressing her lips firmly together and wrapping the thread around a finger tight enough to stop the circulation.

"And now?" I struggle to keep my voice neutral. My fifteen-year-old daughter has had sex. More than once.

"He's saying stuff at school. To other guys. And now, some of them are coming up to me." She places the back of her hand against her mouth.

Accelerated from running, my heart rate now threatens to flatline. The noises of the woods fade back and all I can hear is the child beside me, taking in shaky breaths, scared to speak whatever terrible thing needs to be spoken.

When she begins, I have to lean down so my ear is almost next to her face, her voice is so low.

"The guys are saying stuff like now that Brian's done with me they want a 'go at me.' Some of them write stupid notes and put them in my locker."

She wipes her nose with the back of her sleeve. "You know what really pisses me off? Nobody, and I mean NOBODY, gives a crap that Brian is having sex. It's, like, what he's *supposed* to do. But because I'm a girl? Now I'm the school slut? I don't want to have sex with anybody else. I wasn't even sure I wanted to do it with Brian. But I liked him. *Really* liked him."

The flash of anger is gone as her face crumples again. She looks so young, like the tiny girl I used to carry on my shoulders who yelled, *Run fast, Daddy, run fast,* as she bobbed up and down.

A degree of rage I haven't felt since beating up the Smith boys stirs.

"I was so stupid."

Her voice draws me back.

"You were trusting. You liked this guy and he broke your heart and now he's being a son of a bitch. How old is Brian?"

"Seventeen. His birthday is in May. He skipped a grade in elementary school. I was going to bake him a hummingbird cake for his birthday."

"Too bad he's not eighteen. I'd haul his ass down to the sherriff's."

The corners of her mouth lift. "I'd like to see him in jail. That would be nice." She exhales loudly. "I'm just so sad, Daddy. About Brian. About Mee-Mee."

This is the part no one tells you about. The part where your child experiences pain. It used to be my job to make it go away, to kiss the hurt and cover it with a Band-Aid. Now it cannot be made better. Happy beginning, happy middle, happy ending that never comes. I want it for her, but she has only to look at her parents to see that happily-ever-after can end.

"I'm sad, too," I say carefully, worried about saying too much or too little. This is the longest conversation she and I have had in two years. She has evolved from girl to young woman without my noticing.

"I'm sad the first guy you really liked was a bastard. I'm sorry I wasn't here when all of this was happening. I'm sad about Mee-Mee dying. Your grandmother loved you so much, Honora. I think a part of her will stay with you. I do."

"Don't give me spirit-in-the-sky shit, Dad. God, why do people think that makes you feel better? She's gone. I'll never get to bake birthday cupcakes with her again. She'll never see me graduate from high school."

She pushes off from the trunk and stands up, hobbling toward the road. When I try to help she shakes off my arm at first but then relents. I wrap one of her arms around my neck and steady her so she can hop on the good foot. The rain has stopped.

"You're right. Why would that make you feel better? And guess what? Your uncle died ten years ago and I still miss him. A lot. He would have loved to see you grow up. Your cookies alone would have sent him over the moon."

We rest for a moment in the clearing near the house. Honora leans against me, putting her head on my chest. The wind shifts and clouds mottle the sky.

"Love basically sucks, doesn't it?" she says.

"No, not always. Sometimes love is the best thing in the whole world."

"Until it isn't," she says, challenging me to disagree.

I want to tell her it can work out. That loving the right someone can make you better than the person you are alone. But what proof do I have to offer?

"You left." It is an accusation. "You didn't even tell us good-bye, Dad. What kind of *love* is that?"

This is what looms between us, beneath the pain of Mother's death and the boyfriend's betrayal.

"I'm sorry, Honora. I screwed up."

She looks up at me. "Why is it so hard to love us?"

More than anything else she has said today, these words leave me breathless.

My girl thinks the reason I'm such a shitty dad is something she or Lou did. How could I forget how innocent they are? People say children are resilient, and maybe that's true, but what is not said enough, or at least not by anyone I know, is how small the world is to a child. It begins and ends with her family and when that breaks down somehow—through divorce, adultery, sickness, death—the child loses trust in everything she knows.

"I need you to listen right now. Okay?"

Eye roll.

I step back a little so we can really see each other. "Loving you and loving your sister is the easiest thing I've ever done. I loved you before you were born. Do you know that? Your mom and I had been trying for a while to have a baby, and when she finally got pregnant with you, I couldn't believe how lucky we were. I think you and Louisa are pretty much the best thing on the planet. Everything wrong I've ever done when it comes to you girls has had *nothing* to do with you and *everything* to do with the messed-up person I am. Can you understand that, please? It's really important."

She shrugs.

"I went to Virginia to try and get unmessed up."

This is the short version. She doesn't need the long one.

"Are you home now for good?"

Of course this is the question she would ask. Can I postpone the answer?

"I'm going back to Lacey Farms. I'd like you and your sister to come check it out."

"How long are you going to stay there?"

"I'm not sure."

Her silence confirms my ongoing paternal failure. Next to us is a toppled old oak tree, broken in half. The sun shines briefly and dances across the trunk.

"The gnomes should be up for a sunbath soon," I say.

Honora frowns. "What are you talking about?"

"The gnomes. Remember? You used to believe they lived in fallen tree trunks."

"That was a long time ago, Dad."

But it wasn't. It was a few years ago. It could have been yesterday.

～ Thirty-Eight ～

1985

Honora gets settled on the couch with her leg up on a bag of ice, surrounded by her sister and cousins, one of whom figures out how to connect the Atari game console to Mother's ancient TV. Space Invaders march across the screen.

I catch Jackie's eye and motion toward the door. We walk to the back end of the property line, passing a few left-over pumpkins in the vegetable garden.

"What is it, Zeke? Tell me." Jackie gnaws a thumbnail, her eyes never leaving mine.

"She slept with him. More than once. Then he dumped her. Now he's running his mouth at school."

"Goddamn, motherfucker, son of a bitch." She grabs an old piece of brick off the ground and hurls it at the nearest tree, hitting it dead-on.

"Shit. Shit. Shit. Is she pregnant?"

It never crossed my mind. *Stupid.*

"You didn't ask her, did you? Jesus Zeke."

"I don't think she is. She would have told me." *God, how I hope this is true.*

Jackie paces in front of me, treading a path back and forth between the last rows of Mother's shriveled tomato plants. "We shouldn't have gotten divorced. I shouldn't have married Curtis. This is my fault. I haven't been paying enough attention to her."

"And I've been gone. Look, right now it doesn't matter whose fault it is. What matters is what comes next. School must be hell."

Jackie freezes. "What are you thinking?"

An idea spins out as I speak. "Let Honora come back to Virginia with me. Stay for the rest of the school year. Then she can come back to Clayton when Brian and his loser friends have graduated. Let's give her a chance to get away from this guy."

She collapses into a rusted lawn chair. I kneel down next to her. "Look, we'll figure this out, okay? Maybe Virginia is the right answer. Maybe it's not."

"You're thinking of moving there, aren't you?"

The idea appears to upset her almost as much as the news about our daughter.

"Cousin Georgia has asked me to stay for a while. Osborne's got Alzheimer's and it's getting worse. There are things I could do there. Be of use."

"Why not take Louisa, too?"

It isn't just the girls she's thinking about. The heat rises in my face.

"Jacklynn, you've got no right to be thinking what you're thinking right now."

"And what might that be?"

"You're not mad at me moving for the girls' sake. You're mad because the possibility of a good screw with your ex-husband won't be a phone call away. That's bullshit, Jackie."

She turns her face away, looking back toward the house. Before speaking again, she lowers her voice. "You're not that good of a fuck, Zeke."

How has this conversation become more about us than our daughter?

"I can't stay here. You can understand that."

Jackie walks over to a holly bush and twists off a berry, cursing when a sharp leaf scratches her hand. All must not be well in newlywed land. This is not my problem, cannot be my problem.

"I don't want to take the girls away from you. I could never be as good a parent as you are. I know that. If I could, I'd move the three of you out there."

Her face softens. I put my hands on her shoulders. "Why don't you leave that old car salesman and move out there with me?"

In some ways it would make everything so simple. There is a pull here, a history with Jackie that will not let go. But an image of Elle's face beneath me as we make love appears in my mind.

The wind gusts out of the east and knocks over the lawn chair. I try to give Jackie my jacket but she bats it off.

"I happen to love Curtis."

That she has to say it makes it doubtful, but I keep quiet, trying not to betray the rush of relief flooding through me.

"I'll think about it, Zeke. Okay? Honora won't want to go. But maybe it's the right thing. I don't know what is. Give me a couple of days."

She walks back to the house, leaving me alone in the empty yard. A semicircle stand of poplar trees forms the eastern property line, some well over one hundred feet tall, their tops meeting the sky. I lower myself down on one knee. The wet ground soaks through the thin material of my suit pants. I want to hear the deep timber of my father's voice yelling from the front yard that he needs an extra pair of hands to work on the truck. I want to hear Carter again, the voice most like my own, teasing me for missing a basket. Mother calling to us through the screen door to come in for dinner. Honora's little girl voice at bedtime, *Read one more story, Daddy. Please.*

~ Thirty-Nine ~

1985

Another leaving day arrives. Rosie pitches in to help pack up the shed. The family still calls my former living quarters "the shed," even though it looks like a small house now. Mother put flower boxes under the front windows a couple of years back, and Violet makes sure something is always planted in them. Marigolds this month.

Rosie looks around the living room and kitchen, no bigger than a normal house's hallway, and shakes her head. "How long did you live here?"

"Five years before I got married and then since the divorce."

"Jesus."

What did I need more space for? My daughters never spent the night; Carter had been dead for ten years. It was just me.

"No wonder you've been depressed."

I look at the place through her eyes—the beat-up linoleum floor, leftover pieces from when Daddy redid Mother's kitchen floor twenty years ago, the bare walls, the white paint beginning to peel, the tiny bedroom with a mattress on the floor since I'd never gotten around to getting a bed frame. The fake pine nightstand I found on the side of the road holds a picture of Honora and Louisa when they were little and there is also a lamp with a Budweiser beer–can base. Carter picked the lamp out himself at the Corinth flea market a year after we moved in together.

Rosie calls from the kitchen and asks what she should do with all the pots and pans. I tell her to pack it up; we'll drop it off at the thrift store in Mabry. The only things I want to take with me are my clothes and Carter's. It takes me five minutes to empty the dresser drawers. The hall closet holds Carter's things. It is the only closet in the place, located halfway between the bedroom and the bathroom. My father and I had worked night and day for a week straight putting in the bathroom. Mother kept coming out and saying how silly it was to waste all this time on it when Carter and I could just come and use the bathroom in the house. The thought of having to deal with her every time I needed to piss was enough to make me finish the project as soon as I could.

The closet hasn't been touched in years. I grab a couple of boxes, intending to throw everything in at once. Carter's clothes are on the bottom shelf—jeans, old T-shirts, some socks. I decide that these can go to the thrift store, too. As I toss them into the box, something falls out from between a pair of jeans and lands on the dusty floor. It is a small, infant-size sweater faded to a dull navy color. I remember pictures of Carter and me dressed in matching ones when we were babies. The cuffs of the sweater are frayed, but it's in pretty good shape for being over forty years old. Rosie comes up behind me.

"How cute. What is that?"

I tell her and she reaches out to touch the sweater gently, as if she is afraid it will crumble. "This was Carter's?"

"Probably. Mother told me Grandmother Parker made them for us when we were born."

Rosie flops down on the floor, fingers the material. "You're not going to throw it away?"

I tell her no, and take the sweater from her hands. The afternoon light is fading to dark outside, bringing a chill into the room. I want to finish before it settles around me.

"It's still strange having him gone, isn't it?"

I turn my back on her, letting my silence do the answering.

My sister stands up, hands me an old University of Virginia sweatshirt. "I would like to see Carter at forty-three." She touches the hair at my temples. "I bet he would have gotten really gray on top like Daddy. Maybe a little belly, too?"

I push her hand away from my stomach and she retreats to the kitchen.

After clearing out the clothes, the sight of a basketball at the bottom of the closet makes me smile. Carter used to make me play a game of one-on-one the second I walked in the door from work. When Jackie and I first got married, playing basketball instead of coming in to dinner right away aggravated her. But after a while she seemed to understand it was our way of saying hello to each other after being apart all day.

Not long before Honora was born, Carter came up to Jackie and put his hand on her belly. *I will teach the baby to play basketball,* he said. And sure enough, as soon as Honora learned to walk, Carter took her out in the driveway with a baby-size basketball for her and a big one for him. Her second Christmas we bought a kid-size hoop. You'd have thought we'd given her the moon by how excited she and Carter got. *Look, Uncle Car-Car,* she said, *we can play now.*

Louisa doesn't even remember my brother. He drowned when she was two.

I put the basketball in the save box with the baby outfit, then stand on a chair to check the back of the top shelf.
Shoved in the far corner is an old Dixie Maid cigar box. My
father smoked Dixie Maids on holidays and his birthday, the
only times Mother would put up with the smell of them. The
box feels too light to be holding any cigars. Bits of paper poke
out the sides, and when I open it, some flutter down onto the
floor. A few old newspaper clippings are in the pile.

Carter's wide, messy handwriting fills the pages. A heart
is drawn in the middle of one with the words *Carter loves Jackie*
inside. My hand grips the paper tighter. I knew Carter loved
Jackie, but it had never entered my mind that he might be *in
love* with her. What other women had he really known, though?
I sit on a kitchen chair as sadness steals over me, the ten years
between Carter's death and the present slipping away.

Rosie comes up behind me, startling me. "What are you
reading?"

I pile the papers back in and shut the lid. "Just some of my
old stuff. Why don't you take a break? I can get the rest of this."

She stares me down for a second, smelling a rat. My
sisters always want me to talk, particularly when it comes to
Carter. I have never done so and don't intend to start now.

"Let me get this straight." Her hands are on her hips indi-
cating that this may take a while. "You don't want to talk about
Carter. You already said you don't want to talk about what's
going on with Honora. What the hell *do* you want to talk about?"

I shrug.

"Fine," she says, slamming a box down on the counter.
Before heading out the door, she tosses a can of Budweiser
from the fridge and says I look like I might need it. Her car
door slams with an expensive *thunk*.

"Rosie," I call out the screen door, "don't be mad, okay?"

The words hit her and she rolls her eyes.

"I'll be over at Daisy's when you're done. Going to head back to Nashville tomorrow, so have dinner with us tonight?"

She does not refer to Nashville as home. Clayton is still home for all of us, though, technically, only Violet still lives here. With Mother gone, I wonder if this will change.

I settle myself on the old sleeper sofa in the living room, pop the top on the beer, and take a long drink. The box sits beside me. I finish the beer and then one more before opening the box again, telling myself I don't want to risk spilling anything on its contents.

A paper clip holds yellowed newspaper together. On top is the engagement announcement from the *Mabry Review* for Jackie and me. The next is from the First Baptist newsletter about my going off to the University of Virginia. Carter had circled my name and written *my brother* next to it. He'd never shown me any of these.

It takes the rest of the afternoon to read through all of them, the light waning until the bedroom lamp is required. There are torn-out sections from Captain Marvel comic books, an article from the Tolliver paper on a local boy who made it to the NBA, and a torn-out page from *The Adventures of Huckleberry Finn,* when Jim and Huck begin their adventure on the raft. The passage is about how they fished and talked, took swims to stay awake, and drifted down the river looking up at the night sky.

"Nothing ever happened to us at all—that night, nor the next, nor the next."

And *nothing ever happened to us at all* . . . How I wish that were true.

I place the papers carefully back in the box and put a rubber band around it so nothing will fall out.

After loading up the rental car, I step back inside once more. I stand there, letting the years come back—playing blackjack at the kitchen table; Carter's voice carrying through the rooms as he butchered "Blueberry Hill" in the shower; watching him sleep on the sofa the first night we moved in, one arm thrown across his eyes, the tension finally eased from his face.

The crunch of tires over gravel comes from the side driveway. Jackie walks through the front door, dressed in tight jeans and a sweatshirt with *World's Greatest Mom* written across the backdrop of a rainbow. The girls and I picked it out at the Corinth Walmart two years ago as a Mother's Day present.

"You're leaving us." It is an accusation.

She walks through the empty rooms.

"It's not a home, Jackie. Not anymore."

She sits on the sofa, resting her head back against the wall. I watch her close her eyes for moment. "You made it a home for Carter."

I'm not sure why she is here tonight. We each take a beer from the refrigerator. After opening hers, she takes a long drink.

"Honora got her period this morning," she says.

Our child will not become the third generation of Cooper girls to get knocked up in high school.

"She got lucky," I say.

"She deserves a little luck, don't you think?" She fingers an old throw pillow she must have bought years ago. "Honora will go with you. But only until the summer. She's not happy about it. She doesn't want to leave her friends here, but she understands, at least a little, that she could be better off in Virginia right now."

Relief sweeps through me.

"I'm losing both of you," Jackie says.

I sit next to her, our bodies only inches apart. "You'll bring Louisa to come see us. It's only for a few months, okay? And it's not Mars. Only Virginia."

Jackie jerks herself off the couch, heading straight for the door. I go after her, putting my hand against the door so she can't open it.

"Jackie." My voice is low, shaky. "Please."

Anger turns the color of her eyes a cool blue. "You're lying. You don't plan to be in Bailey for a few months. You want to live there. Can't you see how much Louisa needs you, too? How much she loves you in spite of everything? Everything."

The room presses in on me, making the images come— one after the other, the click-click-click of a camera. The sky wide and blue overhead. The touch of warm October sun on my face. *Swim with me, Zeke,* Carter says.

Jackie's right fist connects with my shoulder, knocking me off balance. "You son of a bitch. Don't you go off into that shut-down world of yours where nobody can go."

She comes at me with both hands now, hitting wherever she can. "I swear, Ezekiel, if you don't talk to me, I'll kill you." Her breath is hot against my face. She is crying.

I hold Jackie's arms against her body. I tell her to stop and I'll talk. Tell her whatever she wants. She goes still.

"Promise?"

We back away from each other, both of us breathing heavily.

"You were thinking about your brother, weren't you? You always get that look on your face when you remember him. Tell me what happened the day Carter died."

It's a challenge thrown up between us, an old one at that.

"I've told you a hundred times before."

"Not the whole story. Ever."

"Yes."

This is not true. The version I have told everyone from Jackie to my family to the police was part of what happened. But the whole truth of that day has been locked up, playing on a constant loop of memory. Ten years is a long time to keep silent. Inside it feels like a thousand.

All that's left is the telling. And when the story's out, what will remain? Could it possibly be less than what I have now?

"Zeke. You're doing it again."

I begin before I can think. "We were supposed to be fixing the roof before the winter rains came. You'd taken the girls into Mabry to go shopping. As soon as you left, I turned to Carter and said, 'Let's go fishing.' The sun was out. Not a cloud in the whole sky. By nine thirty, our lines were launched. I'd never seen Chickasaw Lake look prettier—the water shining so clear you could see straight through to the rocks on the red mud bottom."

Jackie sinks to the floor against the wall, her eyes holding mine.

"We caught five bass before lunch. Took a break to eat bologna and cheese sandwiches. Almost finished a six-pack. We leaned back to rest. The sun warming our faces. That's when Carter asked me to sing our song, Mother's lullaby for us. Something in his tone felt funny."

Moist tracks run down Jackie's face. She loved him, too. My throat begins to close up.

"I cracked open an eye and looked over at him. The scars had healed over, leaving thick lines down his forehead, right eye, and cheek. And while Carter hated the way they made him look—scary, like a monster, he said—I was thankful, in part, for them. They reminded me every day of why I was there, watching over him."

The living room has gone dark and neither of us moves to turn on a light. The small electric heater kicks on, humming near the sofa. Its warmth doesn't reach me.

"What was the lullaby, Zeke? What did he want to hear?"

"You don't remember it?"

She shakes her head.

"When Carter asked me to sing it that day, I said no at first. But I knew he only wanted to hear it when he was feeling sad or afraid or even just tired. I figured what the hell? The beer buzz and the fishing put me in a good mood. So I sang it—'Good night, my sons, the day is done, wait only for angels to carry your dreams.' I forgot the last line. And then it drifted back up through my memory and it was like I could see the words hanging in the air before me—'Let sleep begin, so we may meet again.'

"The singing put a smile on Carter's face. He loved that song, really loved it. When I looked over at him, he just shook his head and said something like *You're all right, Zeke.* But he wasn't done making requests. He got all fired up about going for a swim. Remember how someone floated a small wooden platform in the middle of the lake? Carter wanted me to race him to it, and he stripped down to his boxer shorts before I could tell him no. When I wouldn't budge, he came up behind me, needled me in the back with one of his scratchy toenails."

Jackie laughs. "All the stubbornness of your mother and you rolled into one man."

"Then I got mad. 'Knock it off,' I said, swatting his foot, 'I'll go in the water in a minute. Just give me a minute, for Christ's sake.' All he wanted was for me to go swimming with him, Jackie. That's it. But I was too damn lazy. When I was sure he had gone into the water, I rolled over and closed my eyes. Twenty minutes must have passed, maybe thirty, when a woodpecker knocking in a pine tree woke me up. Three red-winged blackbirds circled the water in the middle of the lake. I said, 'Carter, look at those blackbirds.' No answer. I sat up. He was gone."

There is a welling inside me and I give in to it, letting the cries come, a soft reminder of the ones that echoed around the lake all those years ago.

"I knew he wasn't feeling right, but I didn't do anything. He was a good swimmer, Jackie. How could he have drowned?"

The warmth of Jackie's arms comes around me. She whispers in my ear, shushing me, telling me it wasn't my fault.

"It was an accident. You couldn't have saved him."

A brother should have, I think. It's all I have been thinking for ten years.

She raises my chin so our eyes meet. "He loved you so much. Everything's gotten so messed up, hasn't it?"

The taste of salt comes strong on my tongue. Her lips are soft beneath mine. She pulls me to the couch, trails kisses down my neck, my chest, my stomach. I run my hands under her sweatshirt. The warm feel of her skin yielding beneath my fingers crowds out everything else.

The loving is sweet and rough and fast and slow until we are both sweating and wasted and filled.

The room is dark and cold. I pull a blanket over us. Jackie sleeps against my side, her face relaxed. I don't care that Curtis will be wondering where his wife is.

∿ Forty ∿

1985

When our plane takes off from Memphis, I watch the Mississippi River disappear out the window until it looks like a curving line meandering through a child's model town. The sun is bright and shining, streaming through the clouds as we slice through them. The flight attendant comes to take our drink order. Honora asks for a rum and coke.

"Honora." It is a warning.

"Jesus, Dad, I'm kidding." She raises her voice. "Can't take a joke anymore?"

Heads turn our way and I smile back at them, rolling my eyes. Though I suspect Honora is secretly relieved not to have to face the asshole boyfriend, she is not going peaceably. This I can handle. I think.

Cousin Georgia picks us up in Charlottesville. She is dressed in jeans with creases ironed in them and a pink turtleneck.

"That must be Glinda the Good Georgia."

"Shut up, Honora, and be nice."

Georgia hugs me long and close. "What a couple of weeks it's been for you," she says. "And welcome, Honora. We've heard a lot about you."

My daughter shoots me a questioning look, as though she suspects that I spilled the ugly details of why she's here. I didn't. Only said she'd had a rough semester and needed a break from Mabry High.

Georgia warns me on the drive how Osborne has gone downhill since I left two weeks ago. He doesn't want to leave their room much anymore. Takes all his meals there. The worry weighs heavily in her voice. When I ask if she's taken him to the doctor, she shrugs.

"Won't go. I can't force him. He knows this disease is going to get him, and he doesn't know what to do with himself until it does, so he's scared."

After several failed attempts to engage Honora in conversation, Georgia gives up. Honora clamps headphones over her ears and glares out the window, the muffled, high-pitched squeals of an electric guitar filling the car.

Cousin Georgia clears her throat, and the small hands guiding the steering wheel clench and unclench. She begins talking. Talks all the way to the farm, barely taking a breath, holding up her hand when I try to respond.

"Let me get this out, Ezekiel. I know you've got a lot on your mind right now, but Osborne and I have a proposal. When you came to stay with us all those years ago, you became like a son, and now, with you being back, it feels right for you to be at the farm. We'd like to have our lawyer adjust the estate plans from the farm being shared equally between our nephews and nieces to having you become the sole heir. You'd also get Oz's share of the Lacey family properties. That's not a lot of money up front, but depending on when they're sold, it could go a long way toward keeping this place running. When we die, if the farming life doesn't suit you, you could always sell the property, though it pains me to think of it not being in the hands of a Cooper or a Lacey. In return, I'd like you to help us manage the farm. We'd pay you a manager's salary. Osborne can show you all the things you need to know on the financial and farming side, and I can teach you everything else. We could renovate the guesthouse for you or you could have your own floor in the main house."

Georgia finishes as the car comes to a stop in the driveway. She turns off the engine and settles back against the seat. The proposal stuns me. From the little I know about farm finances, a good year means you make enough to pay the property taxes and break even. Is that the life I want? My father failed at making a living off a farm. But he didn't have the Lacey money behind him to cover the lean years. Cousin Georgia and Osborne have a beautiful if slightly decrepit house and a piece of land any man would be proud to stand on. The offer hangs between us, shimmering and golden.

"Promise me you'll think on it?" Georgia asks, patting my arm. "Don't answer now."

Bailey High School sits three miles from Lacey Farms. The main brick building is a single story, easily half the size of Mabry High. I flinch when the school secretary cheerfully announces that they haven't had a new girl in class for two years.

My daughter wears jeans with one ripped knee and a black T-shirt with Duran Duran on it. As we stand outside the school office, she glances around the empty hallway.

"So, your first class is English. The secretary said that's the second door on the left down there."

Honora doesn't move. Neither of us has ever been the new kid in school. She scuffs the toe of a purple high-top against the floor. Should I have made a clothing recommendation for this day? Like a skirt or something? Will all the Bailey girls be wearing fancy dresses?

A boy dressed in jeans and a pink polo shirt makes his way out of the office, openly staring at Honora. She glares back.

"You catch bus number nine home, okay?" I say. "I'll be waiting for you. Would you rather I pick you up? First day and all. Hey, what about I just pick you up?"

"It's okay. I'll take the bus. See you later."

She heads to the classroom, her small form receding down the rows of silver lockers that seems to stretch on for miles. I catch up to her.

"You're going to be great." I hug her, which is probably mortifying for a fifteen-year-old on school premises, but I do it anyway. "I love you."

Her expression doesn't change. She slips into the classroom and is gone.

The drive back down Tall Oaks Road to Elle's house takes ten minutes. Elle and I spoke on the phone this morning and the conversation felt awkward, distant. Has my absence finished what we had barely begun? At the sound of the truck, she steps out on the front porch. She smiles and my hopes lift. I am on the steps kissing her before we say hello. Her hands find their way around my neck and mine settle on the curve of her waist. The warm taste of coffee is in her mouth. The kiss does not stop until she pulls back.

"Hey," she says.

"Hey."

When I move to go inside the house, she suggests we stay on the porch. "I want to catch up talking first, okay?"

"Right." There are two chairs and we position them to face each other. Her eyes are a clear green this morning, with a shiny kind of happiness. I keep a hand on her knee while relaying the basic details of Mother's death and Honora's situation.

"Was it hard for Jackie to let Honora come out here with you?" Elle asks. "She must miss her."

"We agreed it was the best thing." My hand travels up Elle's jeans, massaging the leg muscles as it goes.

She closes her eyes, murmuring. "I'm glad I get to meet your daughter, though I'm not sure she's going to feel the same way about me. She'll think I'm trying to replace her mother. How was it seeing Jackie again? My ex-husband and I didn't have kids, so I never have to see the bastard again. I don't mean that I never wanted kids—I'm just glad he and I never had any. But it must be important for you and Jackie to stay civil, right?"

"It's complicated." I want to ask more about her ex.

Elle's eyes fly open. "Complicated?"

"A lot of history there, and then, like you said, the girls."

Elle jerks herself out of the chair and is inside the house before I can get up. Through the screen door, she says, "Leave."

"Why? What's wrong?"

She faces me with arms folded across her chest. "When a man says his relationship with his ex-wife is 'complicated,' that means he's sleeping with her. Am I right?"

Elle and I are just getting started. The honest answer won't be helpful.

I sigh.

"Look, some things happened when I was back there, and, yes, we did spend one night together. One. But it's over. We were saying good-bye to each other. I was all caught up in the funeral and Honora and leaving Clayton for good. It will never happen again. Okay? Knowing I was coming back to Bailey, to you, has been the only thing keeping me going."

The front door slams shut.

October passes into November. In the mornings, a fine fog hangs over the hills out my bedroom window. During the second week of my return to Lacey Farms, Georgia, Oz, and I are having breakfast in the kitchen. It's a Saturday and Honora is still upstairs, happy to sleep until noon. Georgia attempts the crossword puzzle in the *Daily Progress* in between bites of grits and bacon. She keeps pushing the reading glasses up on her nose and sucks on her teeth when she can't figure out a word. The sports page absorbs Osborne, whose right arm is still encased in a sling from the car accident.

I clear my throat. Georgia looks up from the paper.

"I'd like to accept."

Georgia puts down her pencil. "Accept what exactly, Ezekiel?" She glances at Oz, who is still deep in the NFL scores. "Oz! Listen up, honey. This is important."

Oz swivels his head in his wife's direction. "What?" he says. "What is it?"

Tucker lurches over from his spot in front of the stove to drape himself over my feet.

"You two took me in so I could go to school at UVA, and all these years later you've taken me in again."

Georgia holds up a hand. "You make it sound like you were an orphan on the street. We opened our home to you because you're our family, Ezekiel."

"Hush," Oz says. "Can't you see the boy's got something to say?"

"Being here on the farm is—" The words won't come. I try again. "Being here makes me remember how I felt when I stayed the first time. You two make me feel like things might still work out. If I can be of use to you, if I can help Lacey Farms in any way, I can't think of any other place in the world I want to be."

I lean back in the chair and realize my hands are shaking. The dog licks the toe of my boot.

Georgia opens her mouth and this time Oz holds up a hand. "Son, we're honored to have you here."

He returns to his newspaper, and after Georgia gives my hand a squeeze, she returns to hers.

Tucker looks up at me but doesn't move. And even though my breakfast is finished, I, too, am content to stay put.

∾ Forty-One ∾

1985

Farm 101 begins. *Can't manage something you don't know a thing about,* Osborne says. He has become animated again almost overnight, anxious to get out of the house and show me all I need to know. *Before I forget,* he says.

Still recuperating from the broken collarbone, he begins each day by calling me into his office to learn something, like how to keep the pests away from the peach orchard or where to buy good fencing materials. There are moments when he stops in midsentence, uncertain which word comes next. He will slam his fist on the desk, trying to force the word out. Most of the time I can help him remember it. When I can't, he gives me a look filled with enough fear and helplessness to collapse a person's heart.

We decide the apple orchard will be replanted, and we spend a week traveling to different apple farms to figure out which varieties to put in. So far, we've decided on the Golden

Pearmains, one of Georgia's favorites, along with Ginger Golds, Bishop Pippins, Carolina Red Junes, Staymans, and Maiden Blushes.

Somehow Osborne and my daughter have become an unlikely pair. They go on a walk every night after dinner. Georgia and I are both pleased. When I asked Honora about it, she told me he was an old guy losing bits and pieces of himself each day and that was a feeling she could understand.

The week before Thanksgiving Jackie calls. Louisa misses Honora and me and wants to spend Thanksgiving break in Virginia. Honora's told her about the horses here and Lou wants to learn to ride. Jackie's voice sounds tight and I ask if she is okay. She snaps that it's none of my business. *Really.* I offer to meet them halfway, but she says the long car ride will do them good. Instant red flag. Long car rides with Louisa are generally only good for headaches, stomachaches, and fighting.

"Will you be staying, too?" I ask, trying to sound neutral on the subject.

"Maybe. I haven't worked it out yet with Curtis. I'd like to, though."

In the end, it doesn't matter. I will have my girls with me for Thanksgiving, the first time since the divorce. Working a double shift at the plant was my normal holiday routine. I figured the extra money would do me good and wanted to avoid spending the day missing them, drinking too much, and feeling sorry for myself.

When I ask Cousin Georgia if Louisa and possibly Jackie can stay at the house, she declares that she will never forgive me if they stay anywhere else. She launches into a campaign of preparations—airing out bedrooms, buying new sheets, and stocking the cupboards with Louisa's favorite foods.

Phone calls to Elle are not returned. Georgia finds me sanding a barn door that won't slide properly and tells me she will be inviting Elle for Thanksgiving dinner. This leaves me speechless. The last people I want sitting down to Thanksgiving dinner right now are my ex-wife and the woman who looks to be my former girlfriend. Is Georgia losing her mind, too?

"I'm not sure that's a good idea, Georgia."

"Ezekiel, I love you, but you can't tell me who to invite to my house for Thanksgiving." She looks at me for a moment before inquiring where things stand between her neighbor and me.

"Kind of a standoff, I guess."

Georgia purses her lips, making me feel two years old. "Tread lightly, please. That woman went through an awful marriage and an awful divorce and deserves nothing but good things. You hear?"

"Tell me about the ex-husband."

"Elle hasn't told you about him?" she asks.

I shake my head.

"Have you heard of Wallace Industries?"

"Nope."

"They grow every food known to man, and even a few new breeds they've cooked up with genetic engineering. Number two manufacturer of farm equipment in the country. Number three grocery store chain in the South. Oz always said old man Wallace would be printing his own Wallace dollars before we knew it."

It takes abandoning the door project and consuming a pot of coffee back at the house, but eventually Georgia tells it all. Elle married Clayton Wallace III after meeting him at the

University of Virginia. At the time, he was called Virginia's most eligible bachelor. They moved to California to start up West Coast operations for Wallace Industries. Elle never told Cousin Georgia all of the details, but from what she gathered from the local papers, who were happy to reveal the gritty divorce particulars, Clay, as he was called, was a mean son of a bitch who fooled around on Elle just like his father and his father's father did to their wives.

The next day, Cousin Georgia informs me that Elle will be joining us for Thanksgiving.

Visions of Jackie, Elle, and the girls seated at the same table make me wonder what kind of holiday lies ahead.

The night before Jackie and Louisa arrive, Cousin Georgia makes me drag the tallest Christmas tree in the state of Virginia into the front living room. It takes Jimmy and me an hour of cursing under our breath to get the tree upright in its stand while Osborne and Cousin Georgia direct us: "A little to the left gentleman. Oh, no, that's much *too* far to the left; let's try it again."

Jackie calls from the Smokies the next afternoon and says they've hit traffic and will be in late. When they are thirty minutes away, she calls again. This sends Osborne into overdrive. He keeps yelling things at Georgia—is the living room cleaned up, where's Louisa sleeping, where's Jackie sleeping? At the front picture window, he places a dining room chair right in the middle and takes up a post, squinting out at the darkness every time the glimmer of a headlight beams in the farm's direction.

"We must seem like fools to you, Zeke," Georgia says. "Making such a fuss. But we're so pleased to have you and your family here for the holiday."

She goes back in the kitchen to warm up dinner, in case anyone is hungry, and makes a fresh pan of corn bread.

"They're here! They're here! Right now!" Osborne yells out. From the kitchen, I hear him scramble out of the chair and throw open the front door.

"It was almost better having him in his room, wasn't it?" Cousin Georgia says.

I feel as excited as Osborne, though, and head to the front door. Jackie appears in the doorway.

"Get your crazy uncle away from the car."

She's never even met Georgia or Osborne. Jackie marches past, saying she's needed a bathroom for miles. Georgia tells her where the powder room is, ignoring my ex-wife's lack of manners. By the time I make it to the car, Louisa has stepped out of it. Osborne is grabbing suitcases from the back.

"Let me do that, Osborne."

"I got it," he says.

Lou unfolds out of the car. I pull her in for a long hug, inhaling the scents of strawberry shampoo and grape bubble gum. Honora offers the glimmer of a smile when she catches sight of her baby sister. My youngest is like one of the yearlings in Elle's stables, all legs and pretty as hell.

Osborne and Honora play tour guide, walking Louisa and Jackie around the house. Looking at Oz right then, no one would guess he was losing his mind. He looks like a man who'd been waiting a long time to share a holiday with young people.

Thanksgiving day dawns foggy and drizzly. Tucker stirs at the foot of the bed when he hears Georgia creep down the stairs to put the turkey in the oven. I can't go back to sleep, so I get up.

The girls' room is down the hall and I can't help myself from peeking in on them. Louisa sleeps sprawled across the bed, legs tangled in the blankets, mouth open wide. As she has grown older, she's begun to look more like her uncle Carter. She has the same sort of shy smile he did. Honora rests on her side with hands held beneath her chin, a tattered purple elephant from babyhood tucked in the crook of her arm. Despite the dyed black hair that hides the same golden brown color as her mother's, Honora looks mainly like a younger version of Jackie. But she's got my dimples—all three of them, one in each cheek and one in the chin. They are so beautiful, these girls. I linger in the doorway.

Tucker wanders past me into their room, though I try to call him back. He gives each girl a quick lick across her face before I can drag him out.

Dinner is set for three o'clock today, though Georgia tells me Elle is planning to come around two. Last night Georgia casually mentioned to the girls and Jackie that Elle would be joining us for Thanksgiving. She referred to Elle as "our dear neighbor and the woman who's been teaching Ezekiel to ride." I kept my head down, not trusting myself to look at anyone. I hadn't mentioned Elle's name to Honora yet, since I didn't want to say, *This is the woman who taught me to ride and is teaching me about love again but isn't speaking to me currently.*

Louisa had wanted to know more about the riding lessons. She made me promise she could take a lesson with Elle while she was here. I didn't say that I doubted Elle would want to oblige me anything at the moment.

Jackie joins Georgia and me in the kitchen, the smell of roasting turkey already filling the room.

I pass her a cup of coffee.

There are dark shadows beneath Jackie's eyes, as if she didn't sleep well.

A strong yeasty odor emerges from the mixing bowl each time Georgia punches the bread dough down. She is showered and dressed in a blouse and skirt beneath an apron with a turkey appliquéd on the front.

"Ezekiel, why don't you take Jackie on a walk around the farm? Show her the lake and the horses."

When I look at Jackie, she shrugs. This could mean hell no, I don't want to go, or I don't care. I ask Georgia if we can help her cook.

"I'm a one-chef kind of woman, you two. The only help I need is having room to move in the kitchen. So go on."

The outside temperature has warmed up to the high fifties. The forecasters got the snow prediction wrong. Oz had said we might take the old sled in the barn out for a run this weekend but it will have to wait. Maybe Christmas. The thought of having Lou and Honora here, snow blanketing the farm, is a good one.

Jackie walks with her hands in the pockets of her jacket. We set off toward the lake. The oaks are bare above us.

"Guess who called the house the other night?" she says.

"No idea."

"That jerk kid, Brian. When I figured out it was him, I called him every name under the sun, Zeke, I did. It felt so good. I don't know why the guy didn't hang up, but he didn't, not until I was finished."

"Why would he call?"

"Who cares? I'm glad Honora's here."

We make a lazy loop around the lake. The loblolly pines damaged in the tornado have been taken out, leaving the depressing sight of empty land surrounding the shore. Jackie bends down to pick up a stray twig.

"Georgia and Osborne have offered me the farm, Jackie."

The twig snaps in her hands. It is dropped back on the ground.

"I've accepted. They've made me the heir of their estate."

"Things seem to be working out for you just fine, don't they?" Jackie says.

She turns away and heads back to the house.

Georgia flutters around trying to get us all to sit down for dinner. Food covers the length of the table—green beans and ham casserole, corn soufflé, yams with brown sugar, mashed potatoes, corn-bread stuffing, ambrosia, rolls. Oz sits at one end dressed in a plaid button-down shirt, his hair still wet from a shower. Several bits of tissue decorate his face from shaving cuts. The arm sling for his collarbone is missing, an act of rebellion sure to provoke Georgia.

A knock on the front door announces the last guest. Elle apologizes for being late, saying one of her horses is sick. The only seat left at the table is the one to my left. Elle reluctantly takes it. Jackie sits across from us, and I feel her eyes on Elle, assessing. Honora appears to be doing the same thing. Only Louisa seems genuinely pleased by her appearance.

"You're the horse woman Cousin Georgia told us about!" she says. "Will you give me a lesson while I'm here?"

Elle laughs. "You must be Louisa. I'll give you two lessons if you work hard like your dad."

My ear is attuned to the unexpected warmth in Elle's voice. Maybe she's not as mad as she was. Jackie shifts her gaze to me. I attempt to keep my expression neutral. *Switzerland.*

With Tucker following behind her, Georgia places the turkey in front of Osborne's plate before taking the seat opposite his. Osborne asks us to bow our heads. "Lord, thank you for this bountiful food and for the good woman who prepared it lovingly for us. Georgia and I are thankful this year for those gathered around this table. Jackie. Honora. Louisa. Ezekiel. Elle. Tucker. We are blessed to share this meal together. Amen."

When I open my eyes, Honora and Lou are both smiling. This is the first Thanksgiving since the divorce when all four of us have been together.

Osborne stands up. He hovers above the turkey, looking at it for a moment before glancing around the table as if searching for a clue of what to do next. His hands clench at his sides. I glance uneasily at Georgia. A minute ticks by. Elle shifts in her seat.

Honora, who is seated to Oz's left, stands up. She hands him the carving knife and fork. "Here you go, Oz," she says, like nothing is wrong.

"Why, thank you, Honora."

And everything is fine.

After dessert Georgia puts Elle and me on dish duty. Elle fills the sink with soap and water while I gather all the dishes. We are alone in the kitchen, standing side by side as I wash and she dries, neither of us saying a word. Our hands bump occasionally when I give her a clean dish.

"I forgive you."

Elle's voice makes me almost drop a china cup. She does not look in my direction.

"But if you ever do it again, I'm gone. And I'll know if you do. Understand?"

I want to face her but instead keep my body forward, though I sneak a sideways glance. She looks vulnerable and hurt and I know I have caused it. Somehow a soap bubble has landed on top of her head and I lean in to blow it off.

"Not so fast. I asked you a question." The bubble pops silently on one of her curls.

"I apologize for hurting you and I promise never to do it again. And I understand the consequences if I screw up. But I won't." My voice is low but clear.

"Good," she says.

By midnight the marathon Scrabble game has finished, sending Elle home and all the adults to bed. Oz takes a large piece of hummingbird cake and a cup of coffee with him, which, my cousin says, as they ascend the stairs, will keep him up all night. My daughters stay up watching *Footloose* on the VCR in the living room.

Jackie and I head up to our rooms and say our good nights. A few minutes later, a soft knock comes at my door. When I open it, Jackie stands there in purple polka-dotted flannel pajamas that look like they belong to Louisa. Her hair is pulled back from her face in a loose ponytail, and the first hints of gray stand out among the chestnut strands. Even in the dim hallway light, the wrinkles around her eyes and mouth are visible. The past few years have not been easy for her, either.

She holds out a photo. "I found this the other day. We took it when we first moved into our house. Remember?"

Smiling into the camera are Jackie, Carter, and me, our arms thrown over each other's shoulders. Carter holds a hand-lettered sign that reads, "Our House!"

I take it from her, and the scene comes back to me. How young we were, still in our twenties. Carter may have been the most thrilled because the new house gave him his own room for the first time in his life.

"May I keep it?"

She nods.

"Thanks. And thanks for bringing Louisa."

It feels natural to reach for her hand, lacing my fingers through hers.

"You always had the biggest hands," she says. Her fingers tighten around mine. "Can we talk? Maybe in your room?"

I hesitate.

"Please?"

In the small confines of the room, she sits cross-legged on the bed while I stand as far away as possible at the window. The moon casts a bright glow across the barn and the old orchard.

"It's not going to work out with Curtis. It was a mistake, Zeke. All of it. Divorcing you. Marrying him."

The words don't make sense at first. A mistake? In the weeks and months after the split, I dreamed of her saying these things, convinced myself that she would realize what we had was worth saving, that I could pull myself together and love her properly. Give her what she needed. Keep our family together.

"I love you, Zeke. Nothing's changed about that. Not ever. I've always loved you."

The room feels too dark and I switch on another lamp. The light touches her face, revealing the hope on it.

Jackie's news doesn't fill me with a surge of triumph. Instead, I feel an odd emptiness. It's too late. For both of us.

"Say something, please, Zeke."

"I love you, too, Jackie. Always have. And I'm sorry about Curtis. I want you to be happy like you deserve to be."

She pulls her knees up beneath her chin, looking exactly like the fifteen-year-old girl I fell in love with.

The sound of our daughters' laughter comes up the stairs and we share a smile.

"We made them," I begin carefully. "Those two amazing creatures down there. Maybe that's what us being together was about. What we have is all twisted up now, Jackie. We love each other but not like we did before. I know we were happy for a long time. You're the only woman I've loved with my whole heart. But Carter's death. The divorce. Curtis. That's become part of us, too. And how can we be good together with all of that between us?"

Jackie bites her bottom lip. I grip the windowsill behind me in an effort to restrain the impulse to take her in my arms and kiss away the hurt. Seconds stretch out.

"It's Elle, isn't it?" she says.

"Yes and no."

The tears start in earnest now, and just as I'm about to say to hell with a decision I'm not sure I've even made, she's gone, the door closing with a soft click behind her.

～ Forty-Two ～

1985

Louisa barges into my room at eight o'clock the morning after Thanksgiving.

"It's time to get up, Dad."

The riding lesson isn't for another two hours, but I get up anyway. We pass Jackie's closed door on the way downstairs and I wonder what she and I will say to each other today.

Georgia is in the kitchen rolling out biscuit dough on a wooden cutting board covered in flour. Louisa watches as my cousin uses an old Vienna sausage can to cut out perfect round circles from the dough.

"Want to try?"

Louisa nods. Georgia tells her to sprinkle a little more flour on top before Louisa uses the can. My daughter beams as she places her first biscuit into the pan.

"You've never made biscuits before?" Georgia asks.

Lou looks over at me, shrugging. "Just the Hungry Jack kind. Where you pop the can with a spoon."

My cousin harrumphs.

After breakfast Lou and I head down to the stables. The temperature is colder this morning, high forties, and we both walk fast to ward off the chill.

"Dad, they must be rich. That's a mansion back there." She jerks a thumb at the house and shakes her head. "I've never seen a place like that. And look how big the farm is!"

I follow Lou's gaze toward the lake and realize I've already begun to take the size of the place for granted.

"It's pretty here," Lou says. "Do you like it?"

"Yes. But you're in Mabry, so I could never like it as much here as wherever you are."

Lou wrinkles her nose, hiding the sprinkling of freckles across its bridge. "That's what Mrs. Hopkins would call an evasive answer."

"And who is Mrs. Hopkins?"

"My civics teacher. She says politicians give the best ones. We've been reading some of them in class."

"You're in sixth grade this year, right?"

"Seventh."

"Right. I can't keep up."

She runs ahead when the riding ring comes into view. Old Whitey has been let out and is standing in the middle looking around as if she's supposed to be somewhere else, like in her stall eating oats.

"Look at her!" Louisa says, climbing up on the ring's fence. "She's gorgeous."

"Now that's a word I don't think old Whitey's been called before." Elle joins us at the fence. She winks at me over Louisa's head.

My palms begin to sweat. Elle wears the usual riding pants and a jacket zipped up to her neck, but I know the lines of her body beneath the material. The traitorous thought comes that if the girls were gone, Elle and I could go back to her house and properly make up.

"Ready for your first lesson?" Elle asks.

Louisa nods, shy all of a sudden.

"Did your Dad give you some tips? He's a pretty good rider now."

I swear to God I am blushing. Louisa peers up at me. She looks at Elle and then back at me.

"Just sit deep in the saddle and don't be afraid, okay?" I say.

Within ten minutes, Lou is leading Whitey around the ring. The horse stops suddenly, needing to scratch. My daughter loses her balance in the seat and tilts dangerously but rights herself just in time.

Elle charges at Whitey and gives her a slap on the butt. "Look, old girl, you don't get to stop when you want."

She apologizes to Louisa and they're off again. I watch as Elle corrects Lou's posture and helps position her feet in the stirrups. Lou listens, learning as quickly as she can. This is the determined child—physical skills come easily to her and she will work until she's mastered them. At nine months old, Louisa decided she was ready to walk and spent an hour one day pulling herself up to stand, trying to take a step, and falling. Over and over she did it, crying, until Jackie picked her up off the floor. Then she wailed to be put down. *Down, down, down,* she said. When Jackie put her back on the floor, Lou took her first step.

"Thanks for ruining everything again, Dad."

The shout comes from behind me. Still wearing her pajamas, Honora charges toward the riding ring. Whitey snorts and starts dancing around.

Elle grabs hold of the reins. "Let's walk him back inside,

Louisa. I'll teach you how to take the saddle off and brush him, okay?"

Lou watches as her sister stomps into view, but she lets Elle lead the horse out of the ring.

Honora is within two feet of me. She is crying. Before I know what's happening, she shoves me with both hands, surprising both of us with the force of it.

"Why do you have to be such a loser, Dad?"

Her voice is so loud Elle and Lou must hear every word.

"Can't you just leave us alone? Stay here and marry that ugly horse woman if you want and leave us the hell alone."

My daughter didn't figure this out by herself.

"Honora." My voice is low.

"I don't care, Dad. I really don't give a shit, okay?"

She drags the sleeve of the pajama top across her eyes. "When were you planning on telling us you're not coming back home? Christmas, maybe? A nice present for Lou and me?"

I touch a hand to her elbow and she shakes it off, stepping back.

"Honora, listen. I planned to talk to you both about it this weekend. This isn't how I wanted you to hear it."

"Hear what, Dad?" Louisa says.

She walks out from the barn and stations herself next to Honora. Lou's expression is hurt but not surprised. They *expected* Dad to screw up again. It was just a matter of time.

"Girls, Cousin Georgia and Oz need help here. Osborne is sick and isn't going to be able to take care of the farm. They asked me to take over."

There is an audience of three for this conversation. Elle is still in the stables. The girls' faces are unchanged and it's clear that the Laceys are not a compelling reason for my decision. Lou's hand slides into her sister's. They face off against me.

My daughters are fifteen and twelve and I have done nothing but break their hearts.

"The past few years have been really hard on you. And they shouldn't have been. It must have felt like I disappeared when your mother and I divorced. And I'm sorry."

"And now you're going to disappear again," Honora says.

I shake my head. "I'm going to live here. But I'll come to Mabry every chance I get. At least once a month, maybe twice.In the summers, I hope you'll think about spending part or all of it here. You could learn to ride and help on the farm and—"

"But why do you want to live here? Without us?" Louisa's voice cracks.

My ex-wife did this to hurt me, with no thought of what it would do to them. *Goddamn, Jackie.*

"I know I haven't shown you very well over the past few years how much I love you. I left Clayton to come here because I couldn't get over the divorce or Uncle Carter's drowning. I know he died a long time ago, but for me, the feeling sad part never stopped. Carter was my twin brother and I don't know if you can understand what it might feel like to lose your best friend and your brother in one moment. I had to find a way to make Carter's death not the thing I think about every morning and every night before I go to bed."

Elle takes a brush into Whitey's stall. The sound of the tack room door swinging shut reaches us.

Louisa breaks away from her sister and comes to my side. She touches my arm.

How do you accept forgiveness when you know you don't deserve it? This girl loves me still. There is a moment when I fear I might abandon any attempt to keep myself together. Can I let them see their father brought low by what he has done and, more important, not done?

In their early years I was surprised by how easily my children forgave transgressions. It seemed to come naturally, as if the burden of holding a grudge weighed more heavily than the hurt. When I considered my own childhood, I recalled that my siblings and I had been the same way. Quick to anger, quick to forgive. Of course, Honora has developed the capacity to stay angry. Does each of us have a quantity of forgiveness allotted to him? And once exhausted, do we lose the ability altogether?

"Are you going to marry Elle?"

Louisa asks the question. Honora looks away. I pause, wanting to make sure I get this one right. For them. And for Elle.

"She and I are still getting to know each other, so I don't know if we'll get married someday. All we know right now is that we like each other. Okay?"

"Thanks, Dad. That's super," Honora says. "We feel much better."

She tugs on her sister. "Come on, Lou."

My youngest pats my arm before following Honora. Their figures retreat over the hill. Lou is only two inches shorter than Honora now. If Lou ends up outstretching her sister, Honora will not be pleased. The girls hold hands and Lou's blonde ponytail sways back and forth against her back as she walks. At least Jackie and I gave them each other.

After my daughters disappear from view, I hear Diamond's bridle jangling like coins in a pants pocket as Elle leads him out into the ring. His head swivels back to the stables, where the rest of breakfast waits.

Elle walks over to the fence. "Are you okay?"

"No. I'm a bad father, Elle. For deserting them again."

"You're not. You're living somewhere that makes you happy."

I shake my head. "Doesn't matter. For them, it's the same thing—I don't love them enough to stay in Clayton. I couldn't love their mother enough to keep our family together."

"Finding out that Dad is living here permanently and shacking up with the ugly horsewoman is a lot to take in."

Tucker joins Diamond in the ring. After sniffing at the horse's hooves and almost getting clobbered, the dog turns around in circles trying to bite his tail. Just as he grabs hold of it, he loses it again and the circling starts over.

"I have to find the girls," I say, pushing off from the fence.

Elle grabs my arm. "They don't want to be anywhere near you right now. Be patient. Let them be angry and hurt for a little while."

What if I do what Honora and Louisa want? Leave Lacey Farms. Leave Elle. Dover Elevator might hire me back.

With some effort, I could get promoted to assistant manager. Maybe shift manager. Make more money. Buy an actual house. In Clayton. Meet Jackie at Motel Tolliver every now and then.

How long would it take for me to start longing again for a trip to Pigeon Forge?

No.

I choose to give them a father who lives in Virginia over a father who is not living.

Honora fails to speak one word to me over the next three weeks. A fourteen-hour drive back to Clayton for Christmas looms. I had hopes the trip would give her a chance to get out all the mad things she needs to say. But my daughter retreats behind the earphones of the Walkman player and speaks only when she's hungry or needs a rest stop. I try a few times to get her to turn off the music but then I give up. Instead, I keep the radio tuned to country stations with the volume high enough to drown out the synthesized beats from the passenger side.

Honora stays with Jackie and Curtis while I freeze in the back bedroom of what has become Violet's home. It still feels like Mother's house since Vi hasn't changed much of anything yet. To reach the creaky rollaway bed, I have to step around silver-wrapped bricks of fruitcake lining the floor. Mother used to call the room her own walk-in freezer on account of its lack of heating.

Louisa invites me to attend Christmas Eve service at Curtis's church, Mabry Methodist. I don't want to go but Lou appears to be making an effort not to hate my guts, so I will. No one bothers to tell me the Methodists like to dress up. I wear pants and a shirt, the only male out of diapers not wearing a jacket and tie.

Before the service begins, the minister asks all those who attended a dad and daughter retreat to come up front. When my youngest and Curtis join the group, I shoot a look at Jackie. She shrugs, but Honora catches my eye and makes a gagging gesture with her finger.

This may be the nicest thing she's done since Thanksgiving.

When we are on our way back to Bailey a few days later, Honora surprises me by pulling off the headphones. We've just passed the city limits of Nashville.

"I saw Brian in town."

My hands clench the steering wheel. If I had seen the boy, the two of us might not be driving back to Charlottesville today. I stare straight out at the road and tell myself to breathe. *Let the girl talk.*

"He was in Grayson's Café. Tried to act like he didn't see me but I know he did."

She fiddles with the buttons on the cassette player, not looking at me either. "He was sitting with all his jerk friends."

Breathe.

"Right next to their table was the bakery counter. And before I knew what I was doing, I had grabbed a whole cherry pie off the top and dumped it on Brian's head. Then I walked out."

I steal a glance at her. A small smile curves her mouth upward.

"I would've paid money to see that, sweetheart."

She shrugs, clamping the earphones back on, but I can tell she's pleased.

❦ Epilogue ❦

1986

The winter was mild. No ice storms or severe snow, as if last year's tornado earned Bailey a break. Spring unfolded and before I had a chance to pause over the sight of the cherry blossoms exploding in what Honora called pink puffball glory, summer arrived.

The plan had been to take Honora back to Mabry when Bailey's school year ended. But somehow, Honora had settled in Bailey. She and Osbourne could be found most mornings walking through the tidy rows of the peach orchard. Georgia was expanding Honora's cooking skills with lessons on meal preparation, something my mother hadn't yet had the chance to do with her granddaughter. At the high school, Honora sang in the performance choir and even joined the home economics club, though she swore it was only because members got extra class credit for baking projects.

"Doesn't sound like our girl," Jackie had said when I told her about Honora's extracurricular activities.

When I suggested that we offer Honora the choice of spending her senior year in Bailey or back in Tennessee, I expected Jackie to tell me to go to hell.

"Fine," Jackie said, her voice hollowed out across the phone lines. "Whatever she wants."

In May Jackie had filed for divorce from Curtis. I did not press for details, hoping my name had never entered the conversation.

"Why don't you and Lou come to Bailey for the summer?" I said.

"What about your new girlfriend?"

"I'm offering you the guesthouse, Jackie. Not me. You need a chance to catch your breath."

So instead of losing Honora, Lacey Farms welcomed Louisa and Jackie. The girls shared Honora's room in the main house and Jackie moved into the small guesthouse.

As evening drops down on the farm, the girls and I meet up on the back porch. Sometimes Osbourne joins us, if he's having a good day. The good still outnumber the bad for now. Through the guesthouse's front window, we can glimpse Jackie bent over a book. She enrolled in a couple of business classes at Piedmont Virginia Community College with an eye to opening her own dress shop someday. She talks about moving back to Mabry or even to Charlottesville. It is an odd arrangement to have my ex-wife living on the property. The moments when Elle, Jackie, and I cross paths remain awkward. But mostly, I'm grateful for the days spent in the presence of my daughters. To his credit, Curtis still keeps in touch with my youngest, though his letters arrive less frequently. The new divorce confused Lou. She didn't understand how her mother could have made the same mistake twice.

She is becoming an accomplished rider, thanks to Elle, and in August Lou will compete in her first horse show. Some days I worry she feels closer to Elle than to her parents. When I mentioned this to Jackie, she said Elle was teaching our daughter things we couldn't and that was okay.

The anger my ex-wife used to wield in my direction has been displaced by a quiet loneliness. There are moments when I find myself about to invite her out for a walk or to a movie. But I don't.

My girls and I watch as the lightning bugs pop out one by one. Elle's slight form moves in the stables as she puts the horses down for the night; Honora and Louisa are in charge of morning care. We count out loud how many times it takes Elle to get Carter, the chestnut yearling Cousin Georgia bought in June, out of the ring and into his stall. Elle still likes to split time each week between Lacey Farms and her place.

Last month she and I had tacked up the horses for a ride and I waved her off helping me up in the saddle. With a faith that had no grounding in ability or past experience, I placed one foot in the stirrup and hopped up with everything I had, throwing my opposite leg over Diamond's broad back in one graceless but effective motion for the first time ever.

Elle blinked twice. "I believe there's hope for you yet."

"Marry me then," I said.

"The only thing you've proved is you can get up on a horse by yourself. Give me a while longer to see what else you can do."

And so I am.

*   *   *

The nightly closing ceremonies are always the same. Honora, Louisa, and I push the swing with our feet, the squeak of the motion now so familiar I refuse to use WD-40 on the chain.

I point up toward the sky and say, "You two see those stars up there? You, my girls, are just as bright as the brightest one. Don't let anybody ever tell you different."

Then they dig their elbows into my ribs and say "Come *on,* Dad."

But they believe it.

Acknowledgments

Before embarking on this book, I thought the African proverb "it takes a village" only applied to raising children. I now know it also aptly describes how a book is brought forth into the world.

I offer my mother all of my gratitude for raising me with such love and instilling a passion for reading and for libraries. She hunted everywhere for kid's books with girl characters who *did* things. As a grandmother she's continued this tradition and spent countless hours watching over my own daughters so I could write. To my father I owe the genesis of this story. I was raised on the tall tales of his own Huck Finn–like boyhood. Dad, thanks for never being too tired to tell the chimney story one more time.

Though Clayton is a fictional Tennessee town, the book serves as a love letter to the place my father grew up and to the happiness I found there during my own childhood. It also pays homage to the memory of my paternal grandmother, Lavice May Paudert, who made the best corn bread in the world, smoked cigarettes in the bathroom so she wouldn't set a bad

341

example for her grandkids, and made strangers feel like family and family feel beloved.

With thanks to my writing family—Santa Barbara Writers Conference (SBWC) founders Mary and Barnaby Conrad and faculty, Squaw Valley Community of Writers, and my local coffee/cocktail klatch writers group. Without the generous support of scholarships to attend both SBWC and Squaw, I imagine I'd still be working on this story in some dark coffee shop.

To the saints among us who read early drafts of the manuscript and whose input made the book immeasurably better—Vicki Dobbs Beck, Ronetta Fagan, Madeleine Kahn, Carmen Madden, Christina Meldrum, and Shannon Pace. And three cheers to Sandra Sommer, Alissa Fencsik, and Nancy Cunningham for helping me figure out how the story should begin.

I owe an extraordinary debt to Elizabeth George and the Elizabeth George Foundation. They gave me a writer's two ultimate luxuries—time and money—in the form of an emerging writer grant. This support allowed me to scale back my full-time work for a year and revise the book.

Thanks to the doyennes of the Pleasanton Library for the use of the study rooms.

To the incomparable Dorothy Allison—thank you for believing in this story before I did; thank you for being such a generous teacher. To Jane Hamilton—you gave me encouragement in the midst of a massive rewrite and inspired me to keep going. To Catherine Ryan Hyde—thank you for telling me I wasn't crazy to quit my day job for a year to write the draft of this book. Your wisdom and example of how to build a writing career have provided steadfast guidance.

Writing nirvana was found at the Vermont Studio Center, which provided a two-week residency that gave me a place to write and allowed the story to grow.

Thank you to Dr. Larry Dobbs for helping me understand Carter's mental and physical issues; thank you to Dan Smulow for consulting with me on how the Smith brothers attack on Carter would have been handled under 1960 Tennessee law; thank you to my fellow Mills College alumna Dr. Anne Reed, DVM, for her assistance with the technical aspects of Tucker's physical condition after Zeke's exit attempt.

I was blessed to find a champion for *Lost Saints* in the form of my agent, Amy Rennert. Amy and her associate, Robyn Russell, gave me invaluable editorial advice on the manuscript. And thanks to her enthusiasm and perseverance, Amy found *Lost Saints* its perfect home at Grove/Atlantic.

At Grove, where the number of dogs lumbering around the office almost seems to equal the number of employees, I have found Elisabeth Schmitz to be the kind of editor writers dream about. Elisabeth's love of the story and its characters allowed her editorial guidance to strengthen the book in ways I couldn't have imagined. Associate editor Jessica Monahan was a constant comfort—she kept things moving forward, never tired of a first timer's questions, and gave the manuscript the benefit of her insightful edits.

Many thanks to friend and book publicist extraordinaire Leslie Rossman, who loves books as much as anyone I know.

The final thank you goes out to my family. My wife, Wendy, was the first reader of *Lost Saints* and her belief in it and in me never faltered, despite mounting evidence that it should. Thank you Wendy for being an exemplary human being and for sharing a life with me.

My daughters have been unceasingly supportive of my writing dreams, even with the hours and weekends away from them it has required. Girls—you are the beginning, middle, and end of my world.